THE ULTIMATE THRU-HIKE

H

WRITTEN BY CHRIS CANCILLA

Humanity gets an Upgrade

The Ultimate

Thru – Hike

by Christopher E. Cancilla

Drawings by

Richard Isbell

ACKNOWLEDGEMENTS

Who to say thank you to....

WOW! I can think of several people offhand, but I suppose I should thank the people who edited my story first—a Big Thanks to all of them for reading and offering ideas about the story and the writing.

<u>**Kevin Carpenter**</u> is my primary editor. He would tell me tidbits like, "That was stupid," or "What does that mean?" and we would discuss how to fix it. In my mind, I know what I wanted to say or see in the story. But on paper, well, it was the equivalent of speaking only one language but talking to someone who can change languages mid-sentence. We often discussed this story, heading out to Camp Durant to teach the Scouts Fishing or Amateur Radio merit badges, or perhaps work in the dining hall prepping, cooking, or serving. OH, By The Way, I strongly recommend editing by reading the words out loud. It brings on an entirely new meaning to editing.

I want to thank **Pastor Brian Metzger** from the Raleigh Vineyard Church in Raleigh, NC. I needed to hold a real wedding in the future, on another planet, with giant animals and a lot of people, so of course, since I had no clue what kind of ceremony or service it would be, I posed the question to him after Sunday service, and he emailed me a template for a generic wedding service where the couple can insert or remove what they wanted. Buffet or smorgasbord ceremony and it was excellent! Precisely what I needed. Using this template, I created a somewhat realistic wedding ceremony.

My list of editors is not tiny.....

...but not all of them really sent back issues or errors.

Some of them let me know they enjoyed reading it, and others let me know I forgot something or maybe I talked about an event that never happened. Either way, I did send all of them the final draft, and they sent something back.

Here they all are in alphabetical order:

Tracey Ayres	John Deacon
Shay Blakemore	Mark Gibson
Shawn Bryant	Gary Henderson
Leanne Bulger	Devyn Isbell
Allison Cancilla	Rick Isbell
Kevin Carpenter	Kirk Johnson
Bob Clade	Brian Metzger
Robert Cook	Brenda Napier
Alyssa Davis	Steve Suzanne
Ben Davis	Astrid Vázquez

Kevin and **Brian**, you know about them already, but my secret weapon is **Shay**. She reads, is an avid reader actually, and is not afraid to tell me something that makes no sense. She may not know how to fix it but knows it needs to be smoothed over.

Astrid is my wildcard. With Spanish being her primary language, I wanted her to read and offer suggestions on the story from the non-English speaker's perspective. Although she speaks fluent English, she admits it is a second language. And since she is living in Mexico with her husband and baby, we talk a lot through IM and text. Her assistance made the story readable and fun for the rest of the world.

The rest of the gang let me know little things, spelling, grammar, and time issues. Hopefully, we got them all fixed, and thanks to them, you get a FANTASTIC experience.

The last person I want to thank is **Jessica Mills**. Her expertise on the trial and willingness to teach and help others was my inspiration for writing this story. A great many folks out there are clueless about what it takes to do a week in the woods, and fewer understand months in the backcountry. Thank you!

I have a simple philosophy when it comes to storytelling;
...a story is nothing more than a random or intentional
collection of thoughts.

So, I hope you enjoy this novel.

My most current collection of random thoughts,

all inter-related and

hopefully entertaining.

The copyrighted

Leave No Trace Seven Principles

have been

referenced in the book

For more information about

Leave No Trace Hiking and Camping,

go to their website

Leave No Trace Center for Outdoor Ethics

The Seven Principles, and their descriptions,

are available on the **Leave No Trace** website
at:

http://lnt.org/learn/7-principles

Enjoy this story. I had a lot of fun writing it, and I sincerely hope you enjoy reading it.

I have had a few questions from my readers, but this is the most predominant. People have asked me how I write and where do I get my stories and ideas.

That's easy. I get an idea in my head, and that idea grows into a thought. Then, that tiny little thought expands into a plot or storyline. Finally, that storyline becomes a movie I get to watch in my head.

After that, I simply type what I see in the movie that plays out in my mind. The cool part is, I can pause the mental video, write what I see, and move on to the next scene.

In closing............

Remember this prologue. I like to call it Chapter Zero. If you are not familiar with hiking at this level, it will help you understand the concepts and terminologies used in this story.

Thanks,

    Chris Cancilla

Chapter Zero

If you are an experienced hiker and/or camper, for that matter, you are most likely familiar with the terms used by someone who partakes in long-distance hiking. And seriously, I do mean very long-distance hiking. A few of the terms like:

1. Thru-hike
2. Section hike
3. Trail Name
4. AT
5. PCT
6. CDT
7. Zero
8. Double Zero
9. HYOH

These terms may be new to you, so let's break them down.

For long-distance hiking trails in the United States, the word most commonly associated with the roughly 2,185 miles of the Appalachian Trail is AT. The 2,663 mile Pacific Crest Trail is PCT. The 3,100 mile Continental Divide Trail is CDT. Other names may also refer to end-to-end hikes like the Florida Trail (1,500 miles), John Muir Trail (210 miles), Hayduke Trail (812 miles), and many others.

There are two fundamental terms used throughout this book that you need to be familiar with, the thru-hike or thru-hiker and the section hike.

What is a Thru-Hike:

The Appalachian Trail Conservancy (ATC) defines a thru-hike as a hike of the entire AT or Appalachian Trail in 12 months or less. A "2,000-miler" is a hiker who has walked the entire length of the AT and reported his or her hike completion to the ATC. The ATC has been keeping records of thru-hike completions since 1937. (The ATC uses the term "2,000-miler" since the exact length of the trail changes regularly due to pathway relocations.) In the process of recognizing 2,000-milers, the ATC does not consider the sequence of sections hiked, the direction of travel, or the speed of the hike. It makes no difference if the hiker carries a pack, meaning either a thru-hiker, a section-hiker, or a day hiker will be recognized as a 2,000-miler. Providing they complete the entire trail. Many groups use this definition within the United States.

The Appalachian Trail travels through fourteen states along the crests and valleys of the Appalachian Mountain Range, from its southern terminus at Springer Mountain (Amicalola Falls), Georgia, to the northern terminus at Katahdin, Maine.

The Appalachian Trail thru-hikers typically take 5 or 6 months to make their way from one end – their beginning – to the other end – their ending. The most photographed area is very close to the midway point. Located in Boiling Springs, Pennsylvania, is the Appalachian Trail Conservancy building, and hikers will have their picture taken in front of the building as they pass the location.

Other Thru-Hike Terms:

Terms like Trail Angel, Trail Magic, zero, double zero, blazer, blue blazer, pink blazer, hiker box, Hike Your Own Hike, Leave No Trace: There are others, but these are a start for you. So let's look at them:

1. _**Trail Angel**_
   a. A person who performs (donates) acts of kindness for the hiker(s)
   b. The trail angel can provide a ride into town for resupply, set up a small kitchen, or cook a nice meal for those on the trail; possibly even stock up (add choice items) to hiker boxes.

2. _**Trail Magic**_
   a. Set up a hiker box (a waterproof cooler, for example) with various coffee drinks, beers, and soda (Pepsi, Mt Dew, Dr. Pepper are fan favorites).
   b. Have a trash bag or container so the hiker can deposit their trash.
   c. Setting up a hiker box with foods, protein bars, chips, snacks, and candy, especially Snickers with Almonds, I hear!

    d. Feeding Hikers is just plain magic.

    e. Allow hikers to stay at your residence.

    f. Any number of "MAGIC" acts of kindness.

3. *Hiker Box*

    a. A waterproof box, usually a cooler or another waterproof container, located on a trail and in plain sight

    b. It can contain the items above plus

        i. Isobutane fuel tanks in case the hiker is getting low

        ii. AA & AAA batteries in case the hiker needs new batteries for a light

        iii. Random foods and snacks

        iv. Tarps

        v. Instant coffee, sugar packets, creamer packets

        vi. Typically, the hiker will search for things they may want and deposit stuff they no longer need. Later, another hiker may find the hiker box and the discarded items and be overjoyed as this is what they needed.

4. _Zero and Double Zero_
   a. Usually, when you hit a town to stay.
   b. A day of rest.
      i.   Do laundry
      ii. Take a real shower
      iii. Eat at a real restaurant
      iv. Have an ice-cold adult beverage
   c. Referred to as a ZERO as in ZERO MILES hiked that day.
   d. Double Zero, two days, no miles.

5. _HIKE YOUR OWN HIKE_ (HYOH)
   a. It means to follow your own path.
   b. Hike at your own pace.
      i. Rubber Neck, look around, enjoy the experience, take in the sights.
   c. Do not let the fact someone else is doing 30-miles a day mean you need to also.
      i. You may only do 10 miles a day or 5 miles because it is **YOUR HIKE**, not theirs you are accomplishing.
   d. Thru-hiking is not a race. Enjoy the experience!

6. _**LNT**_
    a. Stands for **Leave No Trace**
    b. The principles/morales for backcountry travel/hiking
    c. The core belief is:
        i. Take only pictures, leave only footprints
        ii. Leave an area better than you found it
        iii. It means protecting the wilderness and backcountry so future hikers can enjoy what you have just experienced.
    d. Hikers have been known to clean up a trail left littered by day hikers. So leaving that trash bag with a trail angel would be a good day.

7. _**Blazer, Blue Blazer, Pink Blazer**_
    a. Someone who cuts their own path
    b. Someone who thru-hikes but takes a lot of side hikes just to see what's there
    c. There are also other blazer terms like a pink blazer. These are people who tend to follow the opposite sex just to be with them. Nothing terrible, just smiled at, and in some ways accepted, but we will not go into it here. You get the idea.

8. *The Blaze*

    a. A blaze is a paint color on a tree that indicates the trail's path or next section.

    b. The blaze is easily visible.

    c. The subsequent blaze can be seen from the blaze they are standing next to.

    d. This means you do not get "lost."

9. *SPOT or InReach*

    a. A non-terrestrial, satellite-based GPS locator and text-based communications device

    b. Used by hikers in the event of trouble

    c. Connected to someone who is not on the trail. Someone at home, where ever home is.

    d. InReach runs about $400 for the unit and $50 per month and is pretty much unlimited 2-way text communication

    e. Spot X is a tad bit less in cost.

    f. Before deciding on one or the other, DO YOUR RESEARCH

    g. The devices can send a pre-designed set of text messages and possibly in both directions depending on the model, and even a real-time text communication capability.

    h. Accuracy is about one meter, and the refresh rate depends on the level of service you choose.

10. _Stealth Campsite_
    a. To camp in a location with the intention of not being seen.
    b. A stealth campsite is camping in a place you should not be camping
    c. Hikers stop for the night, go pretty far off-trail to avoid the eyes of other hikers, and set up a camp.
    d. No campfire normally, boil water on a backpacking stove, eat, sleep, get up and pack, and move again.
    e. All the while leaving no evidence (trace) they were ever there.

11. _Base Weight_
    a. Base Weight is the weight of the gear a hiker is carrying.
    b. Does not include food, water, fuel, and the clothes on their back.

12. _Cowboy Camp_
    a. No tent camping for the night
    b. Sleep under the stars
    c. Makes for a fast start in the morning
    d. Roll up in a tarp to avoid getting wet from the morning dew

13. _Flip Flop_
    a. Hike a path and turn around and return hike to your starting point

14. _LASHer_
    a. This stands for a Long Ass Section Hiker
    b. Sections are typically done one section at a time, but a LASHer will do a couple at a time.

15. _Trail Name_
    a. Initially used as an anonymous moniker used to identify hikers for the safety of female hikers.

16. _Clothing vs. Sleep Clothes_
    a. When you go to sleep, you want to make absolutely sure you are dry, down to your underwear, especially in colder weather.
    b. Always keep a set of sleeping clothes to change into to crawl into your sleeping bag.
    c. This serves two purposes
        i. It allows to you change all clothing, dry out/off, and not freeze
        ii. It ensures the things you rub up against during the day do not end up sleeping with you during the night
    d. Plant oils, chiggers, ticks, ants, mosquitos, flies, and a great many other things you may unknowingly touch are not terrible, but not great.

What is a Section Hike:

A section hike is nothing more than a portion of the thru-hike. Usually, a trail runs from start to finish and can be more than 500 or 2,000 miles long. Sections can be designated as town A to town B or this mountain to that highway. A section will terminate at a town or road, where it can be, and usually is, referred to as a trailhead.

A section hike, for example, could be from the Beauty Spot in Erwin, TN, to Damascus, VA. This is about 70 miles, so maybe 30 hours hiking. However, used as a 3-day weekend experience, ten miles a day is a relatively low daily mile count and offers the hiker the chance to experience the hike and the beauty of the trail.

A section hike can be as short as a day or two or three, maybe a week, two weeks, or the total time you need to go from where you desire to start to where you choose to end your hike. The only consideration is transportation, getting back to where you parked. *← see trail angel*

You can hike the sections of any trail in any sequence, in any direction. You can walk the trail sections during the year when it's less crowded or even when the weather is better. The only requirement is that you complete hiking the entire trail to be a trail finisher.

Helpful information for the Reader:

The story you are about to read is fictitious since no humans roam around on other worlds *as far as us mere mortals know*. That would be cool, though!

The camping and hiking methods, styles, food, and cooking are based on current or projected reality. That means that I enjoy backcountry cooking and project how, in the future, it could be and how incredible dehydrated and long-term meals can be.

If you are curious about setting up a backpack for a hiking trip, you can find it in this book in Chapter 4. This will give you an excellent understanding of how to rig, set up, and fill a backpack. It also tells you how NOT to set it up for failure.

Even though some of the technology does not exist, I had thought about it when I laid in my tent, in a sleeping bag, on my sleeping pad, and the ambient temp was lower than -5°F, so yes, I have hope!

Hand warmers, foot warmers, and body warmers can be strategically placed in a sleeping back to help you sleep in cold weather, but having the right gear for the weather is always the best option.

In reality, there are blankets you can put inside your sleeping bag; these blankets are self-powered and heated and will provide you with a much colder lower limit for an ambient temperature. But all in all, camping in the cold today is better than it was 20 years ago, or in the 1970's when I was a young scout learning how to camp in my pup tent; imagine what your great-great-grandchildren will be able to experience.

How to eat well.

Food is another story. With the availability of Military Rations (MRE's) and other dehydrated meals, we had come a long way from when I was in Military Basic Training in the late 1970s. Back then, we had what was known as C-Rations. Cans that reminded you of cat food cans or maybe a can of tuna fish that may contain something simulating food and packaged at the end of World War II. I still ate it, though; it did taste close to good. But then again, I was starving.

Today's dehydrated meal packs and the ability to purchase dehydrated anything off the internet give a person the opportunity to buy or make their meals which only need boiling water to enjoy. Mixing a dehydrated vegetable medley with dehydrated meat, toss in a low sodium chicken bouillon cube, add some potato flakes, and you have a really lovely meaty vegetable stew, and all you had to do was add water and let it steep. Meaning clean-up was a breeze. Mix it all in a zip-top freezer bag, and there is no plate to clean up. Cut a small hole in the corner of that bag and squirt it into your mouth and no spoon to clean up. Toss the bag in the trash, and you are good to go!

You get the idea. Cooking, cleaning, meals are limited only by your imagination. Check out Amazon for a variety of dehydrated *anything*. You can most certainly find it there!

Heat Source, as in cooking

Lastly, heating water and cooking uses fuel to keep the water hot while things rehydrate. If you cook in a pot or in a pouch, make yourself an insulated cooking vessel. At the DIY home stores, you can pick up a roll of reflectix, an insulating material. Then form fit it, ensuring it is slightly larger and a little loose, to either the pot, container, or pouch. Once the water is boiling or near-boiling, slip the container into the cozy you made. If you are cooking a dehydrated meal you purchased, slip the pouch into a reflectix 'envelope' while it rehydrates and cooks. It will stay piping hot for you, even in colder weather. This keeps your food toasty warm and ready to enjoy and saves you a ton of fuel because there is no need to 'simmer.' You are now entering the STEEPING zone.

I have plenty of ideas for backpack meals that can be enjoyed simply by adding water—purchasing dehydrated food items/components from the internet, or any company offers you tremendous leeway in designing meals before the hike or when you stop and are ready to eat. Prepackaged meals in this form are available ALL OVER the interwebs. Just look for something that floats your boat.

Personally, a Zip-Top Freezer bag with dehydrated veggies, Jack Links diced up Prime Rib pieces, or any other meat, a tasty bouillon cube, and dried herbs and spices; combined with two and a half cups of near-boiling water and let rehydrate. Then add a couple of envelopes of pre-cooked and ready to eat, shelf-stable, chicken, and enjoy. Believe it or not, the sodium level is not all that bad compared to the prefab meals.

If you choose to purchase and use the pre-made add water meals from the store or the net, be aware of their nutritional values, especially calories and sodium. Please remember that you will be losing a lot of water while hiking, and with perspiration goes the nutrients, electrolytes, and minerals out through your pores. Even though they have a higher sodium content than anything you would typically eat or create for your backcountry experience, one of those pre-packaged dehydrated meal packs may be precisely what you need after a long day of hiking. If you are so inclined, you can also carry a ½ liter generic water bottle to use _**ONLY**_ for propel packets to give you an electrolyte boost at lunch or dinner every day. You can squeeze most of the air out of it and stash it in your bear bag when not using it. The weight is nearly non-existent. Why in the bear bag are you curious? Because it has a smell, the critters of the woods may investigate this new and exciting smell and disturb you during your rejuvenating slumber.

In case I have not said it yet:

1. Never bring any food into your tent
    a. This goes for a liquid "OTHER" than water also.

2. If you spill or splash food on your clothes, they do not come into your tent. Instead, those tasty items of clothing are now placed into your bear bag. For obvious reasons!
3. Critters can smell food and candy through its packaging, so park your backpack outside if you put the candy in your pack.
4. Hang your Bear Bag at least 10 feet up in a tree and at least 10 feet from the tree so critters, not just bears, can't find it and/or quickly get to it.

Chapter One

"I enjoy hiking, especially alone and hitting the trail to who knows where, on a path that takes me through beautiful vistas, across chilly and snow-covered peaks, and into some of the most beautiful landscapes on the planet Earth. There are vistas, waterfalls, and mountain peaks I can scale, descend, climb, pass through, or over, but mostly I get trail experiences. Yes, I said I like traveling the path alone, but there are times I wish I could share it with someone. A common experience, talking about it." He paused long enough to take a breath and continued, "Maybe this is the reason why I signed up for this *adventure* in the first place! I saw the advertisement, you know, the commercial on the way back from my job and thought to myself, this could be fun, getting paid to hike. So how can anyone pass that up!" He paused a moment but never looked at the woman he spoke to; he just kept rambling.

"Perhaps, just possibly, I like the idea of walking through a place no one, no human, has ever walked before. Yes, I will have a permavid implanted in my head, a position tracker, and a communications unit under my skin. All in all, it adds a mere 7 grams to my overall base weight; actually, it adds the weight to my head and not my pack, so not a problem. Give me a couple of days on the trail, and I would never know."

The woman interrupted him and allowed her to finally speak, "Great, yea, thanks for that info." She said after he finally shut up. "All I asked was, are you excited?" The young woman asked. "By the way, you can call me Belle. And you are?"

"You can call me Goose. And yes, I am very excited. But, you realize all the gear they gave us for this trip would have cost thousands back home; I could never afford an auto-set tent and a self-heating bag."

"I know. I love the gear, and we get to keep whatever we want after our 6-month contract expires." Belle looked around the plane. "How many people do they drop off at a time, is everyone on the ship a hiker?

"No clue. As I walked in, I counted chairs, 96 of them. The ship looks full, so 48 teams of two, maybe?"

Looking around the cabin, Goose noticed each set of seats was connected with a bit of distance between the next. Each group of two seats held two hikers. They just looked like hikers, he mused to himself. All of the seats were the same, tan seat, tan back, dark tan armrests. The area between the set of chairs looks like it held a small locker or cabinet on each side and the control center. Controlling the privacy screen and the tv station.

"Teams of two? I thought these were solo hikes." Goose said.

Belle replied, "We hike alone. But we are connected to another hiker through the comm implant in the event shit goes sideways. Someone needs to know where to collect our remains."

"A bit morbid, Belle, but I understand. So I will be connected to someone on this plane. We can have conversations as needed while we maintain a geo-lock on each other for safety."

"Yep, and it will last for the duration of the contract," Belle said matter-of-factly.

"Yea, speaking of which, when the contract expires, will they drop in wherever we are and pick us up? Not clear on that one."

"Actually, yes." She said. "As far as I know, our trailhead will be in a location where we can spend a couple of days with the hiker who has been there for 6-months; once they signal, a ship pops in, scoops them up, and we take over their heading. I heard everyone is going NOBO. They all started from the southern pole, and we are like the fourth or fifth set of hikers."

"Couldn't a planetary scan be easier, or at least faster?"

"Yes, they did that already, but after the last few worlds they tried to colonize and the problems the explorer teams encountered, they want to make damn certain this is a viable planet. Did you hear they are providing us with weapons too?"

"I did. Small plasma pellet pistol and a rifle of some kind. I hate loud noises...."

Belle laughed, "I take it you never fired a plasma weapon."

"Nope, you?"

"Actually, yes. I was a weapons instructor in the military for a couple of years. The pistol sounds like a cross between shooting a rubber band and blowing a spit wad through a straw. The rifle is noisy in comparison. Let's see, ever tossed a large rock into a lake and heard the plunk?"

"Yes," Goose replied.

"Well, not that much noise." She laughed again. "They chose weapons for us thinking about the weight and capabilities, which is the reason we have two weapons. Thankfully, they only provide two clips of 10 for each. The total weight, by the way, is just under 2.5 kilograms for both weapons. Lightest the military has to offer. The rifle, well, if you add a decent scope, it can be an effective sniper rifle. As for the pistol, it will stop anything smaller than a bear with one shot. Two shots if you are excited."

"I have no intention of killing a creature on this hike."

"Nor do I, but if it comes to him or me, I pick me every time." Belle paused a moment. "You need to know all about the weapons. I expect there are predators on the planet who will view us as a mobile meal.

He changed the subject since he realized that a mouse-sized mammal could be as deadly as a king cobra in your sleeping bag on a new planet. "The food, all I heard was they would airdrop us food every five days. Does that mean they will drop a hiker box in our path somewhere, and we need to watch for it or find it, or will they literally drop it on us when we need to restock?"

"You are new to this, aren't you?" Belle grinned broadly. "Essentially military combat rations, 15 packets, one meal per packet. About a thousand calories per meal, packed with nutrients, vitamins, minerals, and electrolytes. I asked for extra sports drink mix and extra coffee cubes, vanilla, of course."

"Don't those military things stop up the plumbing?" Goose asked, smiling.

Belle smiled, "Nope. Old wives tale. Best food in the quadrant." She reached into her pack and pulled out what looked like a small stick. "I brought a fishing pole since I plan to sample the local aquatic cuisine."

"What if it is poisonous?"

"The medical scanner will tell me that, and I'll simply toss it back in the water."

Goose looked at the rod, turned his head to the side like a puppy, wondering what his master was saying. "I am no fishing expert, but that rod seems to be a little shorter than I expected it would be."

Belle laughed, "It is a Tenkara rod. Kind of like fly fishing. Ancient Japanese style uses a collapsible rod and pre-attached fishing line, no reel, and a fly. I brought two in case I break one. A few fly's for each, but I have no clue what kind of bugs the local fishies like to dine upon, so I will make a choice when I get to the water and stir up some muck."

"What?"

"The local fish will eat whatever is in front of them, so when I get to the water, I'll stir up the local dirt and see what kind of water-based larva and bugs are there and see if one of my fly's will match. If not, maybe I will try to use live bait and see how that goes."

Goose looked directly at Belle and asked, "How long have you been hiking?"

"Most of my life. At 17, I joined the Planetary Defense and spent 11 years. During that 11 years, I managed to go through all sorts of survival training, like cold and freakin cold weather, hot and holy shit hot, water survival, and dessert survival. I am so happy we have the K-27 filter system."

"Yea, about that...."

"Let me guess; you never used one?"

Goose shook his head.

"This should all have been explained in the orientation."

"Orientation, yea.....about that; I never actually had orientation. I signed up yesterday afternoon." He looked at her. "I got off the trail a few months ago and went back to work to support my habit and wondered what was next for me. I wanted to do something important, like work for a gear company to make the gear better, safer, lighter, whatever. I was on a transport heading back from an interview at a gear company in Bend, Oregon, hoping they would sponsor me when this ad popped up across from me. **WE NEED EXPERIENCED TRAIL HIKERS,** it said. If you have at least 4,000 kilometers on the trail, your experience and expertise can enhance humanity's capabilities in the colony world services. I thought it was a great ad, besides I hated working in an office and wanted to be back outside; so I tapped the number and got connected to registration. 4,000 kilometers is a little more than the AT, which was my first thru-hike, and I did the PCT and CDT in a couple of years afterward. So I figured I was good."

He paused a moment, "They gave me the interview on the vid sitting in the public transport and told me there was a ticket waiting for me at the port. People around me thought I was crazy but told me to have fun and try not to die. I mentioned that was my first goal." He smiled at her, "That ticket took me to the Atlanta Space Port, where I was supposed to go through orientation and report back a few months to take my place on a team heading for the planet, whatever they call it. There was some confusion since I was supposed to be in the next group, 6-month from now."

He stopped talking and grinned, "I just realized I never told my boss I needed a leave of absence or that I quit. Guess he'll figure it out eventually. I may send him a note later if I want that job when I return, but who's kidding, who? I have no intention of being an office rat for the rest of my life. Anyway, the interviewer said that since several people had to back out from injury or getting married or something, I jumped to the head of the line by default. So I was dropped into this seat with about 20-minutes of orientation with a couple of dozen others. Signed a LOT of paperwork I never got the chance to read and agreed to do my best to not die on the trail. Remember, goal #1 and all!   They jabbed me with pointy things that removed a somewhat large amount of blood and deposited vaccines and devices in my body and under my skin." He rubbed the back of his neck like it still hurt.

Goose took a breath, "Well, I arrived at the Atlanta Spaceport, and they handed me this ticket to sit in this seat, and next thing I know, I'm sitting next to you reading the orientation manual, more of a pamphlet, really. You snore, by the way."

"I do not!! Well, maybe a little I hear from other hikers." She paused. "How long since take-off?"

"Well, you slept through launch, amazed me, by the way." He thought a moment, "I guess your military time lets you sleep pretty much anywhere. To answer your question, almost two hours since we left the Sol system."

"That puts us in black space now," Belle said.

The intercom erupted, "Standby for comm activation. You may experience a sharp twinge or disorientation, but it will pass quickly. A set of chimes and...

"AH!" Goose groaned.

"Holy shit, that hurt!" Belle said.

"No need to yell; I'm sitting right next to you."

"I didn't say a word." They looked at each other. "Can you hear me think?"

"Yes. This is weird!"

"It sure is...."

"Team 103. Are you both online?"

"Belle here."

"Goose here."

"Good, let's begin. I am controller 100. You can refer to me as 100 or controller...."

"Maybe C-Note?" Belle said.

"I like that. Hi there, C-Note!" Goose said.

"Good lord, I love hikers. You people are crazy."

They both said, **THANK YOU**, at the same time.

"The two of you are paired because Belle is the most experienced military survival trained contract hiker to date, and Goose, you are the least. Belle here will give you on-the-job training through the comm, and her primary goal is to keep you alive. You will be replacing a pair of hikers who ended up as a team because of the terrain. You will continue on their path and diverge when safe to do so—Belle to the right and Goose to the left. We are only now beginning to understand the compass of this planet and are in the process of setting up a series of positioning satellites to identify your location. It should be online in a few weeks, maybe a month."

Belle asked, "Who are these hikers?" she asked, "We may know them."

"They are Double Espresso and Belinda Goat."

Belle spoke up, "I know the Goat!"

"I know Double Espresso. We hiked the PCT for a spell. Always had coffee!"

"The Goat and I partnered up on the AT for a couple of weeks till I decided to take a zero......or three. But, man, can she climb!"

"You mean she can climb like a goat?"

They both laughed.

"OK then, you two will need to get 6 hours sleep. That will put you on schedule with planetary time where you will be hiking. Morning for you here is morning there. Once awake and after you eat breakfast, we will begin class, 16 hours of class. Another 8 hours of sleep, then 8 hours of class, and your education is complete. So, in about 40-hours or so, your education and orientation will conclude. We will be giving you information learned from the hikers you are replacing."

Goose asked, "So, how long till we reach the planet?"

"About 100 hours flight time, or 133 light-years if you need to know. We can sustain 1.5 light-years per hour but are a bit slower than that at the moment. So that gives you a couple of days to relax, hydrate, and eat whatever the hell you want. By the way, I know you brought clothing with you, but in the rear section of the plane, there are a lot of clothing racks in case you want to add to your ensemble."

"Did he just use the word ensemble in a sentence?" Belle asked.

"Yes, yes he did," Goose replied. "There may be hope for C-Note!"

Belle spoke, "You know, I can hear C-Note shaking his head at us."

"So can I."

"OK, OK, A few things you need to know. First, any personal gear you do not want to take with you can be left on the plane. There will be a storage bin assigned to you tomorrow morning. That bin will remain in orbit of the planet, and when you return, you can grab the contents on the way home. Also, any gear you use on the trail is – well, used. Therefore, it is yours if you want it. If not, we will just dump it. Old gear makes a beautiful display as it burns up in the atmosphere."

He took a very audible breath signifying something important, "There is an apex predator on the planet that has injured one hiker, so the weapons training, once you hit the dirt, will be of primary importance. Belle, it is your job to get Goose up to at least a minimum trainee level before the team you are replacing heads home. You will be issued additional ammo for this training. Fishing is available in the streams, and so far, no side effects from eating what you catch. Species similar to Earth are here; also, color is unique, though, and they have antlers or horns or something. All we ask is that before you eat it, take pictures. If you find a new species, we may name it after you if you are the first! If you gut a fish, please video the process, and if you want to send one back up to the ship in your supply pod, please do. We always need things to do to feel needed, and I enjoy eating fresh fish."

They laughed at that remark, "Food drops land weekly at sunrise or just after sunrise. As they fall, they emit a smoke trail so you can see and follow them to the ground. They should be less than half a kilometer from you when they land, normally within 50 or so meters. When they enter the atmosphere, there will be a tone in your comms unit. Can't miss it." C-Note paused, "Weekly on this planet is every 5-days. A day is counted by a sunrise. One day is 30 hours giving you more daylight than you are used to, by the way. This planet is more or less in equilibrium since it is not tilted on its axis but experiences all four seasons, just faster than you are used to."

C-Note took a drink of something, "By the way, the star here is closer than Sol but dimmer a bit. You should not notice any difference in the light it gives off, but it also has a much lower effect on the skin. The atmosphere is richer in oxygen than Earth, 31% compared to the 19% back home. The other 69% is inert. Though there are seasons because the planet does not orbit the star at the equator, it is roughly 45 degrees off the orbital plane."

C-Note took another drink of something, "Lastly, there are insects, but we discovered that all insects on this planet are averse to garlic for some odd reason, which is not native to the planet. Kinda odd but at the same time excellent for us mere humans. We suspect this garlic aversion is due partly to the base DNA of the inhabitants of this world. Therefore, you will receive ten garlic tabs in each food drop, and I suggest you start taking them now." A small cover opened in the console between them; it contained four capsules. "Here is your initial dose, take both now, then in the morning, take one, and so on; there is a water bottle in the cabinet next to you." They found the water, and each of them took the two tablets after popping them from a red blister packet with the words initial-dose printed on it. "Two a day is recommended, so breakfast and dinner. The last thing before you get some rest, I need to get the legal crap out of the way...."

C-Note cleared his throat and read from a script. We are not responsible..........held liable........reasonable......etc........

"….Therefore, you are performing this service to the Planetary Expedition Consortium of the Sol military of your own free will as a contractor. All information you gain or learn will be retained by PEC as the sole owner. The PEC will provide you all gear, food, shelter, transportation to and from, and all necessary advice on this contract. No rights are granted to those who make the discoveries."

There was a slight pause, and they knew C-Note was taking in some liquids.

"Great, that's always a fun-filled 10-minute read. Do you both agree?"

"YES," they both said.

"Questions?"

"Nope!"

"One last thing and I will leave you alone for the night; 15 minutes till lights out, by the way. The comm can be turned off; at least the transmit portion can be set to standby. This is to stop you from sending a dream to the one you're connected to, and if we need to speak to you, we can connect the comm from orbit since the receive side is always active. That also means if one or both of you are asleep, the other can wake you up if the need should arise."

He took a breath, "To put the system on standby, tap it three times, holding the third till it clicks. Same to restart it. You should hear a click in your head. Feels odd the first few times you do it, but you get used to the sensation. So give it a try now, off then on."

They did, and they both cringed at the feeling, "That was weird!" Finally, they both said, letting C-Note know they were both back online.

He continued, "The range on the system is limited to a max of 1000 kilometers. As you sleep, the upload takes place, and once you restart the system, a message will be heard if the upload was successful. Same for turning it on, and as it gets familiar with you, it becomes easier." A pause. "Questions?"

Silence.

"Good. Have a snack, hydrate, get some sleep, we will talk tomorrow."

"Not tired at the moment. I wanna go look at the clothes," Belle said.

"Me too!" Goose replied.

"Well, remember you need to get into the cycle with the planet. Talk to you in the morning." C-Note disconnected.

They stood at the same time and grabbed each other. The gravity on the ship is generated from the constant thrust, but it is anything but ordinary. Once they had their space legs, they walked over to the ladder. A sign said four floors down was the storage area.

DING

An elevator door opened next to them, and they both laughed, hopped in, and hit the button.

When the doors opened again, they were in a vast room. Backpacks, all the same, were hanging on one wall. Some already had names assigned to them. It took about 15 minutes, but they each found and adjusted a pack and hung their nameplate above their new backpack.

Goose walked over to a cabinet marked with the words original packs out of curiosity, and he found his pack with his stuff.

"I found my normal pack. There's are a few things in it I want to bring with me."

Belle searched the cabinet and finally found hers. She did the same.

They both looked over the clothing.

"You do realize this winter suit weighs a kilo. What are you thinking for a pre-food pack weight?" Goose asked. "I am thinking 14, maybe."

"A bit heavy, but I see your point. I was hoping to be around 9 or 10 at the most for a base weight. But in a way, we will be free to do as we please as long as we hike. Add the weight of the weaponry and any other gadgetry they may add, and 14 it is." Belle asked, "What special item are you bringing?"

Goose pulled a small black bag from his old pack. Opening the drawstrings, he removed the bag to show a partially rusted, burned, sooty, and dirty can.

"Is that a stove?" Belle asked.

"Yes, it is, my great-great-grandfathers to be exact. It is an original Solo Titan from sometime in the early 21st century. It burns whatever you put in it, boils water fast, and no need to carry any type of fuel either. All you need are twigs and such to feed it. I wonder if they have pinecones on the planet?"

Belle was in awe, she saw them in museums, and this one was in better condition than those, and it was still in use.

"The stove fits into the boiling pot, and all the little fire-starting things nestle in. It is great for cooking, great for just having a small fire to sit near, it is lightweight, burns wood efficiently, has no or very low smoke, and is made of solid steel. I think they called it stainless, but with all its use over more than a century, some stains give it character, and the big dent on the side was from my Dad."

"Gotta be a story in that one."

"Yes, there is, but let's save it for the trail."

Belle nodded. "So, what is the weight of that thing."

"Less than one kilo, and I need no other cooking items. That includes a long spoon, fork, spatula, fire-making items, and a small towel. Under normal circumstances, all I do in the 1.8-liter pot is boil water. "

"Very cool. I carry the autoTabs. Light them, and they burn for 30-minutes. I have a little prop I bring if I cannot find any rocks to mound up around the tab. What's the long spoon?"

Goose pulled a long, very long, handled spoon from a bag.

"Yes, that is one long spoon. I can see it will come in handy eating those military meals, keep the back of your hands clean."

"That too, yes it will." Goose smiled. "He pulled a second set out of the pack, "Here, take my backup. That way, the back of both our hands can remain clean." Belle laughed and accepted the gift.

"What's it made of?" She asked.

"Titanium. These are from my GrandDad or Dad's era. Used to have four sets, but two sets went to my cousin when she started hiking."

"What's her name?" Belle asked.

"Tundra. She is doing her first thru-hike of the AT right now. She did a few sections of the PCT and the Mountain to Sea trail in North Carolina."

"Don't know the name." she paused a moment, then added, "Titanium. They stopped using that metal decade ago." Then, finally, she smiled, "Goose, my friend, you are an anomaly, a true antique hiker anomaly."

"Thank You!" He said and stood up a little straighter.

Belle looked at the clock on the wall. "We got six and a half hours till class time. We can always stop back here and play with our packs after the classes are done."

They headed back to their seats and waited a minute for the elevator. The doors opened on the floor, stepping off and walking back around; they approached their seats and saw someone left a snack and a drink on the table they shared. Pretzels, chips, a Snickers bar with Almonds, a water bottle, a garlic tablet in a blister pack, and a soft drink. Sweet tea, actually, but decaf. "How thoughtful!" Belle said.

They sat and ate their snack, inhaled the tea, drank the water, and started feeling tired. Neither took the extra garlic; they put it into a pocket for safekeeping.

"I am getting tired," Goose said.

"Me too," Belle said. "Time to find a tree and get to sleep."

"Good idea. As I say, my coffee filter is full." He winked at her, and she winked back.

They walked around the cabin and found the restroom facilities. They have been on the plane for hours but had not eaten or drunk anything. It was that time, time to use a tree or, in this case, the restroom.

They each entered one of the 15 or so doors, and as they entered and the door closed, it locked itself; the room sensed someone was inside.

They left about the same time, but honestly, Goose waited for her to exit.

"Nice facility."

"Definitely. Toilet, shower, all the soaps and stuff you would need, a nice supply of towels. Maybe tomorrow I'll take a shower."

They returned to their seats and talked a few minutes about nothing in particular. Then, they both activated their privacy screen, and it cocooned them in their seat. The seat reclined and was very comfortable. The screen made it completely quiet, but without knowing it, they both set the background sound to a forest and fell asleep to the sound of crickets and a gentle wind rustling leaves and branches. The temperature could be set to anything you wanted, so they were comfortable, snug, and secure, and it was dark.

Both of them fell asleep fast.

Chapter Two

"Class time starts now," C-Note said. "Today, we will be learning about the animals - good and bad - on your section of the planet. For example, what is in the streams, and are there any plants you can eat? Also, how to use the medical scanner on a plant or animal you plan to consume, or on yourself, if you are not feeling well."

Goose spoke, "Why, good morning to you to C-Note. Yes, I slept very well; the chairs recline to the perfect sleeping angle. Breakfast, already done, and just WOW! That was some spread they put out for us this morning. Crewman Battery is an amazing cook or chef or whatever."

The Controller started laughing. "Sorry about that; I am not a small talk kinda guy. But you are right. An interpersonal relationship between you and myself is important to good communication during the mission."

Belle spoke, "Well said, C-Note. You make it sound so technical...." She looked at Goose, smiling.

"....I would classify it more clinical than technical," Goose said, smiling.

"You know, I think we're both right. Let's call it clinically technical..... or maybe technically clinical."

"OK, you two. I think you beat that dead horse enough. I get the point."

"So, what's on the agenda for today?" Belle asked.

C-Note cleared his throat. "Let's see. It's an easy day for sure. First, we need to review flora and fauna on the planet. And yes, Belle, including fish. Training in the medical scanner. Pack items."

"Excellent." She said.

"Are the two of you in your seats?"

"Yep."

A screen dropped out of the ceiling between their seats. Excellent visual, and the sound was perfect.

"That is amazing," Goose said.

"The sound is routed through your comms, as are everyone's on the plane, and they are getting this same briefing with the same collection of vids. No need to speak; I can hear you think. We need to talk about two specific creatures and two plants first. This," a still image appeared on the screen—a very clear and very frightening image. "....is what we designated as AP ALPHA. Short for Apex Predator Alpha. At the moment, we think this is the top of the food chain. It attacked a hiker and nearly cut him in two. He squeezed 6 shots from his pistol, and it finally slowed down and died. Granted, all of the shots were in the thing's head, and a couple of them hit its eyes."

"Reminds me of a blue Polar Bear," Belle said.

"Consider this a moment. This thing is so large that a full-grown polar bear could very well be the size of its cubs. And this is what we learned. This is a Daddy Bear protecting his family. The hiker made no sound walking, but the bear sniffed him out as an enemy. No idea why. It could be his fragrance, what he had for lunch, something he stepped in a few miles back. We have no clue." C-Note allowed that to sink in for a few minutes.

"OK, what we know. From the autopsy on the bear, we learned that it is a mammal, male, about a thousand kilo's, arms and legs about 5 meters long each. The only saving grace, it runs slow. About half the speed of a normal human, so add in some adrenalin, and you can outrun it; and from other contacts, we learned it gives up easily. We believe their normal food source is what we are calling AP Beta."

A new image appeared. "That thing is cute!" Belle said. Then it opened its mouth. "WHOA!!"

"Yea, whoa. Those teeth are not just sharp, but there are nearly a hundred of them in its mouth. Have you ever seen a spike tenderizer for steaks? You know, thump it, and it drives a bunch of little spikes in the meat. Well, think of this as a lot more of those. One bite would quite literally shred the meat from the area it sampled."

"Are you trying to scare us to not go?"

"Not at all. I am giving you the information you need to survive. My goal is to debrief you on this plane in 6 months."

"Got a question...."

"Shoot!"

"You said debrief us on this plane in 6-months. Does that mean you are currently on this plane in a forward section, and this plane will remain here until we depart, and if we need to talk to you, we can do so from the comfort of our sleeping bags?"

"Actually, yes. The day before the drop, we always hold a party. We will meet our people then. For some reason, just about all hikers give their controller a nickname...."

Belle cut him off, "Not a nickname, a trail name. You are C-Note to us."

"The best one I ever had!"

"What are some of the others?"

"I'll tell you in 6-months. But we do not stay on the plane. The atmosphere extends about 300k, the orbital norm for this planet, so I will be in a pod station with two other controllers for the next 6 months in a geostationary orbit centered over our 6 hikers but always in comm reach. It may be a small 3-bedroom apartment, but it is personalized. I sleep when you sleep, seriously, the first couple of days are a trip, but we will keep essentially the same schedule. My bedroom is the size of a large dumpster, but I will eat well, and there is a workout area I am required to utilize twice a day for 20 minutes."

"You'll be in zero-G for 6 months?" Goose asked.

"No, the three sleep areas and the workout area are arranged in such a way they rotate around a central hub, creating a form of gravity like on this plane. So, the outside of the circle is the floor."

"What if you have issues with your roommates."

"Not this trip, I expect. Just me and the other two are female."

"Sounds like good math!" Goose said as Belle punched him in the arm.

"It is designed this way. One male and two females in a team."

"You take your shot!" Belle said.

"Actually, before leaving Earth system, everyone got a one-year dose of the sterility vaccine. So, me, my roommates, you two, everyone. But, out here, pregnancy is not possible for that reason, nor desired and for a good reason."

"Understood." Belle winked at Goose, who opened his eyes a little wider, and she nearly fell off her chair laughing.

"Let's continue. Two plants to watch out for and easy to identify. Both are bright red, one has blue fringed leaves, and the other is all red. If you know what poison ivy looks like, the all-red plant looks similar." An image popped up. "Not as bad as poison ivy, but if you see it, stay clear." The picture changed, "The plant that's red and blue, however, reminds me most of a maple leaf but about the size of Kudzu. Both grow in a vine but have been seen as individual plants also."

He paused.

"What do these plants do, you may ask. The blue one has a caustic oil that melts human flesh. We're talking to completely melt your hand; you need to continuously rub it on the leaves for more than a week. But a brushing will sting for several hours. There is cream in the first aid kit. If you do need it, it neutralizes it pretty fast. The container is bright red for a good reason." He took a deep breath, "The all-red, well, the surface of the leaf is covered with barbed, spiked, and nasty little no-touch ums. They each, all of the spikes, deposit the venom, for lack of a better term, just under your skin then fall off. You have no idea they are there until it is too late. About 5 hours later, your skin inflames, pain, itch, burning, and possible infection. If you see you hit one, there are fast-release capsules in the kit to take; the capsules are bright red for a good reason. If you start to feel it happening to you, take three capsules and the red autopen as soon as possible. Contact me, and I will monitor your condition."

"You can monitor our condition from orbit?" Goose asked.

"Kinda. Pulse, O2 level, EEG as in, if you are awake, asleep, maybe dreaming once I see your numbers and get used to them. If you use the medical scanner, it pings the net, and I get a copy a few seconds later. Your scanners are coded to the three of us. Also, a general location is where the two of you come in as a team. Your comms are linked, so you will know how far away you are from each other within a meter and in what direction."

"You can't just see our location on the surface?" Belle asked.

"No, the crazy messed up magnetic fields of this place scramble the location encoding, but thankfully, surface to surface is not affected. We are hoping to get the Geopositioning system running soon, and it will link to your comms." He paused a heartbeat, "From that, we can get a bearing from your location and have a starting point for the search. If one needs help, the other is the safety hiker. If one dies, the other will know the exact location of the remains.

Silence for nearly a minute as they contemplated that statement.

"Let's press on."

For the next several hours, they learned about the medical scanner and each item in the first aid kit, the animals, the plants, and the known fish. It was the ones unknown that posed a threat, a danger.

"Last thing before lunch. I need the two of you to do a deep scan of each other. Full body. I need a baseline for your reading, please."

Belle had her scanner in her hand already, and Goose stood in front of her. She started at his head and went to his toes, lingering at his chest and stomach so the scanner can go a bit more in-depth. They switched places, and Goose used his scanner and scanned Belle. He enjoyed it, actually. He had a glimpse of the inside of her body, something no one had ever had before except maybe a doctor. He did linger at her chest a little longer than he needed, and she shook her head and grinned at him.

"Perfect. According to the reading, you both are healthy; heart, A1c, BP, blood chemistry, and a few other things I know as only letters are all in the normal range. Fine examples of a male and a female human." He clapped his hands, and it made them blink, "Time for lunch. I understand today is build your own sandwich day." C-Note said.

"What are you having?" Goose asked.

"Same as you. We eat and drink whatever you eat and drink." He paused a moment. "Let's dispense with this afternoon's session, and you two head to storage and set up your pack for the trail. We saw you chose a pack already, but if you could please set your pack up in your trail configuration, leaving space or location for food and water, that would be perfect. I would like you two to get what you need, and what you want, before rush hour. Then, when the bulk of the teams head down there, we can have our afternoon session, but let's try to avoid that zoo."

"Wait, question, can you see in real-time?" Goose asked.

"On the plane, yes. On the planet, no. On the plane, we are all on the network. On the planet is another story, at least not until the net is in place, and that's still about 5 months away, I do believe. Why?"

Goose spoke, "Well, a great time for us to get used to the camera. We will activate, and you can watch us set up our packs."

"Great idea. Give you the training to direct your camera at what you want or need me to see. Then, how about we just grab our lunch, and you two head to the hold to eat? Then, I can grab mine and get ready to watch TV."

"OK, 15 minutes."

Belle and Goose headed for the storage area, stopping first to make a couple of sandwiches each, piled on the meat and cheese and a few other things. Then, they each added a couple bags of chips, a liter of sports drink and headed down to the hold.

Grabbing the table nearest to their packs, they sat and started eating. "Turn on the camera and the comms." Belle said, touching both devices.

A few minutes later, almost one sandwich to be exact, C-Note joined in.

"I see Goose on Belle's camera and Belle on Goose's camera. The audio is perfect. I am going to record this so I can make up a report later."

"OK...."

"Very rare to see an initial setup. Make for some great reviews when we all get home."

They talked while they ate, and once done, Goose cleaned up the plates and tossed them into the recycler. Next, he moved the remainder of the drinks to the center of the table, so each takes an end to work on their pack.

They were not the only people in the hold; two other groups were far enough away, so none of them could hear each other. With almost 50 teams on the plane, only 3 units to be doing this seemed a bit odd. They started collecting clothing items and stopped, "C-Note, can you give us a weather report for the next couple weeks where we will be walking?"

"Sure thing." There was a pause. "Possible rain on 3 of the next 21 days and high temp around 15°C. Mostly sunny the first week. End of the second week, colder weather moves in. Possible rain, sleet, snow."

"Great. Perfect hiking weather the first week or so. So warmish clothes, rain protection, UV protection. That end of second week part, how cold?"

"Well, estimates are in the negative teens for a low. One forecast thinks a lot colder."

"Great, sunbath, then deep freeze," Goose said.

"Oh actually, UV is not an issue. The atmosphere filters near all UV light with the higher Oxygen level and more ozone at the higher altitudes, leaving it only visible. So, good sunglasses are needed. Go over to the wall next to the cabinets."

Belle and Goose walked there, and the wall popped open. "These are new for this trip. Grab a stylish pair and try them on." So they did, and they fit and felt great. "Let me activate, ok, uploading."

"A little green light appeared in the upper right."

"The little green light means message waiting. I can send you voice messages, text messages, or upload maps and other things to you. Even books if you want something to read. Look at each other; I uploaded the mission database."

They looked at each other. "Wow. Jaclyn 'BELLE' Reynolds, born....You just had a birthday, and it seems we share that day in common, down to the year: height, weight, favorite foods, allergies, and the works. There's a complete bio and the trail log. Did you know you have 18,241 kilometers under your belt? AT, PCT, CDT, Florida, and quite a few others."

"Pity, you have a mere 17,991. I WIN!"

"300 kilometers, wow, there's a huge span."

"It is Mr. Gilbert 'GOOSE' Gossling." She laughed. "Now I understand the trail name, GOOSE! We traveled a lot of the same paths, it appears."

"Now that you know about Goose, you'll need to tell me about Belle?"

"I'll save it for the campfire." She said and winked at him.

C-Note spoke again, "Now, for the real reason you have these. Look at something in the room. It will identify it. If it is unknown, it will perform a deep scan and may request you to do a medical scan of an animal or vegetable. A medical symbol will appear in the upper left corner if it needs you to do a scan. Keep the medical scanner easily accessible and the glasses either on your face or hanging around your neck. Now, look at the far side of the room, at one of the other teams. As you look at something, slide your finger from the back to the front of the left temple arm." That zoomed in to the person and displayed the bio of the person focused on.

"Cool," Belle said. "How far can we see?"

"No clue, but a lot. Slide your finger from the front to the back to pull back or tap the back three times to go to normal view. The right stem is the control. You saw the green dot; when you see that tap, the front joining, the hinge area."

"It says I have three messages."

"Slide your finger from front to back a little to scroll. Then, when you stop on a row and raise your finger, it will open."

They read or listen to, or watch the messages.

"OK, On and Off, and recharge," Goose asked.

"Easy stuff, Goose. On and off, when you put them on, they sense the comms implanted near your ear and activate, take them off, and they shut off. Their function is tied to the comm unit: recharging, they auto regen. Leave them in the case at night, and you are set for 36 hours of continuous use. 1 hour off equals 4 hours of run time. Night vision mode, infrared mode, link mode. In link mode, you can see what your partner is looking at. This way, when you are separate, you can share the experience to some extent."

"Now, grab a case and put them into your pack where you plan to carry them," C-Note said. "Tinder bundles. The cabinet marked 1."

They looked at the other teams, and both sets were looking at them, so they just got their glasses. Belle and Goose both waved like tourists. The other groups laughed and waved back.

Closest to the cabinet, Belle opened number 1 and grabbed two of a few things in the cupboard.

"In front of you are tinder bundles, sparkers, fold-up stoves, mess kit, and water boiling pot. We recommend boiling all your water to be safe even though the water appears safe to begin with. It is another planet, after all. 3 minutes, rolling boil. Let it cool before drinking. Pour it into the water bottle through the filter to remove sediment. You can make 2 liters of water at a time. The micro Lattice cup will hold everything. Total weight, less than 250 grams."

"OK, next up. Do you like the pad, bag, and tent?"

"I do, but I need something a little longer," Goose said; Belle agreed.

"Cabinet 4. Tent. Pick the blue one, my favorite. Weight is .87 kilograms: 2.2-meter square base, 1.5-meter center height. Contains built-in regen heat you can set; sorry, no AC. Controls are near the door, recharge is in sunlight. An hour a day will run the heat for the night. Stop for the night earlier than you would normally, and I do not recommend hiking at night anyway. That is the main rule. No night hiking. This way, you can always set it up and let it charge before sunset. Temp differential is ok, I guess. If the external is zero, it can keep the inside around 5°C. If the outside is -40°C, the inside max warmth is a toasty -20°C. Remember to set up early; it is not a race. It's a survey, be thorough. Besides, the tent is bright red, just the bag is blue. This particular tent survived a class 5 monsoon; it is extremely waterproof and self-sustaining. But it is not a submarine! Please keep that in mind."

"Gotcha," Goose replied.

"The bag should be good, it is several centimeters longer than you are tall, but the sleeping pad is another story. The team assembling the kits were not backpackers, let alone hikers. All they did was surf the net and pick the stuff that was pretty or cool looking. Gotta admit, though, the bag fits the bill just about perfectly, but the sleeping pad, well, open cabinet 5."

Belle was closest, she opened the cabinet, and as the door slid to the side, there were rolls of pads; each of them had a length below its cubby.

C-Note continued, "OK, first off, I used to hate a shorty pad; my legs would freeze in cold weather, so you each know your height, pick a pad several centimeters longer than you are tall."

They did, silently, and put the tent, pad, and bag on the table next to their pack. Since they were close to the same height, they both selected the longest sleeping pad available. It was several centimeters longer than they are tall, so they will be comfortable.

"A not about the sleeping bag. It has self-contained heat coils that are battery, as in power cell, powered. Any time a resupply is received, there will be a set of replacement power cells, and you can drop your old cells in the box for return. So if the outside is -40C and the inside of the tent is -20C, the bag should be able to compensate and give you a comfortable night's sleep." He paused.

"Rain gear."

"We selected a set last night," Belle replied.

"Good." The image went to his monitor. "Believe it or not, you picked what I was going to suggest." He paused a moment. "This is also what I suggest for a winter coat. Rating to -15°C but not recommended much colder. If it gets that cold, hunker down in your tent for safety. This planet has a COLD but short winter. Winter, the coldest section, is about two weeks, then it starts warming up again quickly."

He had a drink of something, "Let's recap. You picked a 70-liter pack in red, and it weighs in at 2-kilograms. I would suggest red because the animals on the planet know the red plants can cause pain, so you may be safer in a red tent and/or wearing the red pack. Speaking of the tent, the bag and pad together weigh about 3-kilograms. Therefore, the essentials total about 6-kilograms. With no heat activated in the bag and tent, you should be good to about -10°C as-is. With heat running, -30°C easy, maybe a bit more."

Belle and Goose put the items into their packs into the configuration they customarily used. Bag and pad in the lower section. The tent is in the left pocket and strapped to the backpack. They put their pillows inside the bag with the sleeping bag; they were the size of a fist when deflated. And weighed nearly nothing. They grabbed a scale and weighed the rain gear, 400 grams. At the same time, they went to their respective garment rack and picked two wool sweaters, one hooded. Next, they selected a pair of shorts, a pair of long pants, an extra set of sleeping clothes, 4 pairs of socks, with one pair reserved only for sleeping.

C-Note asked, "OK, why 4 pairs of socks?"

Belle replied, "A pair only for sleeping, a pair to wear, a pair in reserve in case my feet get wet, and the last pair to hang on the outside of the pack to dry if I rinse them out."

"Logical. You realize the raingear is also a -10°C cold suit. Zip it all up, and you can be somewhat comfy at -10°C."

"Good to know."

"By the way, there is a red dot on the left chest," C-Note added. "Press it, and it has a set of heating coils that will run for 8 hours off the battery pack. This is a standard power cell, so you will need to carry spares or not use them for 8 consecutive hours. I can send spares in the resupply when the weather warrants. So grab a few extra power cells; they are universal and weigh about 150 grams each, so grab a few."

After weighing everything, "My weight is up to 13-kilograms." Goose said.

"Mine is just a hair less than 13 kilograms; let's call it 13 also."

"First Aid Kit. In the red cabinet and you each get a pack. You can put it in your pack, strap it to the outside, or strap it to your thigh. Whichever way you want to carry it. On your leg, though, it will allow you to have fast access to the medical scanner inside the pack. We'll go over the scanner operation more in-depth in the next session."

"OK, hiking poles. I think you will both like the bright blue ones. Made of a new alloy, never broke one, and they can extend pretty far, 80cm to 200cm range. Since the tents are free-standing, no need to use the poles for anything but walking. I know you both have a favorite knife you carry, but there is a bright yellow one in drawer L."

Goose opened the drawer, "I like it!" He grabbed a couple and handed one to Belle.

"Perfect for making a fir stick or filleting a fish. Utility knife made of Nitinol 517 so you can reserve your personal knife for food; this way, you know it will not be contaminated if you use it to cut meat or fruit or veggies or something. Besides, it is a 25 cm blade, but it's sturdy enough to use as a hatchet. If you need to, find a large stick, and you can beat it through a tree with no blade damage and not lose its razor edge. You can wear it on the pack strap, designed to attach that way, so the butt of the knife pulls down. The sharpener is in the handle."

"Put it on the right strap, Goose." Belle said. "The left strap is where your pistol is going to go."

Goose asked, "OK, what the hell is Nitinol?"

"You may know it as the SM-100 process or the SM100 metal. Essentially, it is a 60 - 40 mix of nickel and titanium, 60 percent nickel, and 40 percent titanium. So strong that it holds an edge forever, takes weeks to sharpen but so worth it. Every hiker gets one because it will last forever. This knife costs more than most of your gear combined, but it is a safety factor we think is worth the cost."

"Cool!" Goose said.

C-Note continued. "Now, Belle, stopover at drawer J."

She opened the drawer, "Lights."

"OK, gear guy, which do you suggest?" She asked C-Note.

"Grab two orange pouches." So she did and handed one to Goose.

The number 300 was on the outside of the pouch. Opening them, they saw it contained 3 different lights: a headlamp, a tactical light, and a small lantern-type lamp.

"Let me explain. The headlamp can throw a strong beam nearly half a football field on the brightest setting, but the battery will last only a few hours. On the lower settings, you can get around 5-days. In your food drops, I will include fresh power cells. We designed the cells to fit everything that uses power cells. By the way, the total 300 is the weight, including a complete spare set of batteries for each light. Light is white, red, green, and blue with a variety of intensities. Rotate the knob to set the color, press it to change intensity. It always starts at the lowest level of red light since you will most likely be turning it on when it's dark, no need to blind you. The small lamp can be used as a reading light or pullup on the beam head, and it becomes a mini lantern, one light level, about 40 lumens. It is just a low-level torch that is perfect for inside the tent when looking in your pack. The battery will last about 100-hours of run time. If you need a new cell for it, let me know in your nightly report, and it will be in the next gear and food drop. Better yet, there is a box in the food drop containers; I will make certain a few power cells are always in there. Leave the old ones in the container, and we will clean up your trash." He paused, "The tactical light is another animal. One setting, Holy Shit **ON**!" He said with force. "Brighter than a star, but not as hot. You should get about 3-hours of continuous run time, and the throw of the light is a full kilometer. Next, the switch flips from white to infrared to ultraviolet. Use the glasses in night vision mode and turn the light on to the IR setting, and you are golden. White light is always the first in the rotation."

"Perfect for getting away from a nocturnal critter, too," Belle said. "That beam will blind them for sure!"

"Maybe, but always remember you have the pistol. Although it is a last resort, please do not simply dismiss its use. If you do dispatch a creature, it will be extracted within a couple of hours. The plasma round sets off a tell-tale ping locator in the monitor satellites. The tactical light also has a 40-Watt laser, which you can use for location at night, shine it into the sky, and if you are being searched for, they can follow the green beam to the end, which is where you will be resting. Will also start a fire in a minute or two. Use the tinder I gave you."

"C-Note, I understand the need to be weapons-capable, but I also know there are alternatives. The creatures in this world have been here forever. We are the aliens, the invaders. We are the conquerors. I hope to bring an understanding and peace and calm to this world rather than randomly exterminating the current inhabitants."

"Sounds like a plan, Belle, but please remember if it comes to you or him, please pick you."

Goose added, "That is exactly what she said to me yesterday. So I think it's all good, C-Note."

They packed their packs in trail configuration, leaving space for food and water. "Oh, one last thing. The light blue packet - grab 2 each. In the event you need a drink, it is a filter straw. Stick the red end in the water and suck on the green end; Green Good – Red Bad." He laughed at his joke. "For bottle quantity, use the FlowKleen 27. Lightest and easiest to use. It will filter a liter in a couple of minutes. I recommend you each take 2 water bottles, 1.5-liter each, and drink at least that much water a day." He smirked through the comm, "Besides, it is a great way to verify you are not dehydrated." He chuckled, "Do you need a urine color card?"

"NO!" Belle said in reply.

"What's left?" Goose asked.

"For tonight, nothing. Your pack is packed and ready for the day after tomorrow. When you return to your seats, there is some paperwork, food items, likes, and dislikes mostly. I will keep you gastronomically entertained. Who knows, maybe some candy once in a while, ice cream if I can think of a way to transport it to you." They closed their packs and hung them up on their hooks next to each other.

C-Note said to both of them, "OK, let's review.

1) Navigation is taken care of
2) Sun protection is not needed
3) First Aid
4) Knife
5) Shelter/sleep
6) Fire
7) Clothing
8) Food
9) Water
10) Lights

You are set. Open cabinet Z please, the code is 12345."

"Really?"

"Yep, that is the code it came with, and we left it." The wall opened, and it revealed many pouches, backpack meals, boil water and eat. "Pick 7 days' worth of food, and yes, you can mix and match. Always, always carry extra food if possible. Resupply is every 5-days, so you should always have an extra 6 or so meals on you."

For the next half hour, they selected 21 meals, 3 per day for 7 days, and a few to use as walking snacks.

"Oatmeal, cool. I like to soak it and eat it cold," Goose said.

"Not me; I like it piping hot with cinnamon and sugar and butter."

As they selected meal choices, they put the meals into a waterproof bag. The dry bag will protect them in the event of wet weather but also served another purpose. It kept everything in one place. Food, utensils, condiments, and like items were all in the same place. Meaning one single location when it came time to eat or hang the bear bag.

C-Note said, "Pull open the drawer on the left." So she did and found small packets of Ghee, clarified butter, very flavorful. Next to it were packets of cinnamon and sugar, hot sauce, and other food enhancements, condiments, and additives.

"Goose, you like coffee, right." She grabbed a box of coffee cubes and tossed him one. "I figured you for an espresso guy." She also took a box for herself and a box of decaf black tea for something warm at night but will not keep you awake.

"You figured right. These are my favorite!"

"Cabinet K contains a mess kit and small pot/fry pan. Perfect to pan fry up some fish. Grab a handful of Ghee butter, and you are set. I think there are packets of lemon there also." He paused a moment and added, "I was very worried you would pack your fears. You know, just in case I need it. Never a good sign. Use what you have, have what you use. If something goes unused a few weeks, toss it in the box when you pick up a drop. I am adding the new alloy multitool also, just in case. It weighs 100 grams, so no big deal. As I said, it is not a race; it is a survey. The goal is not to get to the end; the goal is to not die. So be smart, be safe, perform the survey and if you think about it, have fun."

They all laughed.

"OK, now the personals. Belle, head to the white cabinet, Goose to the black."

They opened the cabinets, and it was proper gender-related toiletries. They each selected a toothbrush and powder, hand/face cloths and people soap, antibacterial wipes, a couple of towels. They each also picked up a packet of clothes soap, so 6 laundry days were taken care of in the packet. Belle thought about it and realized she did not need feminine products thanks to the shot she got on Earth, but she put a couple of items in there just in case; if worse came to worse, they could be used for severe bleeding wounds. She laughed to herself at that, but she did add an extra packet of wipes and several waterproof, airtight zip-top bags to put it all in and a small shovel and toilet paper.

Goose grabbed the shovel and paper also along with the soap and wipes, but he also grabbed an electric razor that was out of his price range back home. It should last him a decade. Uses the same power cells as everything else, but he figured one cell should last three months.

"I know it does not need to be said, but I am required to say it. The latrine shovel never comes into contact with 'the stuff.' As such, the paper is 100% biodegradable and can be dropped into the cat hole. A new pack of paper will be in each food drop.

OK, so you both remembered to add underwear, t-shirts, extra sox, your boots, winter weight long underwear, and a pair of moccasins for around camp? Also, I suggest a zero once in a while, double zero if needed. If you find a nice place, stay an extra day and rest." He paused, "I hear from other controllers there is an odd weather cycle. Winter hits fast, and it hits hard. There are a couple of weeks when it is dangerous to hike, so hunker down, set up the tents in a shelter of some kind and stay safe. You have everything else you may need. In the paperwork, you will see in a bit is reading preferences. Let me know, and I can send you books in the upload; you can lay in your bag, put on the sunglasses, and read. Previous groups did not have this tech, so your group is the first to use them. By the way, the glasses are the display, the comm unit is the computer. Together they give you a lot of interesting tech."

They hurried and collected what they missed. The additional items weighed only a kilo or two, so not too bad.

"OK, stuff everything into your pack, add three of the black blocks. They will simulate 3 liters of water." They did. "Now, weigh your packs on the hook hanging from the ceiling."

Belle walked to the hook and hung her pack. 18 kilograms. "I can live with that!" She spoke.

Goose did the same, 21 kilograms. "Acceptable!" He said to no one in particular.

"Now, the others will be here shortly; clean everything up and close all the doors. Hang your packs back on their designated hooks. Did you remove the black blocks?"

"We did," Belle said.

"OK then, tomorrow is an easy day for you. We will go over protocols, talk more in-depth about the medical scanner, review the reporting features, review the toys implanted in and on you, and watch some low-level, 50-kilometer altitude, drone footage of the path you will most likely take. Belle, you will break off in a few weeks and head on your path, and Goose will just press on. From what we can determine, you will never be more than 100 kilometers from each other. Yes, far away, but close at the same time. If one of you gets sick or hurt, contact the other immediately. Upload a report, and I will get it pretty fast. If medical professionals are needed, we can have someone there in less than 90-minutes. Now, go do your menus and relax. I left something on your seat."

He was gone, leaving them alone in their heads and the room.

"Elevator or ladder?" Goose asked.

"Elevator!" and she pressed the button.

Chapter Three

Returning to their seats, they found a small box with their name on it. They opened the box and found an icy cold beer, a tiny bottle of tequila, salt, and a wedge of lime; also a sampling of chips, nuts, and pretzels.

Belle rubbed the lime on her hand, sprinkled it with salt, and covered that spot with her mouth. Then, opening the bottle, she drank the entirety in one sampling. It was a single shot bottle, after all.

Goose watched her smiling and put the lime in his mouth, covering it with his lips. He looked at Belle and waited for her to look back at him. When she did, he smiled, and all she saw was the lime. She shook her head and smiled at him.

Removing the lime from his mouth, now just the rind remaining, he opened the bottle and drank it down.

They both opened the beer and tapped them together.

"To the hike!" They said at the same time. Then, they took a long sip and looked at the snacks.

They found a datapad under the box of snacks, and when activated, it was the menu selection, allergy information, likes and dislikes for food and drink, reading preferences, and a note from C-Note.

It was a gold 100-credit bill he made and printed for them. Written on the back was, "TAKE ME WITH YOU!"

"OK, let's see. What foods do I not like?" Goose said out loud.

Belle laughed and replied, "Anything that tastes good, I suspect."

"Oh Ha Ha..." Goose replied, then added, "Let's see, favorite food. Uh...Peanut butter and liver sandwich with onions."

Belle laughed out loud. They chatted a bit as they hit new and interesting questions. Finding they had a lot in common. Reading materials, vids, foods, and drinks, to name a few.

They had been in the cargo hold for a bit more than two and a half hours, so a large group will take 3 or so hours, maybe longer. They also learned that each seating section was divided into 4 with their specific area, so no more than 25 people were in a single cargo hold.

That is the reason Belle commented she counted only 13 tables in the room. They were both glad they were not mixed into that cluster fuck. "25 people all heading to the same cabinet or drawer at the same time; C-Note did us right."

"Sure did. HEY C-NOTE, you still there?"

A moment later. "I am back on. What's up?"

"The other two teams who were in the hold with us, can I assume they were with the two other pieces of your triad?"

"Good guess, and yes. We talked about it yesterday and decided to do it this way. These two teams or the two tracks on your left and right. We got better and quality time with you compared to the mass hysteria happening at the moment."

"Nice, you three did us right by setting us up early. I bet it is a real orgy down there."

"Well, not really; an orgy would be fun. This, well, is a cluster fuck!" They all laughed, "Gotta run, paperwork to do for your weapons and a few other things."

"OK, we need to finish up the forms."

"Later, dudes!"

Finishing up the menu survey and other stuff took nearly 90-minutes. So, it was a tad early, best he could figure about 8 pm or so, but he was getting tired.

"I wanna meet C-Notes roommates hikers," Belle said.

Goose did not say a word, just nodded and stood. They walked around the plane and found three women and one man talking near the café, so they stopped.

"Since the six of us are the only teams on this floor, and since I remember the four of you from the gear room, can I assume your controller said to dispense with the afternoon classes and go set up your pack?" Belle asked.

"Good guess," the guy said.

"OK, Names!" Goose pointed to Belle, "This is Belle. I'm Goose...."

"I'm Flambe; this is Chisel, Reena, and Toonist."

They all shook hands, a few hugs. Then, Belle asked, "What did you name your controller?"

The four shook their heads, "They said to call them controller, so...."

"Well," Goose started, "Ours is controller 100, and we named him C-Note."

Reena said, "Our controller...." Then, pointing to Toonist, "....is controller 111, so maybe Trip?"

Toonist voiced up, "No, Triple One!" They both nodded in agreement, and all of them looked at the last two.

Flambe spoke, "Our controller is 105; what can we make of it."

"Is there something special about her?" Belle asked.

"How did you know our controller was a woman?" Chisel asked.

"Well, C-note told us he will be roommates with two female controllers for the next 6-months. And since C-Note is a male, it stands to reason both of your controllers are female.

"Let's see, I know she likes to fish a lot. Her favorite food and hobby." Chisel said.

Flambe said, "Bass Master?"

"Revelation!!" Chisel said, and they all nodded. "Bass Master it is!"

"Now, let's see if our controllers are still awake. Here's what we can do. Let's all get online, and each of us looks at the other teams, so when they start vid on their end, all of us will be on screen waving to them."

"I love you, Belle; you are devious!" Chisel said.

"Just think, she and I are a team." Goose said, "This is going to be interesting."

At the same time, they all started their comms, their respective controllers all came online, then they all began their vids.

"This has Belle written all over it," C-Note said.

Goose nodded. "Any way to make this a party line for you three and us six," Goose asked.

"Give us a minute," C-Note said. After a minute, all nine of them could hear each other.

Belle started, "Yea, well, we were discussing C-Note, and these other teams wanted to know who that was, so we explained C-Note is our controller, we named him...."

Goose took over, "Now, understand these poor other teams wanted a real controller, one with an appropriate name and not 111 or 105."

The three controllers chuckled.

"Well, we came up with an appropriate name for you 105...." Chisel nodded to Flambe.

"You are now and forever named Bass Master," Flambe said.

"So...." Toonist started, "We have a name for you too. 111, or one-eleven or a hundred and eleven is sooooo boring. Therefore...."

Reena finished, "We named you Triple One."

"So there. You all have names, and tomorrow night we expect to see the appropriate name tags worn!" Belle finished.

The nine of them all chatted for about 20 minutes. Finally, triple One said, "They are just about finished in the hold, so may I suggest you six hit the shower and catch some Z's."

"Good thought; I need to hit the hay. I am exhausted for some reason."

"Me too." They all said, "But a shower first is perfect, then sleep."

"Great idea." Belle and Goose left their triad group but heard the rest of the teams returning.

Chisel yelled as they all started to disperse, "The last one to Katahdin wins!!"

"Exactly." They all yelled back.

Goose added, "H-Y-O-H!"

Toonist said, "Hike Your Own Hike, my friends."

The other 4 also took showers. These six hikers would be the first in line to get ready for bed tonight. There was a fresher unit in the shower room. Pop your clothing in there for 15 minutes or so while you are showering and, although it is not completely clean, it is the next best thing.

They all knew from experience the showers on the plane had all the soaps and towels they needed and a toothbrush for single-use, so they headed for the center section and into the shower rooms. Entering the room, they locked their respective door, so it displayed OCCUPIED on the outside. The toothbrush and powder tasted good, and the shower felt excellent. Fragranced soap and shampoo. Used the facilities and put the towels in the wall bin. Donning the refreshed clothing, they made the room ready for the next person. There were even mini deodorants, and although Belle does not use them on a hike, she used them today and loved them.

Belle left the room after Goose and returned to her seat, where Goose already had the privacy screen around him. She saw the light of the vid around the edges, so he was most likely watching something on the vid and using the earphones for the sound, privacy mode. She did the same and flipped on the news channel.

All of a sudden, she got a wave of anxiety, fear, apprehension. Did she want to do this scary thing!

She opened her privacy screen, and Goose was looking at her; his earphones were off.

"Are you OK?" He asked.

"Why?"

"You were shaking so much I felt it through the seat." Since the seats are set as two's, the next set of two seats was 50 centimeters away, so the dual seat system, they figured out, meant each set of chairs was a team; this way, the controller can easily teach the classes needed. In addition, the screen would drop between the seats so both team members can see it clearly and not disrupt the others.

"I got scared for what we are about to do. Like I was going to die here. The weirdest feeling I have ever had, and so real." He held her hand. She looked at it a moment then decided she did not mind. "I can hike a trail at night in bear country with a light that needs new batteries while eating a PB&J and not feel scared. But this is different. This is another world. I have no frame of reference here!" He held her hand gently but firmly, patting the top of it with his other hand.

"Whatever happens, we are in it together till the end. So I expect to be sitting here with you telling tall tales on the flight home."

You could see she was feeling better and started to relax, "What are you watching?"

"Music vids mostly. Found a channel of comedy shows, wanna watch one together?"

"Yes, please." She replied.

He connected his vid system to hers, so it played on both screens at the same time. Goose set the privacy screens to merge so both seats would be encompassed by the screen. She felt better just seeing him there. She reached out and held his hand. He would hold her hand as long as she needed; she was beginning to feel better. This may just be a good arrangement, she thought. He is caring and empathetic. She likes that. She feels safe again. She felt cared about, something she has not felt in a long time. The upside and downside are that she did not know it was missing until this moment.

While they slept, the vid realized it was not being watched and turned itself off. After a while, they let go of each other's hand, but it was a while after they had fallen asleep. They dreamed of hiking together. True friends, maybe more. But it was not that kind of a dream.

It was a dream of reality. It was a dream of truth, truth to oneself. Truth to those you care about. It was wonderful. In their dreams, lying on those seats on a plane heading for a distant world, they were both smiling and happy. They were content.

~~~~~~~~~~

Belle opened her eyes and retracted her privacy screen. The hustle and bustle of the day jarred her into reality. The compartment's volume level was loud compared to being asleep, surrounded by a noise and light blocking privacy screen. She tapped the button to put her seat upright, in the sitting position, and as she did, the smell of breakfast permeated her nose.

As she sat up and got her bearing, Goose returned to his seat with a breakfast sandwich and a large cup of coffee. "Good morning, Sunshine." He said to here.

"What time is it?"

"No clue, no clocks, remember. I woke up, was hungry, smelled coffee, and found this lovely breakfast package in the café. You may want to head that way yourself."

"First, a nature stop. Then coffee and food."

She returned a few minutes later with two coffees and a bowl. "Open your mouth," he did, and she shoveled in a large spoon of cinnamon sugar oatmeal with raisins leaving her spoon in his mouth. "So, what do you think?"

"Well, you were right. It's not terrible." He grabbed another spoonful as she playfully pulled the bowl away. "OK, I like it." He said to her.

"This is another black coffee for you. I already had an iced coffee in the café. Sucked that bad boy down without a breath. But, man, it hit the spot this morning. This is a hot coffee with vanilla cream, so we each have two in preparation for today's education."

"I may go get another!"

He stood and walked to the café. He passed by several of the other teams, a few he realized looked a little familiar, so they most likely met on a trail somewhere.

Every seat looked the same. Every set of hikers looked pretty much the same. Finally, he stopped at one group and looked at them. Two men, he realized, looked more familiar than any of the others. He thought about it a moment, and they looked at him.

"GOOSE!" One of the men, the darker one, said.

Goose had started walking away, but when he heard his name, he stopped dead and turned around, "Ace of Spades! It took a moment to remember your face. You're a little darker, let me guess. You finally went and hiked around the Med like you talked about."

"Good memory, and yes, I did. This is Ace of Clubs, my husband. We met on the trail a few years ago and just finished the Med together as a honeymoon."

"That's one hell of a honeymoon, what, 5 months on the trail?"

"About that. But it was worth it. I learned a lot on the trail, and besides, like you kept telling me, you'll hike far enough to meet yourself one day when you're hiking. Did you ever get to meet yourself, Goose?"

"I did, not ideal conditions, but we had a long talk, and it cleared up a lot of things." Then, he looked around, "I need to head to the café and get a coffee for my partner and me before class."

"Who's your partner?"

"Belle."

"Heard the name on the trails, but we never met." He extended his hand, but Goose gave him a hug.

"Nice to see you Ace, or maybe Ace's." He extended his hand as Ace of Club's, and they said their goodbyes.

Goose headed to the café to grab a third coffee. Without thinking, he asked through the comms if Belle wanted anything else. She replied another cheese danish, so he grabbed a couple and some napkins and headed back to their area. He did have the oatmeal while waiting for his coffee. It was a big bowl with butter, cinnamon, sugar, and raisins. He hates raisins, but in the oatmeal, it is pretty good. He saw someone adding granola, and as he had a spoonful left, he added a sprinkling. Meh! He thought to himself. He tossed the empty bowl in the trash and headed back to his seat.

Handing her the danish, he sat. "Had a bowl of oatmeal in the café, Belle style, I added raisins, cinnamon, sugar, and butter: even tried a little granola. It was delicious."

"Granola, huh. WhatCha think?" Belle asked him.

"Meh!" He replied.

As if on cue, C-Note popped in. "That was nice last night. The girls appreciated it, as did I. I know you two were the ring leaders of that communal activity."

"Well, I figure there may be times when you are not available, and one of your roommates may need to talk to us, so hey, let's get to know each other. By the way, what do they look like?"

"An ogre and a troll," C-Note said.

Belle started laughing, "Oh poor C-Note, his roommates cut him into little pieces and tossed him into space when they heard what he said about them."

"If you ever tell them I said that…..."

"Our secret, but it now means you need to be nice to us," Goose said.

"So, is blackmail just a hobby or a way for you two."

"We'll let you know in 6-months," Goose replied.

"Touché!"

"So, what's on today's agenda?" Belle asked.

"I think we can finish it all up before the party, big dinner and all. You were in the hold and noticed 13 tables, one per team. As we speak, the tables in the hold are being arranged into a triad—three controllers in the center and the six hikers on the outside. We are being served meals developed from the list we filled out of our likes and dislikes. So no, no one but the galley crew has any idea what anyone is eating. During the meal, the nine of us will all be linked to talk without screaming at each other. Most of the ship's crew, and the resupply teams, will attend also; they will be interspersed with the teams. And before you ask, I have no idea who we are eating with."

Belle asked, "So what do you know?"

"That you will be dining with the best people on the ship this evening."

"Agreed!" Both Belle and Goose said to him.

"Now, I need to educate you …. PEOPLE …. HIKERS …. Whatever!" He loudly inhaled, "First on the list is a tour of the medical scanner and the first aid pouch." It was already on the screen between their seat as it lowered into place.

"Look at the pretty lights!" Belle said.

Goose added, "OOOOOOOO…...AAAHHHHHHHHH"

C-Note said, "Good lord!"

~~~~~~~~~~

Belle and Goose exited the elevator and saw someone waving at them. It had to be C-Note since they noticed his **PROPER** nametag. He introduced the ladies, Triple One and Bass Master. Chisel and Flambe were already there, and a moment later,

Reena and Toonist walked into the room after climbing down the ladder.

They all hugged, not communal, but a heartfelt 'I care about you' hug. Then, the lights flickered, and the room quieted; the ship's captain appeared on a HUGE screen.

"Teams – today is your final dinner with us. Tomorrow you can check, double-check, and reset whatever you need to prep your pack. Then, just before the next planetary sunrise for your track, you will be dropped off. Some of you leave in 19 hours, some of you a bit later. You know who you are. For the past few days, you have been living close to the same schedule as those you are replacing, more or less. Kinda interesting as to how you are getting down to the surface, and we wait till RIGHT NOW to tell you. Does anyone in this room have experience or know what a drop ship is?"

Belle and three others raised their hand as she spoke under her breath to her triad. "Good lord!" Goose looked at her side-eyed, as did the other two teams and the controllers. "Just wait," She said through the comm connection. Since they were talking through the comms, no one else heard her.

"Those four must be former military and most likely have taken a fair bit of survival training. Let me explain." The screen changed to a small box, 3 by 4 by 5 meters, with four seats located in the center. One wall had cargo mesh, and an opposite corner had a locker.

Belle spoke to her triad members, "Squad of 4 straps in with all gear stowed securely under the cargo mesh, weapons stored in the lockers. Strap in tight, hold on, try not to toss your cookies." She said to everyone she was connected to. They all looked incredulous at the idea of falling 250 kilometers, then trusting the motors to land you softly on the ground.

The Captain began, "This is a Drop Ship.", He paused for a dramatic flair, "They are used to deploy a squad of 4, all their gear and weapons quickly and easily to a pinpoint location in a record time." The video of 4 people entering, stowing their weapons and gear, strapping in, played on the big screen. "Once secured, they ensure the craft is airtight, and they are ready to drop; the pod does just what you think, it drops off the mother ship and falls into the atmosphere where several minutes later, 4-minutes, in this case, it touches down softly on the surface of the planet." He said that with a smile. "We are at 300 kilometers above the surface when you drop; it will take you four minutes to touch down. The last 45 seconds are the most fun. Landing rockets fire and slow you to touchdown."

Belle had her elbows on the table, holding her head in her hands.

"Where are my four experts? Please stand." The Captain said.

They all stood, he pointed to each, in turn, starting at the far left of the room, most distant from the entrance area, "Number of Drops?" The Captain pointed to the woman first.

She said, "4, Captain." She said with pride. The second guy said 6, the third guy said 3, then he asked Belle.

"I made 12 drops Captain, 11 successful." She replied.

"What happened on the unsuccessful drop?" The Captain asked as if he already knew.

"It was a night drop, and the light-R failed. We hit rather hard and rolled onto our door. It took us 3 hours to get out, but I have to say, there were no injuries."

"May I ask how you extricated the pod if it was lying on the door?"

"That was my idea and a lot of fun. Always wanted to try it too. The pod had a ton of extra ammo for the rifle, and plasma is an efficient digging tool. So we donned our breathing gear and shot a tunnel, or rather burned a tunnel, straight down and out of the pod."

"Creative! What did your CO say about the misuse of his ammo?"

"The 4 of us expended almost 200 rounds, two clips each; we took turns because of the heat in the tunnel." She grinned, "Let's just say the Colonel did not appreciate it. Nevertheless, all 4 of us received a commendation when we made it to the rally point. We got there first, by the way."

"Can I assume you are Master Sergeant Jaclyn Reynolds?"

"Yes, sir, how did you know that?"

"I am the general that authorized and signed those commendations for your Colonel; I believe his name was Renk."

"Yes, sir, it was….is."

"Who is the other half of your hiking team?"

"That would be me, Captain; the name is Goose. Belle's partner."

"Well, Goose, if Belle is your partner, I know I will see you in 6-months. And trust these words, hold on because it is going to be a wild ride."

The room erupted in laughter, cheers, and applause. The captain explained a few things, but C-Note had already briefed them on it, so Belle sat there contemplating another drop. Not her favorite pastime, but not the worst way to get there either. After a few minutes, the crew members joined the Captain. He introduced the crew, spoke about their commitment to the mission and to the hikers.

The crew dispersed across the room and sat in the three empty seats around the triads. The Captain approached their triad, "Ladies and Gentlemen, I am Captain Robert Marless. Crewman Maria Wills and Lieutenant Victor Marchetti are both from resupply, and by chance, they are responsible for ensuring you eat for the next 6-months. You can call me the G-

MAN. I got that name from the first set of hikers about 2 years ago, and I like it."

He looked around the tables, "I see the controllers have been properly tagged. C-Note, Triple One, and Bass Master. I like it!"

A moment later, the crewman, Lieutenant, and Captain joined them on their channel. "Now we can chat properly!"

Goose spoke, "Crewman, Lieutenant. May I say you are my favorite people for the next half year."

Maria looked at Victor, "Lieutenant, I believe he wants something?" She paused, "I believe you are correct. Should we find out what special items he wants?"

The Lieutenant said, "We were told not to make eye contact; it makes the animals restless."

Maria looked at Goose, "OK, Goose, what is it you are looking for to be added special to your snack pack?"

Goose grinned from ear to ear, "Orange liquor, brandy, single malt scotch, rum, vodka." He paused, "Take your pick, mix it up."

The other five hikers all nodded emphatically. Maria and Victor shook their heads, but they were chuckling.

"6 random bottles of 'something' every third or fourth drop." Victor looked at the Captain, "Sir, do you have anything to add?"

"I do. In Belle's drop, two months from now, I will add a bottle of champagne in honor of the anniversary of receiving that commendation. It needs to be cold."

"We can handle it, sir," Maria said. Victor winked at Belle.

"So, Belle, you sound like someone I may need to keep my eye on. We are always looking for talent to recruit as a controller." He looked at Goose, "You too, by the way. If she rubs off on you, you may end up being good." He looked at the three controllers, "Which is their controller?"

"I am Cap; they call me C-Note, controller #100. This is controller 105, known by her team as Bass Master, and this is controller 111, known by her team as Triple One."

"The fact you three have gotten to know your teams, and the other two teams in your...."

"We call it a triad, sir." Triple One added.

"Triad, I like that. Lieutenant, make a note to call the three-team groups a triad from now on. Let's everyone know you are a team, controller, and hikers."

"Sir, to that end, perhaps they can be referred to as Triad 100A, B, and C, for example."

"Excellent, Victor," He squinted his eye a little, "Are you bucking for a promotion?"

Victor smiled, "Maybe...... Sir!"

Chisel spoke up, "Captain, during our hike, is it possible for the six of us to be connected in the evenings, for a few hours around dinner time. We may be eating alone on a new planet in harsh conditions, but if I learn something significant, telling it to the others over dinner may protect them if they run into it also."

"Nice thought, we will explore it. If the teams agree, controllers connect them at dinner—the biggest rule on this planet, no night hiking. Too many drop-offs, and since there is no real moonlight, it is dark. I wanted to see for myself, and I am considering implementing this for all controllers, to spend 5 days dirt side so when you speak on a subject, you know what the hell you are talking about."

Toonist asked, "You camped a week on the planet, sir?"

"I did. Called it a vacation. Brought a few of the crew with me, 8 of us. We hit the southern pole during the summer and explored out about 15 kilometers in just about every direction you can think of, and it is a beautiful planet."

"What about the critter?" Reena asked.

"Blue Bears are annoying. Just as quick to eat you than to ignore you. Pistol round just below the eye will drop them instantly. Come to learn their brain is unique, and that is a kill shot that can save your life. Seriously, one solid swipe from a blue bear will kill a human. Their paw is just a little smaller than most human torso's, and they have claws." He was about to change the subject, but C-Note spoke up.

"Captain, I would enjoy a hike on the planet for a week to make me more credible to my team, but I would not want to do it alone. Mainly because, well, I know how to camp, but this is way more than next-level camping. Backcountry has nothing on this little trek. If I could go to the surface for 5 days, one of the ladies could take over my reporting duties. Then, when I return, one of them can do the same and so on."

"OK, Mr. Experiment. Done. Ladies take over his duties for the first week, and C-Note, you'll drop with your team. Team 103, your job is to keep your controller alive." He laughed. "If this works out, we can implement it next cycle. Triple One and Bass Master, figure out who are second and third, you will meet your team when C-Note returns."

"Since the first week is being dropped and hiking to the old team, then a flip flop back to the pod, I would get maybe 3 days in each direction."

The captain looked at the 6 hikers. "Teams, and controllers, in the morning, can you please set up controller 100 with everything he will need to survive the hike. I already know he is physically fit enough for the hike but is he ready for it."

C-Note shrugged and opened his arms. "OK, what the hell just happened?" C-Note asked.

Belle replied, "Well, C-Note, you popped your foot out of your mouth just long enough to say something that makes perfect sense; therefore, as a proof of concept, you are the guinea pig."

The captain applauded. "Master Sergeant Belle. You are so correct!"

C-Note just shook his head, and the ladies, the other two controllers, did not say a word. They were next, and they knew it. Thankfully, controllers are required to have a minimum of one thousand kilometers on the trails. So, at least they have a clue.

The food arrived, and Belle's plate was dropped off first. Fried catfish, hush puppies, corn casserole. The Captain's plate was dropped off at the same time, his plate looked just like Belle's, but instead of hush puppies, he had cornbread.

"Well, cap, looks like a fine choice. The cornbread looks good."

"Jalapeno cornbread actually, make you a deal, half the cornbread for half the hush puppies?"

"DEAL!!" They swapped their food and sat and waited for the others to be served.

The controllers all had the same thing. Breakfast for dinner; crispy hash browns, 3 strips of bacon, spicy sausage, caramelized onions and peppers on top, and three eggs, still very runny, sitting on top of it all. C-Note had an English Muffin, Bass Master had an Everything Bagel, and Triple One had Cinnamon raisin bread. All perfectly toasted and properly buttered crust to crust.

Reena asked, "Is that a standard controller meal or something?"

"Actually, no, it is just my favorite meal." Bass Master said.

"Mine too." The others added.

Goose received lasagna and a few sides, Reena got sushi, Toonist was excited when she got a colossal everything burger, and by a strange coincidence looked like what Chisel received. Flambe received her plate last; southern fried chicken, scalloped potatoes, corn casserole, and a wedge salad.

The captain spoke, "There is an in-depth psych eval done on controllers. They all need to be compatible, making sense they would have many of the same likes and dislikes. So they will be locked up together as roommates in a closet for the duration of your hikes." He looked at Flambe, "Tell me you got blue cheese dressing?"

"Yes, Captain, I did. With a drizzle of balsamic vinegar." Flambe asked. "Are all triads one male and two females?"

"Actually, yes. But it is organic and not by design. There are always 96 hikers on the planet. Therefore we need 48 controllers. At any given time, we will have 16 male controllers, and the remainder is female, so the ratio in a triad is always 2 to 1." The captain grinned. "Makes for an interesting half year, and for some, it develops a unique relationship. In the total time running these hikes, there has never been any negative occurrence. We match personalities, hobbies, attitudes, and several other factors, but I have to say, the thought of living in a closet with two women is not all that appealing to me. Their entire apartment will fit into this half of the holding area with more extra space if you can call it that. Besides, women can live with each other easier than men. However, put a man into a situation with two women; well, he will always be gracious and kind."

Toonist added, "What about, you know, the male and female dynamic?"

"Well, all controllers are adults, all controllers had a shot as you all did before leaving Earth system, and if they want to engage in recreational activities, well, it is good for the spirit, the soul, and the emotions. Not something we talk about, we know it happens, and it should. Nothing has ever gone wrong. A few hikes ago, we had a triad that married. I conducted the ceremony, and it was amazing. They married when their teams all made it back to the ship to stand up for them as witnesses. That was one hell of a party."

"Yes, sir, and we cleaned up after it for days. Unfortunately, my head still hurts from the hangover." Crewman Maria said.

"Maria is our events coordinator for the ship. These parties, a few other things. On your birthday, she sends you a gift in the resupply drop."

"Captain, this is a first. Belle and Goose share a birthday." Maria said.

"Good to know. Thank you." The Captain paused and ate some of his meal, "I will tell you that a few of the controllers reported by the end of the 6-months they just stopped wearing clothing. They can adjust the environment controls as they wish. Since most monitoring and reporting activities are written reports, they each have their own suite, desk, and computer system. There are no cameras in the apartment; it appears to just be easier for everyone. They interact with each other at their convenience. As you call them, most controller groups, or triads, make it a point to have the evening meal together. Cross-pollination of the information collected from their team."

The three controllers did not say a word.

Both women were knockouts, dark hair, brown eyes, well proportioned, and very evident, well-toned muscles and perfect physical condition. Their forms were flattering. C-Note was no different. He also had dark hair, but not as dark as the ladies, a medium brown with a few well-placed light streaks. He wore a somewhat tight shirt, as did all of them, but he also had on a light jacket with a logo of an outdoor store. His stomach appeared to be well-defined, thanks to his clothing. Although his muscles were not massive, they did, at the same time, seem a tad larger than an average person of his stature. All three of the controller were not as tall as Belle, who was roughly 185cm. But they were all maybe 178cm, give or take a couple.

Reena added, "A lot less laundry to do also!"
Everyone laughed at that thought.

"Where did you hear this?" Goose asked.

"At the end of the time frame, a 100-question survey is provided to all, hikers and controllers. Sex has about 11 questions, and it was anonymously reported that multiple teams were nude when working on reports or monitoring their teams. The dynamic survey further asked if being nude around the others created anxiety or a sense of security. All reported they felt comfortable, safe, and relaxed. No pretense, deep trust. So, all in all, the controllers can do whatever they damn well please as long as I get their reports on time each day. As I said, never been an issue."

The remainder of the meal was laced with conversations, and the captain asked Belle about her service. They had been to the same places, at different times, and through a lot of the same training. Knew some of the same people too. They also learned that Goose has never fired a weapon, so he will need to be instructed.

"Captain, has anyone ever needed to use the rifle on the planet?" Belle asked.

"To my knowledge, no. The pistol is usually all they needed; why?"

"I would like to not carry the rifle on this trip but rather carry a second pistol. Same for Goose. I can teach him to use the pistol easier than the rifle, and I feel the rifle, on this planet, is a bit of overkill."

The Captain thought about it a moment, "Well, if you feel it would be beneficial, then I authorize it."

"Since we are talking a close-range weapon, I do not expect to ever require a DMR," Belle said.

"I think you're right; I approve." The Captain said.

"Us too?" The other two teams voiced in.

Toonist asked, "What's a DMR?"

The captain replied, "A DMR is a Designated Marksman Rifle. A long-range weapon and Belle is correct. There is never a need to hit a target a kilometer or two away. Every instance of a weapon fired to date on the planet has been less than 15 meters. Average is 7 meters, so no more rifles for the teams is actually an outstanding thought."

"You mean a sniper rifle," Goose asked. Belle and the Captain both nodded.

Belle spoke, "Bulk and weight of the rifle vs. the pistol is a good trade-off. Additional clips are smaller, and we can carry extra and save more than a kilogram of weight and a ton of space in and on the pack. I propose a holster on your dominant thigh and on the opposite shoulder strap of the pack."

"Good thought," Victor said. "I will get the holsters to you in the morning, and you can all attach them to your pack strap when you set up C-Note for his trip."

"One holster for him, please. He's just a tourist." Goose said.

Everyone laughed, including C-Note.

Victor added, "So nine thigh holsters and six holsters for the left pack strap?" He thought a moment and asked, "Left or right-handed? If you are left-handed, please raise your hand."

There were two lefty's, C-Note and Bass Master. "Excellent, that makes my job easier."

Dessert was served, chocolate-chocolate chip cake with chocolate buttercream frosting appeared at the table with a nice cup of the best-tasting coffee.

After they had their dessert, the crew members left the table and disconnected from their channel.

"So, C-Note, ever been on a drop-ship ride." The look on his face told the story. "That would be a no." Belle laughed.

"Well, let's all meet here tomorrow morning and find him what he needs for his adventure." Bass Master said to the group.

They all disconnected and went back to their standard comms. The party was beginning to break up.

The three controllers left together and went into the elevator, and were gone. The six hikers sat at the table for a while and got to know each other better.

Chapter Four

All six hikers in the triad, and all three controllers, were standing in the cargo hold. Belle pulled out the note she received from her controller, "Did you all see this?" She showed them all the gold notecards he gave them. When they flipped it over, they saw it said, 'TAKE ME WITH YOU!' and they all chuckled.

Toonist added, "Well, C-Note, it looks like you got your wish."

"Yay me." He replied. He was excited to be going, but at the same time, scared to death. He liked camping and hiking to some extent but had not ever done either at this level before.

Victor and a crewmember walked into the hold. "Ladies and gentlemen of the hiker persuasion, may I present to you all your new holsters." The crewmember put a box on the table. Victor handed C-Note and Bass Master their holsters, "And for our out-of-the-ordinary controllers, the few South Paws on this boat, we have yours too."

Belle went and retrieved her pack. In seconds, she attached the holster to the left strap and strapped on the leg holster nearly as fast. Then, she looked at Victor, "Perfect!" She said to him and smiled like a kid on Christmas.

"Excellent. If you need anything else, please let me know." They left the room.

Chisel walked over to the extra pack area and grabbed one off the shelf. "Now to make certain of a proper fit." He walked over to C-Note.

Goose grabbed a pair of sunglasses for C-Note but put them on and looked around. He scanned each of the people in the room, saw their real names and their bio. He did not say a word just looked like he was playing around.

First, he looked at his partner, Jaclyn, of course.

Then there is Todd Chizzelski from Marengo, Wisconsin.

He looked at Toonist; her name is Devyn Jade. It has her being from Hong Kong, China.

Reena's real name is Wanda Renaldi, from Cleveland, Ohio.

That left Flambe from Dijon, France; her real name Claudine Blanchet.

He looked at the controllers next, William Franklin from Rome, New York. He got it now, Ben Franklin, a C-Note. Goose was glad he ran with that thought.

He looked at Bass Master from Providence, Rhode Island; her real name is Tammara LaRue.

Then lastly, he looked at Triple One, whose real name is Yvonne Dominguez from Butte, California.

They set up C-Note and Bass Master, and Triple One simultaneously since they would be doing this in weeks. The gear can all be gotten when it came time, but an improperly fitting pack meant exhaustion, tired back, pain all over, and learning to enjoy the suck. But, as a base, a pack that fits appropriately meant enjoying the hike and not feeling the weight you are carrying.

"OK, you want to put the pack onto your shoulders, then fit your backpack from the hips up, starting with positioning the middle of the hip straps directly on top of your hip bones. Many new hikers have the misconception that most of the weight of your pack should rest on your shoulder straps—these are the people who feel pain and exhaustion a short way into their hike. Instead, 80 to 90 percent of the weight should be on your hips and the remainder on your shoulders. This is because your hips are where your center of gravity is located. Therefore, it is the most stable and powerful point on your body — take advantage of it." Belle helped Chisel adjust the length of C-Notes pack. Then, they reset the hip straps and roughly set the shoulder straps to something close.

"Now," Goose took over. "Your shoulder straps. To properly fit your shoulder straps, pull the straps forward away from your body and then down toward your hips to get a natural fit. Do not overtighten; this will cause the straps to dig into your shoulders." He worked the shoulder straps a few minutes and discovered the torso was set just a hair too long. "Take the pack off, please."

He readjusted the torso, so the length was a few centimeters shorter.

"Let's give this another try." He loosened the shoulder straps, and C-Note clicked the waist. Goose talked as he worked for the benefit of C-Note and the other controllers, and so they all knew what he was doing and why. "When the fit is correct, the straps will hug your shoulders from front to back without any gaps, especially between the shoulder strap and your back." He tugged a bit and adjusted, "Now, that is a good fit."

Chisel and Reena walked up and took over, "Two major, but minor, adjustments left for you. The load lifters and the sternum strap. Both are essential for a comfortable fit, and both are essential to have a good day on the trail. The load lifters lift your pack to a comfortable position on your back. First, pull down on the tab until the straps make a 45-degree angle. You know it is too tight if the top of your shoulder strap pulls away from your body." He adjusted the load lifter.

Reena took over, "The sternum strap keeps it all together and secure. Needs to be tight enough to be effective, but not so tight it restricts your breathing. The strap should be a few centimeters below your collarbone." She smiled and said, "Ladies, please don't squish the girls. That would be considered a bad strap position." She adjusted C-Notes strap.

"You buckle the strap and grab the loose ends and tighten until the strap slips through your fingers. Hold it firmly but not a death grip. If you make the sternum strap too tight, you'll see the outside edges of your shoulder straps begin to lift off your chest. Its job is to keep the shoulder straps in place and very snug, not to molecularly bond it to your body." Everyone laughed.

Toonist took over, "We grabbed the gear you will need," It was all laid out on a table. It looked like a lot, but it will fit into the pack and be a dream to carry. "....and here is how to pack the backpack properly." The other controllers took a table, and the hikers made a display similar to what they saw in the C-Note staging area. Toonist continued, "Thankfully, these packs have a lower compartment, so the sleeping bag and pad in the lower compartment, pillow too, please. This way, you always know where it is located, and it will not get in the way if you need to dig through your pack for something. It serves two purposes in the lower compartment. First, your tent is outside the pack for easy access and set up in other than perfect weather. The tent can get wet, so outside, the pack is fine. Second, in the bottom compartment, your sleeping stuff is away from any location where water will hit it. A wet bag is unusable to sleep in!" She stuffed the bag and pad into the lower compartment. She added a pair of socks, a pillow, and a long-sleeve T-shirt, and sleeping pants. "Anything you will use INSIDE your tent, a dry place, needs to go into this dry place so, sleeping clothes, pillow, bag, pad." She stuffed and zipped the lower section. The pad and bag were just a hair larger than a water bottle, so it all fit well, and the sleeping clothes packed around the items perfectly.

Continuing, "Putting the bag and other softer stuff in the bottom of the pack means your lower back will have less strain, therefore less pain. The main and lower compartments are somewhat separate, and in the main section, you put the food, stove, extra clothing stuffed in such a way as to fill in the gaps. A bear bag is good here, and even though there are no bears, you get the idea. Put all your food and trash in the bear bag to keep it all in one place. Easy to get to, and easy to remove and hang when you set up your site."

Chisel interrupted, "I put an extra dry bag in my bear bag, which is also a dry bag. Albeit a smaller one, but only for the trash. When I get to a place, I empty it, rinse it out, and flip it inside out to let it dry completely." He looked at the controllers, "If you can drop a few extra dry bags in each drop, we can swap them out as necessary?"

Bass Master took notes, "I like that idea. Consider it done."

Reena took over the main presentation, "As for the tent, all six of us seem to use the left pocket and a strap at the top to hold the tent in place. Therefore, all of you will be doing it the same way. Call it our standard triad configuration." She winked at them all. "Water bottle goes in the right pocket." She looked at the lefty's, "Any issues pulling the bottle with your wrong hand. Do you need it flipped?"

They both shook their heads, so she continued, "You can grab it and sip on it as needed. Swap it out with the one inside the pack, which is always filled and ready to use, when you finish the one in the outside pocket. Always prep both bottles in the morning and finish them during the day. When you find water, refill both bottles as needed." She smiled and said, "I also carry a rain catcher. Essentially a huge collapsible funnel and a one-liter bladder. If it starts to rain, I set it up. A small filter in the bottom of the funnel to stop sediments like leaves and dirt. Empty into a pot, boil the crap out of it and filter it again, and you get clean water. Ever tasted ozone? That smell after it rains. It is amazing."

She put it all together for him, and the others all helped the girls set up their packs the same way.

"Now, one last thing," Belle said, and the others began unpacking all three of their packs and laying it all out. "You need to pack it yourself, so you know where everything is in the pack."

It took them about 15 minutes to pack it all back, and there were a few errors, a few mistakes, but all in all, they did well. "One more time."

They removed everything, and this time they managed to get it all in the right place.

"FOOD!" Bass Master said.

"You know the cabinet. Pick a week's worth of items and put them in the bear bag, then put the bear bag into the center of the main compartment of your pack." Goose said.

C-Note, Bass Master, and Triple One walked over to the cabinet and took a while to determine what they wanted to eat. Omelets and oatmeal for breakfast, Asian and Mexican for lunch, Italian and American for dinner. All dehydrated and all tasty. They grabbed a few protein bars and a couple of candy bars—coffee, enough for 3 a day, for each of them. Goose gave them the thumbs up.

"Pot roast and mash potatoes rehydrated together is a fantastic meal, and easy and fast too. You can use chili and mashed taters for a backcountry shepherd's pie or any soup and mashed taters. Dehydrated potato flakes are a blank canvas and can become anything, literally.

"OK, it looks like your packs are ready, one last thing. Clothes, are you happy with the clothing choices we made for you all?"

C-Note asked, "Do I need a set of bedclothes?"

Flambe replied, "No, actually—underwear, clean and dry, and a t-shirt. I recommend a pair of socks you use only for sleeping which is in the lower compartment already. I put on fresh underwear in the morning when I get up. Then, when I go to bed, I remove everything and let it all air out...."

Chisel said, "Good to know!" He looked at C-Note, "Unless it is colder outside, I am in underwear and maybe a t-shirt. Then, as it gets cold, I change into a long-sleeved t-shirt, then into a hoodie. After that, I have flannel pajama bottoms. Always sox, I hate when my toenails get caught on the sleeping bag.

That reminds me, in the toiletry kit, make damn sure you have nail clippers. Foot maintenance is a daily thing. Those puppies are your greatest asset on the hike. Treat them well."

Flambe shook her head and smiled at him, "Anyway, do what you feel is comfortable." She said.

"OK, skivvies it is." He grabbed a few boxer briefs, rolled them up, and put them into his clothing dry bag.

Something they did when packing clothes was to put the clothing in a dry bag. Sleeping stuff went into another dry bag and food into a third dry bag. As they said, never know when the monsoon will hit.

"C-Note, the boxer briefs are the best. Helps with chafing when walking." The ladies did the same. They grabbed underwear, and what looked like bicycle pants is the recommendation from the other women in the room.

C-Note managed to get it all packed up for the fourth time. Food, water, everything. His pack weighed 12 kilograms, but as he ate meals, it would lighten up. The ladies' pack weight was similar. They did not need much equipment since they would be traveling with the teams, and the teams all had the equipment they needed.

"The last thing, let's check the straps and verify a correct fit with a full pack. Now, put it on and click all buckles."

They all did, and after a few tugs and tweaks, it was perfect. "Now," Goose said. "Since nothing in this pack is perishable, and your water bottles are empty, you can either hang the pack here or take it back with you and store it where you are living. If you are going to the pod station, you may want to take it to your room now. That way, it is not lost or emptied. Just remember to fill your water bottles **before** you drop!"

The other hikers added full water bottles to their packs and made sure everything was in the bag, tight, closed, and ready to rock and roll. Then, to verify, they each, all six of them, completely emptied their pack and repacked it again. The controllers were amazed at the speed they could pack their backpacks and how they knew exactly where everything went, where it fit perfectly.

"Well, that's it. You are ready to go out with us." Goose said. "I take it the pod will launch and head back to the ship with those we replaced and our spare tire?"

"Yes, it will. What can I expect in the dropship?"

"Never been in one before?" Belle asked.

"Nope."

"Do you like roller coasters?"

"Yes, I do."

"Great, this is the ultimate rollercoaster ride that lasts only 4 minutes. You'll love it."

C-note and the other controllers left and returned to their cabins, taking their packs with them.

"OK, really, what can we expect on the drop?" Chisel asked.

"As I said, no matter what you think or feel, it will be over in 4 minutes. It will not kill you even if there is a highly unlikely malfunction, and I think it is fun."

She elaborated, "As you hit the outer atmosphere, you'll feel the G forces hit with a thud, and the closer you get to the ground, the more your stomach will try to get into your chest or throat. When the landing rockets fire, it all stops with a punch in the ass, literally. 45 seconds later, you are on the ground. 5 days later, we put everyone back in the box, the door closes, and someone presses FIRE. Launch rockets fire, and it heads into orbit where it is picked up by the ship, and you head home or back to where ever."

"OK THEN!" Reena said, "I guess we are free till the morning. Good breakfast, extra coffee, and drop out of orbit. The contract starts."

They spent nearly 5 hours in the hold with the controllers and watched other groups walk in and out during that time. After that, they all went and had lunch, relaxed, and did pretty much nothing for the rest of the day. Then, in the morning, the adventure will begin.

~~~~~~~~~~

"TEAM 103 plus 1, report to Drop Pod Zulu. You drop in 20 minutes."

"That's us, shall we," Belle said, putting her coffee on the table, not happy she did not get to finish it. She stopped a moment, then headed to the cooler, opened the door, and grabbed a bottle of cold-brewed coffee with cream and sugar. Popping the top, she turned it upside down and drained the bottle in one breath.

Goose saw her and did the same. "Great idea!" He said to her as he wiped the coffee dribble off his chin.

C-Note walked into the café at that moment and grabbed one also. He finished it, "Well, it looked like a great idea at the time." He said to both of them.

"Holy crap, I am scared of the drop but feel fine about the hike," Goose said.

"Me too," C-Note said.

"Trust me, this will make number 13 for me. I am at the 'whatever happens' point flying in these things. To help your stomach out when you feel gravity again, scream or grunt, it does help. I grunt."

"Let's do this."

They made their way to the drop deck and spoke to the lead. She pointed to a pod, and the three of them started walking to the pod. "Will! Are you really going to hike?"

"Yes, Mable, I am. God help me, but I am. Please pray for me!" C-Note said.

Mable laughed and, in a loud voice, "DEAR LORD!" The rest of the crew joined in and repeated her words. "Watch over my brother William. Don't let him get eaten by anything or fall off a mountain or something. Send him back to us when his adventure is over. And the Lord's people all said."

"AMEN!" Every crewmember yelled.

The deck broke into applause, and the team entered the pod.

"Looks like you, sir, are a celebrity!" Goose said.

As they entered the pod, C-Note was already grabbing the 4th position. Belle took the 1st position. The one with the control interface. Goose sat next to C-Note and behind Belle. The box was configured with 4 seats, two by two, in the center. Position 1 has the controls, which are actually located between seats #1 and #2. Behind Belle was Goose, position #3, and next to him was C-Note in #4.

A top bar provided structure in the event of a missed landing and the 5-point harness to hold you in place. The straps cinched themselves tight when the FIRE button is pressed. The crotch strap pulls the thighs apart some, and when the fire button is pressed, the ankle biters pop off the floor and keep your feet and legs from moving in positions they are not supposed to move.

All gear is stowed on the walls behind unbreakable metal fiber mesh. The weapons are stored in the locker, welded to the wall, and bio encoded to those in the pod.

Belle walked to the gear and made sure it was secure. Then went to the weapons locker and opened it, verified the six pistols were unloaded, safe, braced, and secured, and the ammo was in its proper place. There were also a couple rifles in the locker and a few clips.

She then sat in her seat and activated the control interface. Next, she pressed the big button that said talk, "Pod Zulu prepped."

"Pod Zulu, drop in 4 minutes."

"In 8 minutes, we will be on terra firma." She said to her team of three.

"Pod Zulu, arm drop system."

Belle flipped a couple of switches and pressed the talk button. "Pod Zulu armed and ready for drop."

The Captain spoke next, "Pod Zulu, Master Sergeant Belle, it is so nice when the pod operator has a clue."

"Pod Zulu thanks you, sir. Drop at your convenience."

A minute later, the Captain's voice came on again, "Pod Zulu, drop in 3........ 2........ 1...... DROP!"

Belle pressed the DROP button.

"OUCH!" the guys said at the same time. "What the hell is that?"

"Those are what we call the ankle biters. They keep your feet and legs from breaking.

A moment later, the biggest clunk was heard....felt, and the up and down no longer meant up and down. The OMS fired and moved the pod into position.

After thirty seconds, "What was that?" C-Note asked.

"That was the OHMS," She over-pronounced. "O-M-S, orbital maneuvering system. Tiny little gas nozzles set us into the correct entry position. They keep us on course."

"Oh, OK," C-Note said.

A minute into the flight, "WHAT WAS THAT?" Goose asked.

"That is what it feels like to hit the atmosphere at an insane velocity. We'll be on the ground in three and a half minutes."

They felt G Forces now. "Pod Zulu, control, three minutes till dirt."

Belle yelled over the noise, "Roger Control!"

About that time, they felt the free fall. C-Note and Goose started screaming, yes, like little girls. But Belle could tell it was all good, laughing and screaming. Although she could not see them, she knew they had a smile on their face simultaneously. She did not yell, but she did grunt effectively. A couple of minutes passed, and the landing rockets fired. A few seconds later, they were on the ground. No movement at all.

"We landed; you can stop screaming now." They all started laughing!

"Control, Pod Zulu. Landing joy. Putting the pod to sleep, heading out."

"Pod Zulu, nice flying with you. Have a great hike." A pause. "Control out.

"Not as bad as I thought it would be," C-Note said.

"Agreed," Goose added.

"Take-off is even more fun!" She said, looking at C-Note. He looked worried.

Belle stood and nearly fell. "Forgot there was real gravity."

"And if I remember right, it's about 85% Earth-normal," C-Note added. "By the way, other hikers report a nasty smell in the air. Some of the plants are nasty."

Belle went to the weapons locker, opened it, handed out two pistols to Goose and one to C-Note, and took two for herself. A holster for the right thigh, a holster for the left pack shoulder strap.

She grabbed the door latch and swung it open. "WHAT THE FUCK?"

The smell wafted through the pod. It was nasty.

Belle started laughing; Goose asked, "What's so funny?"

"I guess after a few days without a shower, I can blame the trees!" They all started laughing.

Grabbing their packs and leaving the pod, they put on their pack. They put the pistols into their holsters and the extra ammo in the pocket of the backpack, they headed out.

Goose said, "OK, it smells like a....a...."

"Say it," Belle said.

"A tuna factory."

"Nice save!" She said.

"Wait, now I smell ass," C-Note added. "Possibly horses ass, to be precise."

"Chicken coop?" Belle added.

"This is one weird place. You never mentioned the sunlight has a green tint."

"I had no idea."

"I wonder if the reason the light appears green is the pollen or chlorophyll in the air refracting the light. I bet it is not there after it rains." Belle said.

"OK, let's head south," Goose asked. They all looked around, "Which way is south?"

Belle thought a minute and pointed in a direction. There were no trails or blazes to follow; no one, no human, has ever stood here before. "I think that

117

way if my orienteering is sound." She removed a compass from her pocket and looked at it. "Well, it tells me this way is east. Therefore, the magnetic north is not at the top of the world here. But it does give us something to follow. I know we are heading east, and that is all I need to know. If we do not run into the other team in 3 days, we can all head back to the pod simply by going west."

"Good thought. I had no idea the first hike was this disorienting on arrival. The positioning satellites should all be in place in the next month, and we can put locators in your weekly drop. They will be about the size of your thumb, and you can clip it to your belt and not even know it's there. Then, at least, you will know where you are....or were at least." He looked at Belle, "How do you figure the direction?"

"Well, in all the simulations I saw, in all the drops I made, the pod orients itself – at least on the Earth – so the door opens to the east. Which means standing at our door and looking out would be south. My compass, which is an Earth compass, tells me that direction is east. So here, south is east. We head east!"

They walked till near dark, twilight. "Camp setup," Goose said. "Besides, I'm hungry. I want dinner, and since we missed lunch because we had such a huge breakfast, I may eat both for dinner."

Belle got a campfire started, and Goose pulled out his antique stove, collected some twigs and stuff, and got that fire burning. He put a couple of liters of water on to boil, and after maybe 12 minutes, all 2 liters were boiling fine.

They all pulled out a random meal, put the requested amount of water into the packet, and let it rehydrate; 15-minutes later, they were eating a nice dinner.

"Belle, Goose, can you hear me?" It was Reena

"We can. How was the drop?" She asked.

"I screamed like a little girl!" She said to Belle.

"Mee too!" C-Note and Goose said at the same time.

"Well, our site is set up, meals are hydrating and heating; at the moment, I am eating a Snickers as an appetizer," Reena said.

"We are all set up as well. Water just came to a boil, and we are cooking." Belle replied.

"Us too! I guess all of us are on this channel and can talk during dinner. Hey, C-Note. Is there a way for Triple One and Bass Master to join in on this?" Chisel asked.

"If the captain will authorize the use of the active dish for an hour a day, yes. But if not, all we can do is review your reports."

"This is Bass Master; can anyone hear me?" She spoke.

C-Note perked up, "This is new."

"We can. Is Triple One there also?"

"She is. The captain liked this option, and maybe not every night, but this could be a good thing on a rotating basis. Casual conversation."

For the next hour, they talked about the drop, and their dinner, and a few other things.

"Any idea where the team is located that we are going to replace?"

"Hang on a sec."

A few minutes later, "OK, Belle/Goose, your end game is 44 kilometers south, which would appear to be east if you looked at a compass. However, I see the pod is located 19 kilometers opposite, so you traveled right. Good pace too."

"All downhill." Belle smiled, "I did get to verify that C-Note rolls like a snowball."

"Oh my god, I do hope you got pictures!" Triple One said.

"I did just happen to be recording also; there is a video you will get in the upload tonight."

"Hey Belle, let me teach you how to perform maintenance on the file structure of the comm unit later," C-Note said in jest.

The ladies all laughed but continued, "Let's see, Chisel/Flambe, your team is located 33 kilometers in the direction you are currently traveling, and Reena/Toonist, your team is 40 kilometers away. I estimate 2 days, and you will meet up. 3 days to return to the pod. So stuff them in, press the button and get rid of the dead weight and get to work."

They all ate, and before they disconnected, the roommates asked a straightforward question. "So, did someone verify C-Note knows how to use his new home?" That was Bass Master.

"Well, he watched Belle and I set up our tents, inflate our pads, layout our bags, and grab a lamp. He is an excellent follower. Before we crash, I plan to show him the internal heat controls. Temp here is dropping, maybe 7°C, and it looks to get below freezing tonight. The sky is so clear so, no nature's blanket."

"Well, here it's 12°C ...." Chisel said, "....and the cloud cover is low and thick, so we should be warm for tonight at least."

Toonist spoke, "We have the same weather as you, Goose; clear, cold, and crisp."

"Thankfully, there is a lot of deadwood around......"

C-Note chimed in, "Please be careful with the wood. If it has those red plants on it, it is not a good idea to burn it or touch it for that matter."

"Never thought of that. Thanks for the tip."

"So, roommates, how's your weather?" Belle asked.

"Hot, the thermostat is stuck on hot. We are sitting around naked. A shame C-Note is not here." Triple One said.

C-Note shook his head. Goose said, "Dude, looks like you may have a hobby for the next six months…..." He paused a moment, and Belle looked at him. He smiled and said, "Keeping your roommates happy! Belle can offer you a few notes, as can the others…... Me, well, I do what I can…." He put his hand on his heart and got hit in the chest full-on by a flying trashbag. Belle is a good throw.

"Well, by best calculation, the sun will rise in 9.5 hours." Bass Master said. "I need a shower, a snack, and some tea. Look forward to your uploads tonight. I will review them in the morning and pass around one specific video. Not sure if this evening link is permanent or not. If it is, that's cool. If not, well, we'll let you know before they cut us off. If worse comes to worst, we can connect the land teams on a recurring timer. We just need to figure out the best time and what time it is so…."

"Can it be set to sunset plus a couple of hours?"

"I think it can. Let you know tomorrow. Have a good sleep!" The orbiting controllers disconnected, as did the other two teams.

"Looks like we are alone in our heads. I am getting cold, but I want to set the fire up for the night." Goose said. He put his sunglasses on, "I like these; the Infrared mode is great." He looked around and stopped on an area, "We got a heat source over there. Small, like a hamster." He watched it a minute, and the other two put their sunglasses on, "You two see it?"

"Yes, I see it," Belle replied.

"So do I," C-Note said.

"Wait, it's flying," C-Note said.

"It is a cold-blooded bird that picked up our little mammal friend, so I cannot see what picked it up, and it's too far away for the low lux setting. Can you say dinner is served?"

Goose saluted the little rodent, "For those of you about to die, we salute you." Then, he removed his shades and turned to C-Note, "let me give you the once over on the tent and bag. Then we can get some sleep. Primary, keep a light next to you at all times at night. I put mine in the pocket of the sleeping bag, so I know where it is."

C-Note said, "Roger that!"

"You know how to use the tree, right? " Belle asked.

"I think I can figure that out."

Chapter Five

"According to the distance calculation from the roommates, they are less than 3 kilometers from us, but that was at breakfast; we have traveled at least that far. Did we pass them?" C-Note asked. They had been hiking for the past couple of days, getting to know each other and teaching C-Note about backcountry camping and appreciating where you are, and not taking any aspect of the hike for granted.

Belle said to him when he looked tired the second day, "OK, let's stop for the night."

"Why?" C-Note asked.

Goose said, "Killing yourself will mean tomorrow will be worse, and the next day, etc.... So, if right now you need to stop, STOP. Instead, set up camp, relax, chill, make a snack, have dinner. This is not a race. It is a survey!"

C-Note responded with a smile, "Touche, brother Goose." Then, he removed his pack, "Camp time it is."

On night #1, Goose asked him if he knew how to use a tree, and he gave him a look. But a few hours later, the other thing made him ask about digging a cat hole.

Goose told him to find a not too huge tree to hold on to in front of him, dig a hole maybe 15 or 20 centimeters deep and big enough around so you won't miss when you drop the bomb on the target. Use the paper, put it all in the hole, put water into the hole, and cover it up with the dirt. Jab a stick in the freshly covered package to mark the location.

Well, it took a couple days, but he needed to test the process. The group stopped for lunch, and C-Note actually went into the trees and disappeared into the woods. A little time had passed, and they were getting concerned he was not back yet.

He was gone almost half an hour. When he did come back, he pulled the fresh bottle of water out of his pack. They had just refilled a couple hours ago, so they asked where his water went. They laughed when they discovered he poured the entire liter and a half into the hole. They need to be specific; Belle said, "Use a couple of glugs, not the entire bottle. The idea is to get it wet, not float it in a pool."

"Wait….," Goose stopped and dropped his pack. "What the hell is that sound?" Looking in the direction of the sound, he followed the smoke trail and estimated the intended path. He pointed but at the sky. He found a huge rock and climbed on top of it.

"What the hell is that?" Belle asked.

"That is a resupply pod. Essentially a 75-liter airtight cooler with landing and take-off rockets."

"Take off?" Belle said.

"Pack out your trash, right?" C-Note winked at her.

"Oh, I get it. So what we don't or can't burn we put back into the cooler, and it blasts off back into orbit."

"Exactly. Once there, it makes its way to the orbital station in polar orbit, and the trash is consolidated. Then it's all put into one pack, compressed, and mag shot into the star. Efficient! We determined that resupply costs us about 8 credits per team every 5 days. Expensive but worth the price. Can you imagine the cost if we had to land a shuttle, unload a single box, launch and get to the next location?"

Goose returned, "Saw the hiker box land over there. I guess maybe 15 minutes away." He put his pack back on. "Shall we?"

They found the place the cooler landed and smelled smoke, campfire smoke. It must be the gang they are replacing. Nowhere near evening, but maybe they hiked differently.

They saw the other team sitting at the fire, and Goose let out a whistle. All three of them waved their arms, and the other team acknowledged by waving theirs. A few minutes later, they became a team of 5.

"BELLE girl! Not who I expected to see. How the hell are you?"

"Fine, BG, I am just starting on my contract and replacing you."

"Damn, just figured out who you are, Goose!" they hugged a moment, "You owe me a coffee if I remember right."

"I do, DE, you're right!" Goose reached into his pocket and pulled out a metal can. "Been carrying this for a few days. It is really heavy but worth it to see the look on your face when I pay up my wager."

Handing it to Double Espresso, DE pulled the tab, and the aroma of hot fresh espresso filled the air. A minute later, after taking a tentative sip, "THIS! Makes us square."

Belle spoke, "Belinda Goat, Double Espresso, this is C-Note. He is our controller." They both did a double-take.

"What the hell is he doing down here?" DE asked.

C-Note explained, "I commented to the captain it would be a good idea for the controllers to hike a short time to understand the hike and the process. He agreed. 48 hours later, I'm in the drop pod screaming like a little girl."

"Me too, the screaming like a little girl part." Goose volunteered.

Belle added, "All true. I don't think there is a situation I would let out a scream like that, but you can tell they had fun doing it."

They all sat around the fire. "Talk to us. Is there anything important we need to know?"

"Not really. How far away is the pod?" DE said.

"Two or three days, maybe. We made it in 2 and a half but was mostly down-slope." Belle said.

"Excellent, 5 days, and we'll be back on the ship heading home," BG said.

"5 days?" C-Note said. Knowing he had only 2 days of food left in his pack. His fellow hikers had the same amount.

"We always take a double zero on drop day. Gives us a chance for a couple of day hikes left and right. Found some amazing waterfalls, a beautiful valley, and a perma-fog covered field."

"Perma-fog?"

"Yup, the field is in a place where it is never in sunlight, and the temp inversion holds a layer of fog about 2 meters above the ground. We watched it a few days, placed a camera, and in the past few weeks, perma-fog according to our controller."

"Well, the three of us have maybe 3 days of food left."

"Never fear, they just dropped us 7 days knowing that (a) you will be here with us and (b) we will be taking a zero at least."

"Hey girl, join me. We'll make dessert." The Goat asked.

"We will?"

"Yup."

They walked off into the woods, leaving the three guys at the fire.

"So, you glad to be heading home?" Goose asked.

"Yes and no. I love this planet. I would live here if I was able." He paused a moment, looking at the fire. Watching the smoke trail go up a short way, apparently seeking out C-Note. "Belle and Belinda are going to look for a fruit we found. We planned to bring it back with us; it grows everywhere. We found critters eating it, so we scanned it. I like it raw; I like it cooked. Reminds me of a cross between an apple and a mango, but it's blue. We call it blue fruit, no idea if it has a real name yet or not. I like to make hand pies out of it and have them later. My controller drops us a couple of pizza dough balls, making a bunch on drop day or the next. He also puts a large pot and some cooking oil in the drop. We make the fruit compote on drop day, that night, and after breakfast the next morning, we make the pies. We have a couple of containers they fit perfectly into and get a pie a day till the next drop. With the air cooling off like it is, it is easy to carry cooked food things for a few days or so."

"I heard nothing about the blue fruit, but I am willing to try it and bring it back for analysis." C-Note said, "Does it grow on trees?"

"Sorta. Underground at the base of the nasty red plants. You just need to be careful collecting it. We figure the plant found its way there, knowing the locals are afraid of the red plants, so it would be safe." He took a drink, "We saw the Kitties eating them and decided to try one. They are excellent. Med scanner has it green."

"Kitties?" Goose asked.

"What you were told was apex predator beta. Nice little things."

They talked for another half hour or so, and the light began to fade. Then, finally, Goose stoked the fire again – well, a few times – and the girls returned.

"Do you have any idea where we retrieved these morsels?" Belle asked.

C-Note replied, "Well, judging by the look of this fruit, I would say it was buried in the ground at the base of those toxic red plants." He paused, and Belle just stared at him. "Am I close?"

Belle looked at Double Espresso and simply stared.

He replied innocently, "What?"

The guys started laughing. Belle and Belinda went to a small tree stump and used it as a table. Cutting up the fruit and sprinkling it with a bit of bourbon.

"Macerated Blue Fruit. A staple for us." Belinda Goat announced. "Contains 35 grams of protein, 8 carbs, 6 sugar, and 5 fiber, with various nutrients. Each whole fruit has roughly 130 calories, so like a protein bar but better tasting. We make them into fried fruit pies and one a day is awesome."

"Wow, looking forward to trying these things." She looked at the fruit. "So, I guess the medical scanner told you what's in them?"

"Precisely. So far, these little fruits have scanned identical, so we can assume that the bush that produces them is all the same, hopefully, planet-wide. Like a plum tree in one country will produce a plum very similar to another country. Just an ever so interesting difference in flavor we are attributing to the soil it grows in."

"FIRE'S HOT!" Someone yelled.

"That means we can put on a pot of this stuff and cook it down. It loses about half its weight in water, and the nutrients and protein diminish when it's cooked, so we reserve one fruit and fine dice it, then adds it after it is cooked. Normally, 4 to 1, as in cook 4, add one later."

"Is the ratio important?"

"No, just that after cooking it down, that is the perfect amount for the two of us. No waste."

"Gotcha!" Belle winked. "That's why we are cutting up a dozen of them."

"Exactly," BG said.

They talked for about 5 minutes and slowly made their way to the fire, placing the pot, which has seen better days they noticed, on the embers.

"Oh crap!" BG said to the group.

"What?" DE replied.

"I forgot to reserve fruit for dicing up fresh."

"We'll get some." He told his partner. Looking at Goose, "You still got that antique boat anchor of a stove?" Double Espressos asked Goose.

"I do." He pulled the black bag from his pack. "Need hot water? We can play with it if you want?"

"Like for making a coffee?" He grinned from ear to ear.

"Save enough for a cup of tea, please," C-Note said. The other two guys just looked at him. "I lived in London for 5 years, gimme a break!" They all laughed.

They all collected small twigs and things and started a fire in the center of the can. After 5 minutes, it got hot, and they added larger sticks and twigs and stuff until the flame was dancing barely out of the top of the can. Finally, Goose filled a small pot with water and balanced it on his little antique stove.

"Coffee in 6 minutes!" Double Espresso said. "If I remember my timing correctly."

"Pretty close," Goose replied.

The cloud cover was starting to roll in, and it made night arrive a little early. The temperature cooled off fast, making them all happy they had the fire to stay warm. Goose and Belle brought something special; a reflective sheet. It was two meters tall and twenty meters long, wrapping around the group. Giving the inside of the heated circle a diameter of about 260cm, enough room for everyone to sit comfortably around the fire and warm up. It increased the heating factor of the small fire tremendously.

"You know, who would have ever thought a tiny little shiny metal fiber sheet could make so many people a little happier," C-Note said. "You know I'm taking notes here to make a few interesting recommendations on future hikes."

"We figured. I wish we had this thing a few months back when we were in the mountains. It would have made life a little bit better!"

"Better, huh," Goose said. "What would have made it most bestest?"

"Better food!"

Everyone nodded.

Goose spoke, "When these heat reflectors came out, I sent a couple of them to friends who were hiking a trail somewhere. I worked with the company to help them gain traction with hikers, and they paid me by giving me a dozen of these things. So I mailed the reflective sheets out to the resupply drop for a few friends in an envelope. Got a call the night Bucky received his, and he laughed at me. I told him what it was and how to use it; he thought I was kidding."

Goose sipped his water bottle, "A few weeks later when he played LASHer on the PCT and hit a freak snowstorm.... a freak arctic blast. He wanted to get ahead of the herd and started thinking he would be fine starting on the trail a few weeks early. He was almost to Truckee, and the temps dipped well below 0. After a few feet of snow, he said he thought he would freeze to death. Then, he remembered the sheet and remembered how I said to put it up around his campfire. He was, by no means, hot. But he did finally warm up. Before the end of the storm, 5 other hikers showed up at his campsite. They saw the light from his fire, he said it was a bit larger than it needed to be, and he opened the circle. To this day, he tells me they survived that hike because I thought to send him something weird, new, and cool. I told him if I find something that works great, takes up almost no space, and has almost no weight, I will always pass it on."

Goose paused and had a sip of coffee that Double Espresso handed him. "Thanks." He continued. "Can't beat micro metal mesh, ever. Wind-proof, heat reflective, very lightweight, and strong. I dare say it would be hard to cut this thing with a knife."

"Goose, my brother, I cannot tell you how Bucky talked about the crazy man that sent him the shiny thing. He complained he carried the extra 40 grams in his pack because he would feel bad tossing it in the trash. Now, I cannot remember the other hikers there, but Bucky I remember. He is right. Saved our asses that night. BTW, we all took a triple zero in Truckee after that experience. We walked past the state cops' place, and one of them saw us and pulled us into the building to warm up, have some coffee and a pastry. One of them, trail name PoPo, sat, and we talked for a while a few minutes later. Then, her partner joined us and told us rooms were waiting for us at a hotel for 3 nights, paid."

He paused a moment, "We all had a room, nice room really, at the Knox Bed and Breakfast. The owner was Joanne, and she and her husband Mark turned the family home into this amazing refuge for hikers and travelers. The food was better than anything we could have imagined. The house has been in the family since the early 2000s since her great-great-great-grandmother or something moved there from New England to teach. If I remember right, it was English or something. So the six of us helped them with chores around the house during that time and woke up to bacon frying every morning."

He looked around at the group, "The officer that dropped us off popped in a couple times and had a few meals with us; she told us that in three days, once the weather broke, they would pick us up and bring us back to the building we started, and we can continue NOBO on our merry way." He looked at Goose, "Brother birdman, that was by far the best zero set I ever took. Bucky is a nut job. We all had a blast. To this day, I get a card every year from the Knox family on the anniversary of that triple zero." He paused very reflectively. "I definitely need to head back there and visit with them."

They sat and chatted a while and realized the weather was taking a turn for the nasty. Everyone quickly cleaned up and hung the food in the trees nearby the site. C-Note piled a few smaller tree limbs onto the embers, and they lit, but not in a large fire. Small finger fires and essentially just embers. With a bit of hope, it will be fast and easy to light in the morning.

Everyone went into their tent, and after getting nice and warm in their bag, the link activated.

"Can anyone hear me?" they all heard as Triple One connected.

"Oh yes. Why so late tonight?" Belle asked.

"There was an incident." She paused and took a breath. "A hiker on the other side of the world from you ran into a flock or whatever you call them of the APA's, tore her to bits. She has been recovered, and the last thing she could do was contact her partner to let her know where she was. It was getting dark, and the weather was getting worse, so she hiked through a clearing, hoping to take shelter in the trees. That's where they all had the same thought. She killed 3 of the creatures, a male and two females, so we assume that she walked into the middle of a family, and the parents were protecting their offspring. This is the reason we tell hikers to not hike near dusk, feeding time. So please, all of you, set up camp well before dusk."

They were all silent for a long time.

"What happens next?"

"A special forces squad was dispatched to make their way 30 kilometers further down the trail. They should meet up with the new team on their way to meet up with the old team. Once they return to the pod, the SF's and the lone hiker will head up here and home."

"Thanks. If you hear any more, please let us know. But for now, we will disconnect. The weather turned cold, and we are ready for sleep."

"We see a cold front moving in, and it was not there four hours ago. I love the weather on this planet." She paused and read more of her screen. "Let's see. The forecast for the next 60 hours is cooler temps with a high around 11°C, and lows peaking at about -5°C. Sorry guys, but you can expect liquid precipitation mid-day tomorrow and last for about 16 hours so, I guess you can expect snow tomorrow evening. Glad you chose a heated tent and bag!"

"Me too!" They all said.

Everyone was in their tent, in their bag, and the wind picked up. Then the rain started, light rain, but it made for a good night's sleep as the raindrops fell on the tent. They are in a clearing, so there is no chance of a widowmaker or a limb falling on their tent. The night was uneventful, just rain, wind, and more rain.

Morning came, and the sun shined very brightly this morning. Double Espresso was up first and got the fire started. The temperature was about 7°C, so he was somewhat bundled up, jacket open, though.

Belle crawled out of her tent next and less bundled but dressed warmly nonetheless. She went and sat by the fire and plopped a cube into her cup, and filled it with a ladle of hot water. She drank her coffee black and loved it. It had a vanilla flavor to it, and besides, black coffee is lighter on the trail since there are no accouterments needed to have a coffee.

They have not spoken yet, typical trail life. Enjoy the moment, talk later. C-Note got up next and joined them all.

"Hi everyone. A wild storm last night; kept me awake for quite a while. The lightning was impressive though, kept thinking I was about to be turned into a smoking hole. Oh great! You have hot water already. Let me grab my coffee cubes and a cup. I'll be right back." He went back to his tent.

DE looked at Belle, "Is he always like that?"

"Yup." She replied. "But all this is new to him, so we just let him experience it."

"Well, 4 days and he'll be back on the station, you and Goose will be hoofing it through the planet, and the Goat and I will be on the plane heading home."

"Will you miss it?"

He thought for a minute. "Yes, a lot. I may sign up for another hitch, but they have a rule, one hike per Earth year. So maybe in a year, if I still want to come back. But I have a recommendation for the powers that be, teams of two instead of one. I hiked alone for the first two and a half months, and Belinda ended up on my trail because her trail petered out. Looked like the Grand Canyon, she said. She would have spent 6-months walking through a 50-kilometer stretch because it would have been a lot of climbing. Her control said to head this way, and she met up with me. Honestly, at first, I was annoyed, but to have someone to share this experience with is priceless. We talked about becoming permanent hiking partners."

"As in......"

"Yep. As in...." He paused a minute. "You and Goose stay together as long as you can; trust me, you will be better off. Goose is an OK guy. Almost too nice, but he compensates for it by being empathetic. Anyway, there was a time those bear things were stalking us, I was oblivious, but Belinda's female intuition kicked in or something. She knew exactly where they were, and we kept an eye on them. They knew we were watching them too, and they will only attack under three circumstances. If they are cornered or if they are protecting their young, or if they are stalking food. The first two are SURPRISE!! The last one is hard to determine. Those things, as big as they are, are quite silent. We have seen them attack and feast as a family unit on smaller creatures, not the Kitties, mind you, but things that look like large hamsters and birds of vulture size. Devastating is too mild a word. The sightings of them are infrequent. If you see them, look directly at them. Stealth is their high ground, and if you see them, know they are there and let them know you see them, well, you are less likely to be attacked."

"Have you had to shoot one?" She asked.

C-Note returned.

"No, we probably should have on one or two occasions, but a couple of rounds in the tree next to them stopped them in their tracks. They are skittish, afraid of something they don't understand. I think in a few millennia, they will become smarter, but now, in this time of the history of this planet, those things are the smartest thing native to this planet."

"WhaCha talking about?" He asked.

"Blue bears." Belle replied, "Just got a lot of insight into them. Not as scary as I first thought."

C-Note asked as he was sipping his brew, "What about the little razor spiked mammal? Seen any of those?"

"They're everywhere. Here, watch...." He pulled a whistle from a pocket and blew on it, it made no sound, but the tree line could be heard rustling. A few of the little critters came to the edge of the trees, just as Goose and Belinda exited their tent."

"Calling the babies?" She said to DE.

"Yep." A minute later, they scampered to the fire and stood near it, and felt the warmth. Goose just looked at the critters.

Belinda reached in a pocket and pulled out a protein bar, and unwrapped it. She walked over to them and handed the bar to the closest one. The largest one. That one broke it apart and gave it to the others, and they sat there and chomped on it like a rabbit chewing on a carrot.

Belinda said, "Family unit, we think. The largest one, we figure, is the Dad, and the next largest is the Mom. The others are the kids. At least we think. Never flipped one over and looked. They are less afraid of us, but we realized they are afraid of my pack. It's blue, like the bears."

The Dad finished his piece of protein bar and looked directly at Goose for a long minute. Then, dad walked casually over to Goose and rubbed his leg with the top and side of his head. Then, he looked up at Goose, "I swear he is telling me he likes me."

"Try to pet him on his head. He will not bite you. If he does not want the touch, he will just bat your hand away."

"OK." Goose reached slowly to Dad and stroked the top and side of his head. Dad looked like he was enjoying it for a couple minutes. "WOW! Is he soft!" Then the kids made a commotion, and Dad looked at Goose, who withdrew his hand, and went back to his family.

The rest of the Kitties finished their snack, and they all scampered off back into the woods.

DE said, "In an hour or so, they'll return with a gift. They return the favor, we fed them, they'll feed us. I think they know we like the blue fruit as much as they do."

They made breakfast and talked about the trek so far. Exciting things like the critter stories and the birds. Beautiful birds that like people. "If you camp near a tree and there are birds in the tree, you know you are safe. If the birds, all of a sudden, take off into the air, grab your pistol, and get out of your tent. The birds are sensitive to the bears, and it all revolves around the bears on this planet. They are at the top of the food chain. No creature on this planet can take one of them out, except for us and our toys."

As they were cleaning up, the little critters returned. Each of them had fruit in their paws and placed it at Belinda's feet.

Dad walked over to Goose, who was sitting on the ground. Dad handed the fruit directly to Goose, who accepted it. He rubbed Dad's head and stroked his back a moment.

Goose pulled out a bar, unwrapped it, and handed it to Dad Kittie. Dad accepted it, and all of them went about their business. After they all left, he tossed the fruit to BG, and she went to dice it up for the pockets.

After they made the hand pies, they packed it all up, killed the fire, left the place like it was before they arrived, and headed west by the compass, north to the top of the world. They walked in relative silence.

Even C-Note remained quiet. He was beginning to understand the hikers' connection to the planet—the relationship to all creatures to exist in this small and very new world.

Small talk, mostly about life before the planet, while they hiked. Aspirations in life, direction, the future.

They each had a hand pie for lunch, so they wanted to stop early for dinner. A few hours before it started to get dark, they heard a stream not too far away from where they stopped.

"OK. Everyone, I hear a stream over that way, and I got a few 5-liter water holders. I need someone who wants to go to the water with me and carry them back."

C-Note volunteered, "I'll go with you, Goose."

"Excellent!" Goose replied.

They headed to the river and filled 20 liters of water. Goose did not want to carry them, so he found a large stick and pulled a coil of rope out of his pocket. He tied the rope to the limb and put a carabiner on each water bottle handle, and they were secure. A slight sway but more or less stable.

"OK, here is how this works. This is about a 2-meter tree limb, and if we put the end of the limb on our shoulder, we will never even notice we are carrying about 20 kilograms. But if we tried to put 10 kilograms in each hand and walk back, we would not be happy campers."

"Smart Goose!"

They put the log on their shoulder, Goose in the front, and C-Note bringing up the rear. "Make sure it extends a little past your shoulder. The edge would not feel good digging into the soft part of your body."

They walked back a little slower but realized walking in step is not the right thing to do. The containers swung crazy. So random walking worked the best.

"So, how are you surviving this trek?" Goose asked C-Note.

"Better than I thought, actually. I was scared to death of doing this, but now I am kinda happy about being here. I know the girls will love it when they get here. It is just a new thing, and new things are scary."

"I felt like that on the plane. I thought to myself, what the hell am I doing? Hiking randomly on a planet, an alien planet with humungous blue beasts and little razor-toothed critters. Am I nuts?"

"Yes, you are. But that's the reason this is right for you. You survive to be on the adventure. You love the experience, the newness. You are an explorer. Me, I'm a bureaucrat. I organize, I structure. I budget, and I make meetings. That's what I do, and now, I have a greater and deeper appreciation of what you hikers do. I understand."

"Thanks, dude."

"No, you don't understand. I am not in my comfort zone. You are in yours, and I am with you. I am with you, Belle, DE, and the Goat. You people find this fun. Me, personally, I find it a lot of work. How do you do this so easily?"

Goose stopped and took the pole off his shoulder, and they put the water on the ground. He walked over to a large rock half a meter away and sat down. C-Note followed him and sat on another rock.

Goose pulled out a water bottle and took a drink, and handed it to C-Note.

"My friend. You need to know this is easy for us because we have done this for years—me and the rest of us, maybe over a decade. When we started off hiking, I knew less than you know right now. A few hikers let me follow them and showed me the ropes. I made some glorious mistakes, made many people laugh, but they showed me what I did wrong and how I needed to correct it. Never made that error again."

C-Note shook his head, "But, I am always afraid I am going to do something stupid, and someone will get hurt."

"No, we would never let you get hurt."

"Not what I mean. I am afraid my being so naive is going to get someone else hurt or worse. That is what I'm afraid of; if I get hurt, well, as long as it is me and not you or Belle or the others. I could not live with that."

Goose looked at him sideways. Something was going on in his head. Something new and not quite right. "C-Note my brother, let me tell you this right now. Watching you these past few days, I would hike anywhere with you, except on a mountain. I'm scared of heights." C-Note laughed. "Let's just restate the obvious; in the last couple of days, you learned a lot. Not because you had to, but because you wanted to learn and get good at being a hiker. Even for a few days."

He saw a smile on C-Note, and somehow he knew he was feeling better.

Belle broke their reveries, "Goose. C-Note. Are you two OK. Been a while, and we wanted to know if you need anything or are you just taking your time."

"Goose, I heard her. Tell her we are on our way back. Thanks though, I feel a lot better about a lot of things, decisions, stuff in general."

"OK, let's head back."

"Hey Belle, we'll be there in a few minutes. Sorry, I had my comms off. Did not realize it."

"No worries. See you guys in a few."

They stood and hugged a moment. "We good?"

"We are good."

They picked up the limb, put it back on their shoulder, and headed back to the campsite.

By the time they returned to the site, the tents were all set up, and a fire was going. There was a pot of water starting to steam a little already.

"Perfect timing. We all realized we had just enough water between us to fill the pot. Now we need to filter and refill our bottles."

"Then I am glad I suffered carrying this extra 45 kilograms to make your lives easier," Goose said as he and C-Note dropped the water near the fire.

"You're all heart, Goose!" DE said.

"I got my filter here; let me filter enough for a bottle each. We can do the rest later." C-Note said.

"Thanks, Dude!" DE said.

C-Note filtered 5-liters, a liter each, for dinner. He finished just as the water was boiling. "You guys get yours first. Almost done here, and I'll get mine."

Belinda Goat grabbed her meal and C-Note's and got them made up. She resealed them and let them fully hydrate. C-Note finished and handed out the bottles, about a liter each at the moment. He realized his meal was made up and thanked whoever did it.

Belinda went over and kissed him on the cheek. "For a controller, I like you. You have heart, spirit, and a need to do good. So don't sweat the small stuff, and always remember, HYOH!"

"Thanks, but what is HYOH?" He said to the group.

"It means HIKE YOUR OWN HIKE. Don't try to follow in someone else footprints. You may be on the trail with four pretty experienced hikers, but you are C-Note. You are not Goose or Double Espresso. I can also say for a fact you are not BG or Belle; I like looking at them." Double Espresso said. "So, HYOH. The unwritten rule when traveling in a group is to hike at the speed of the slowest. It gives everyone the chance to take in the sights."

Time for dinner, coffee, and campfire stories.

C-Note sat against a log and started eating his meal, "I wanna know something?"

"What?" BG asked.

"How did you all get your names?"

"Let's see," Goose said, "Mine first." He cleared his throat. "Since my last name is Gossling, Goose seems natural."

"You named yourself?"

"Not really. I got the name Goose in college. Had it forever." He looked at Belle, "You're next up, Belle."

"Well, I am from the south, Prattville, Alabama, and I really love to hunt and fish. That Tenkara rod has traveled thousands of miles, literally, on trails, mountains, and streams with her. It weighs a few grams and can easily be used to fish for fresh food on the trail, which she has done quite a bit. I got my name when I was with a group of hikers in the Rockies. I had a good day fishing and caught enough to feed the entire group. Found some fragrant herbs and vegetables in the woods on the way back to the campsite. When I got back, one of the hikers said, "She is no Southern Belle," and the name Belle just stuck. Since that day, I have fallen in love with the name."

Chapter Six

"I see it, almost directly above us," C-Note said.

The cooler drifted off-center a little, maybe sensing lifeforms in the spot it originally planned to land. No one moved, and the cooler touched down as intended a dozen or so meters away. They all strolled over to it a few moments after the engines went to sleep, giving it ample time to cool down.

"Here's how to open it." DE pressed a few buttons, and the lid popped; he swung it up and to the right out of their way, revealing the internal contents. On top of everything was a handwritten note. "Hi Gang," He read out loud. "Please send our roommate up to us in one piece. We look forward to his stories. Oh, by the way, we added a little gift to this drop. Signed, Bass and Trip."

"OK then, what is the special gift," Goose asked.

DE rifled through the container and revealed something, and gave the widest of smiles. "Found it." He said.

Pulling out a large plastic bottle of whiskey and 5 glasses, he turned to the group. "DESSERT!"

Belle spoke up, "Whatever we don't finish tonight, Goose and I can use to macerate that fruit and ourselves."

"Nice idea!"

"OK, let's get camp all set up." Goose said, "Get some fruit prepped and hot water on the fire. C-Note, would you be the keeper of the flame?"

"I would be honored." He had done this so many times over the last week he was getting good at it. In a few minutes, the fire pit would be ready for a pot of water. Then in about 15 or 20 minutes, dinner.

C-Note sat near the fire, finding 5 hunks of a tree to use as seats. So much better than on the ground. The air was cooling again, maybe 7°C now, and with the sun dropping fast, the temperature would follow. Goose pulled the big tarp out, and the two of them set it up around the fire pit, leaving an easy entry point facing the tents.

Belle, in the meantime, climbed into a tree facing the large rolling hills, wearing her glasses. She set it to all options, and there was nothing around on any spectrum. So she climbed down and made her way to where Belinda was cutting up fruit and, putting the diced items into a zip-top bag, added the whiskey and a few packets of sugar.

She removed as much air from the bag as she was able and then dropped it into the boiling water to cook it in a seviche-type method, at least that's what she called it. "20-minutes, and we toss it in the frying pan with the spices."

"Just did a security scan, nothing of note," Belle said to the group. "But I have this odd feeling like we're being watched. Not only that, but my brain believes the woodland creatures are talking to me or something. Just an odd feeling I have."

"Good, time to relax. Dinner will be ready shortly." C-Note said to DE. "The cooler had five packets of thanksgiving dinner, so I guess this was intended for tonight. It contains Turkey Tetrazzini, mashed potatoes, or yams. It seems there is a choice, and the others can be packed by Goose and Belle for the trip. Also, green beans in a cheese sauce and fiesta corn."

"Fiesta corn?" Goose asked.

"I don't make them. I just read the labels." C-Note replied.

"What about dessert?" Belle asked.

"Fruitcake, believe it or not. By the way, the fruitcake is my favorite." Goose said.

"You can have mine!" Pretty much everyone said.

"Not mine!" Belle said, "I like the fruitcake."

Since Goose was cooking, DE set up his tent for him. All tents and beds were ready for the night. Goose walked away from the fire and realized it got colder. Then he saw it in the twilight, snowflakes. "Uhhhh gang, it's snowing."

They sat and started eating, and the orbital team joined in, "Are you getting snow?"

"Yes, we are, light flurries at the moment, why do you ask?"

"Hang on a sec," Trip said. A moment later, another voice was added to the call.

"Hello?" The new voice said.

"Who's this?" Belle asked.

"This is Skeeter. I am DE and BG's controller. This is rather cool. We never spoke, only texted, over their time on planet."

"So nice to speak to you finally," DE said. "You have a nice voice. I forgot it since our last dinner."

Belinda added, "Skeeter if you could see the smile on his face right now...."

Everyone laughed, and Skeeter sounded a little embarrassed. "Anyway, we can meet tomorrow for the debrief. After that, we have about 100 hours on the flight home to talk. But, is there anything you need to say now?"

"Actually, there is." Belinda said with confidence, "DE and I started our contracts like any other, alone. We were forced to become a team through the sheer accident of the terrain getting all fucked up. I need to admit; first, I was a little miffed at being with someone else, and I am sure DE felt the same way, but we did more and saw more as a team than we could have alone. That is why my strongest recommendation for all future teams, including the current teams, is to be teams of two. There is a lot to be said for being together. Sharing experiences, sharing jobs, and sharing emotions."

C-Note added, "After being in this little group a few days, I understand and endorse that opinion. However, if I had it in my power, Belle and Goose and the other teams would remain as teams of two."

Trip added, "I sent that as a report to the Captain. It's up to him to make the call. I think he will, though." She paused, "Besides, if my math is correct, the current teams will all be the last. They should hit the north pole in less than the contract time."

Goose said, "Now that is a milestone." Everyone was silent for a moment, "So, about the weather...."

"Well," Trip said, "Looking at the radar, you have a major blast heading your way. Possibly half a meter by morning."

"Wonderful." Belle said, "Looks like we found the winter season."

"Not really; call it fall." Belinda started, "We hit this same weather about four or five months ago, I think. It seems to be on a 4-to-6-month cycle, so in a couple of months, the temps may hit 40°C. Remember, this planet is not tilted in the least. It has a somewhat long day and a shorter year. It is not a full circle. There is a slight wobble on the ends, so winter and summer are the wobbles, I guess?"

C-Note added, "I remember this. The equatorial plane, like Earth, is how our home planet revolves around the sun. Here, it is not a flat orbit, here it is 45 degrees off the orbital plane. So making it summer in the north and winter in the south at the same time. But I would suspect right now it is warming up in the south because it is getting colder here."

"Excellent explanation C-Note," Belle added.

"True, so I guess in 6-months, you will experience a complete revolution around the star," C-Note added.

"Works for me," Goose said. Belle nodded.

Skeeter added, "One last thing you forgot to mention. Because the orbital plane is so screwed up, the spring and fall have equal light, and the summer and winter have a lot less and a lot more sunlight. You are in what we call the NORTH, so winter is approaching."

"Glad I got my winter stuff in the pack now," Belle said.

"So, those tents and the bag. How well does it heat when the air is at its coldest?" Goose asked the other team.

"There were a couple of weeks when the weather was frigid, hit -30°C and colder for 5 days straight, not much warmer during the day. Not a lot of sun to recharge the tent or bag either, so we used one tent for those nights."

"Did you put the bags together and share?" Belle asked, grinning like the cat that ate the canary.

"We did and yes, it was what saved us. Hope you don't mind sharing." She looked at Goose and Belle.

They both just smiled at the thought. Of course, sleeping in the same bag as Belle made him happy, but the fact the air was going to be so cold, well, may take the fun out of it.

"OK." Goose said, "Let's eat!"

Dinner went well, and DE pulled out the remainder of the bourbon he had stashed away. The bottle had just enough for each person to get a couple of finger's worth and gave its all to the cause.

C-Note spoke up as the last of the elixir left the bottle. "To the mission! Surviving the hike, learning about this new world, making new friends, and happy times like this meal. To the memories."

Everyone said, "To the mission and the memories." And took a sip. It was excellent.

The other groups came online, and it became a party. The next couple of hours were filled with conversation, joking around, and yes, even a little information about the planet. Skeeter mentioned this is a great idea and wished the tech had been available to speak to her hikers on occasion.

Once it was just the 5 of them, plus the three in orbit, "So, what are tomorrow's plans?" Skeeter asked.

Double Espresso said, "I figure we get up at sunrise, have a good breakfast, verify the integrity of the pod, disperse anything we have you guys may want, and head up."

"Solid plan," Belle replied.

Goose added, "WhaCha got I may want?"

"Well, not to spoil the surprise, but the cold snap is hitting in less than a month. This is like fall. Winter is around the corner. I recommend a portable recharge unit, an extra sleeping bag to use as a quilt, few extra days of food in your pack at all times. Food that does not need boiling water, so at least 7 days of hot tab food packs. We can talk about a drop in the morning. Morning temp should be warm if we wait about an hour after sunrise to get up."

Trip said, "I just put in a request to drop ASAP the week of hot tab meals. I copied this report to all controllers to look at the weather patterns and drop the meal packs if their hiker's weather is about to take a dump."

"And on that note, I'll be filling my bag. I'm beginning to get cold, and I hate being cold," C-Note said.

The others all agreed and decided to leave the heat reflector up for the night. The fire should be hot enough to get going quickly in the morning.

Double Espresso, Belinda Goat, and C-Note all went to their tents to rest, sleep, and warm-up. Then, those in orbit disconnected and went to do what they needed to do.

Goose tapped his neck just below his right ear, the off spot for the comms unit. Belle saw and did the same.

"What?" She asked him.

"You still ok with all this?"

"Yes, I am. Not sure why but it does not seem dangerous or threatening like on the plane. It seems surreal now, but after spending a few days with the other team, I see they became close and plan to make it a permanent arrangement. Who knows?"

"I know. They paired us up well. We hike similarly, eat similarly, and have things in common already. But at the same time, you are the yin to my yang." Goose said.

"Well put, did you know I have a master's in eastern philosophy," Belle said.

"No, did I use the reference correctly, professor?" He laughed.

Belle smiled, "You did, but in Ancient Chinese philosophy, yin and yang are a concept of dualism, describing how seemingly opposite or contrary forces may be complementary, interconnected, and interdependent in the natural world. So the relation between the two diverse ideas is the answer, not the question."

"Cool!" He smiled at her and winked. "No clue what you just said, but you said it really well. So I say we do not diverge when we get to that point." He took a breath. "I like their idea of a permanent two-person team. I think it is safer, and besides, I like a shared experience."

"So do I. Not so much for safety, but as a male and female, we see things a little different, so what one misses the other sees maybe."

"Agreed. I need some sleep. I'll set the fire up for the morning and hit the hay myself."

"Good night." She said to him and left the circle. She walked to her tent with no light. The sky was phenomenal this evening, and she stood there and just looked up, trying to put Earth references to an alien sky. Her eyes adjusted to the darkness quickly, and she thought there was someone or something in the tree line.

She reached into a pocket and put on her sunglasses. Resetting to low-lux, then IR, she saw a very large Blue Bear looking directly at her. It did not appear aggressive; it was just watching her, the bear knew it was being watched, and Belle knew the bear was watching her. She realized there was no anxiety, fear, or any sense she or her fellow hikers were in danger. She nodded to the bear, and the bear dipped its head and turned around, walking away into the woods quietly, and Belle felt calm.

There was something about this event, she cannot put her finger on it, but she felt as though the mutual respect she felt for the bear and the bear felt towards her were genuine. It was almost as though she felt it in her mind, in her heart, in her being. Then, shaking herself out of the deep contemplations, she looked around one last time, and there was nothing in her view.

She walked the few steps to her tent and crawled in, setting up the inside the way she likes it for sleeping.

She heard footsteps, Goose she realized. She listened to his tent zipper – twice – and knew he was in his tent and getting ready himself. She removed her clothes and put on a pair of flannel pants, a hoodie, and a favorite pair of wool socks. These were her favorite garments. Again, she felt reminiscent of her family. The sleeping clothes she used on the trail, have used for years, were a Christmas gift from her mother many years ago when she started hiking. Mom always said if you can sleep comfortably, life has a way of working itself out.

At the moment, she is very happy to not be a very well-endowed female. A very tight shirt, or maybe a sports bra, is all she needs. There are times, though, when she wondered what it would be like……..

As she wondered what a larger chest would be like, she fell asleep. Her dreams made her smile.

~~~~~~~~~~

Goose laid there in his bag, all snug and warm and comfortable. He has been awake for just a few minutes when he heard a tent open, footsteps, noise near the fire, footsteps, and the tent closing. He started to smell the smoke of a campfire. Goose did not realize it was C-Note heading back to his tent to get the bacon.

"OK, I am guessing someone got up and prepped the fire?" He yelled.

"Guilty as charged," C-Note said. "I give it a half-hour, and you should be good to go, the embers were cherry red when I got up, and the wood I tossed on smoldered fast."

"OK, sounds like a plan," Belinda said. "You're OK for a controller, C-Note!"

"I agree!" The others all said.

Over the past couple of days, the group of five people became friends. Good friends. More to the point, they became one group. An hour before sunrise, C-Note woke up and got a fire going good. He had the coffee ready when they all woke up. He did not tell anyone, but since this is his last day on the surface, he has been carrying something special. He is making breakfast for everyone.

His secret, he has bacon in his pack and egg crystals. So he grabbed a few frying pans and started frying the bacon, and surprisingly, that woke everyone up.

They all asked, one at a time, 'Is that real bacon?'

He had crystalized whole eggs and powdered milk; he planned to make cheese omelets, but after trying to make the first one, he realized scrambled would be a lot easier and actually they would look better. Unfortunately, it seems that egg crystals do not turn into recognizable omelets, but he did eat that first experiment and found it quite good. The omelet was actually eggs scrambled with cheese.

He made sure some of the potatoes were fried crunchy, rehydrating hash browns and frying them up for everyone. The cheese would melt well over the top of the eggs for the scrambled eggs just by laying the cheese over the eggs and covering them, so the heat melts the cheese.

This is a special day. He is going back into orbit, off the planet, and away from a place he now adores. Maybe they'll let him come back again.

A few days ago, he felt like he was a nuisance. Like he had no purpose, or business, being here. But now, he realized from the campfire conversations that each person, each and every hiker, hikes their own hike. At their own pace, in their own time, in their own way. Take in the sights, the sounds, the smells. Yes, there are a few exciting smells to take in, but he realized, flipping hash browns, that he is going to miss even the aromas of a campfire, food rehydrating, even the nasty plant smell when they first arrived - a scent they are all mostly nose blind to now. But, ultimately, the trail ends, and you return to what you were, remembering the time on the trail with hope, kindness, adventure, and joy.

Yesterday afternoon they made it back to the pod. The group camped the night near the pod, which is 75 meters away. As they were setting up camp last evening, the resupply cooler was heard.

It was nice of the girls, the roommates, to pack and drop a bon voyage gift.

Sunrise came and went, C-Note watched it. It was a spectacular last-day event for him!

He has been up for more than 90-minutes prepping for a great breakfast. None of the others wanted to get up. The air temp was bitterly cold.

About 30-min later, the ambient temperature increased, and the smell of bacon cooking filled their nostrils. The hikers got up and dressed in less than a minute and made their way to the fire. Taking the same seats as last night, they looked at the spread C-Note laid out for them.

They looked over at the controller in their midst, and he finished up preparing the fresh coffee, scrambled eggs with cheese, perfectly cooked hash browns, and bacon. Freshly cooked, almost crispy bacon.

"OK, what gives?" BG asked.

"Well, for half of this trip, Belle and Goose kept me alive. For the second half of the trip, all four of you kept me alive. So this is my way of saying thank you for not letting me die down here." He paused, "Well, dig in. I made enough for ten hikers, so you got your work ahead of you!"

They all grabbed more than their usual amount of bacon since the packets came in a kilogram pack; he fried up an entire kilogram of bacon. They sat in their same seats again, like they were assigned, and had a chat. It did snow, but not much, a heavy dusting. Inside the reflective ring, the temp was so warm all the snow melted already. The seats were mostly dry, but a small plastic layer C-Note put on them last night ensured they did not get a wet butt.

"I thought the cold was not for a while," Goose asked.

"We gained about 1500 meters over the last few days. Higher altitude, different air temp, different weather pattern." Belinda said. "You got a couple of thousand more meters before you hit the top, and there looks to be a path if you keep heading in the same direction."

"So.....cold!" Belle said to be funny.

"Yes. Cold. But it's a dry cold!" Double Espresso replied as a joke. Everyone laughed at that joke.

"I'm wondering if holding up for a month up the hills would be safer than hiking in sub-zero days and more suber-zero nights," C-Note said.

"Well," Belinda started, "We were about this altitude during the 2-weeks we had to hold up because of the coldest weather. The snow and wind were horrible, but we were both in one tent, bags on max heat, and zipped together at night, making it tolerable. We devised a lean-to shelter that broke the wind, reflective material in the shelter's back, fire in front of the shelter. It made it tolerable during the day, and the night in the tent was not bad since the bags and tents are heated somewhat. There was one day we did not leave the tent or the

164

sleeping bag with very few exceptions. Air temp, wind, snow, overcast. You get the picture. But we survived and actually would not give those days up for anything."

She paused a moment, "Since we had nothing else to do, we talked. Got to know each other better. This was a week and a half after our trails merged. We knew each other, talked a little, but by no means knew each other well enough to sleep in the same sleeping bag. We traveled for a week or so together, so we were beginning to get closer. But, when the weather turned deadly, the survival instincts kicked in. It was freakin cold. We lived on protein bars mostly. We shared the few instaheat meals from the bags, sitting in the tent or completely submerged in the sleeping bag. As it started warming up, the tent would compensate for the extreme cold outside, and we used our packs as back support. Seriously, that was the best week of my life!"

DE added, "During this time is when the Kitties started to visit more often. We fed a few of them, and they brought us food: the blue fruit, potatoes, and the onion balls. We never felt threatened by them at all. A few of them even cuddled like cats, and at one point, we protected them from the bird dog. I think they look at humans like protectors, and I believe the odd sounds at night are them talking to each other. Like a continuous messaging system. One starts, and the next and the next; it sounds as though they send the same message around the planet at night."

"There was one time," Belinda took over, "they passed on a message they heard while they were in the area near our fire. At one point, at the coldest timeframe, there were a dozen of them at our feet. That is the largest group we saw. A few of them stayed in our tent one night. It was like having a pet. When they wanted out in the morning, they made a sound, and I swear they asked us to open the zipper. The sound was like music, and the words, if you can call them that, like lyrics. We recorded the received sounds from far off in the distance and recorded their sounds after hearing them. The match was 98%. Those creatures have rudimentary intelligence; I call them space Kitties, but pure instinct in the blue bear. Nothing cuddly about them. If they see you, they either try to eat you, or they ignore you."

"Did you send the recordings to your controller?" C-Note asked.

"We did. They ran it through whatever they run things through and told us except for the pitch, the two sound clips are nearly identical."

"I may need a copy of that when I get back upstairs," C-Note said to the group.

Belle added, "Last night, as I was heading to my tent, I heard something. I used the glasses and saw a blue bear staring at me, but I felt a peace and a calm coming from her."

Goose added, "Her?"

"Yes," Belle said. "Somehow, I know it was her, a female blue bear." She sipped her coffee, "We looked at each other for a few moments, then she nodded to me and turned back into the woods."

"Wow," DE said after a few moments of silence. "Also, there are some cool-looking birds you will see when it warms up a bit." DE added, "Mostly blue, but some are red. Not sure if they are the same species or not. There is one other creature, a bird .... well, sorta. It is about the size of an eagle with both fur and feathers; it takes off like a Goose, not you brother, with a larger wingspan," Everyone smiled at the joke, "which lets it float on the air easily. Their face looks like an animal, close to a dog, I think. The only one we saw had been dead a while, and it was nibbled on so...."

"Ah! Bird-Dog, I get it now. You saved the Kitties from them?" Belle asked.

"Yeppers!" DE said.

The next few hours, they rifled through backpacks and stuff, and the old team passed on information and gear to Belle and Goose. Goose had extra space in his pack, so he took C-Note's sleeping bag as a spare. In reality, it was only a week old. Belle grabbed the 7 spare power cells and carried them in case they were cut off from the sun for a while in bad weather. Finally, the three departing hikers pulled out their remaining food and gave it to them, who packed it in their packs. Fortunately, the pod they dropped in on never went back up, so no one knew C-Note had a special package in it.

He went into the pod, returned with a couple of bottles, and gave them to Belle and Goose. He handed them a half-liter bottle of scotch and bourbon. They also had the remaining whiskey from the other gang, so they were set.

"Excellent, thanks. We are set for antiseptic!" Goose said and received groans from everyone.

Stowing their remaining gear in the pod, they all hugged each other and wished them all well. Then, the three entered the pod, with Belle and Goose standing at the door.

"OK, who's taking seat one?" C-Note asked.

DE said, "Odd hiker wins." C-Note felt good about that. He actually felt like a hiker now. He put a fist into his other hand, and the others followed. At the same time, they slapped their fist into their other open hand, and on the third one, they extended either one or two fingers. C-Note and DE had a 1, Belinda had two. "I guess you get to press the button."

Belinda sat in seat one; the others sat wherever. "BYE GUYS, Be safe, have fun, let's meet further down the trail." She pressed the closed-door button. Belle and Goose stepped back about 5 meters.

A minute later, a loud beeping as the ship enunciated an impending launch, each beep a higher pitch and a much longer beep to announce the launch. Then, finally, the engines fired, and the pod jumped into the clouds. They could almost hear C-Note screaming.

"Well, now what?" Goose looked at Belle.

"I know, wanna go for a hike!" She replied.

"Great idea; how about that way?" He pointed in the correct direction. They picked up their packs and put them on, and started walking into the hills.

Chapter Seven

Stopping for the night was a great idea. When they finished setting up, it was just beginning to get dark, and the wind was calm, and the air temperature was about 10°C with clear skies. So, a clear sky means no ground blanket, so the air would cool off considerably.

They started a small fire since it was just the two of them and heated water for dinner. Then, they made a nice cup of tea and ate a meat meal, supposedly pot roast, rehydrated.

"Add the mashed taters into the pot roast, add more water. Make it a backcountry shepherds pie, sorta," Goose said to Belle, who was tending to the rehydration.

"Good idea; I got a few ghee packets also. That should help too." Belle answered.

About the time they started eating, the comms turned into a party line.

"Well," said Belle, "We survived a whole day alone, just the two of us." Then, she took a bite, "Holy crap, this is good!"

"What did you make?" Toonist asked.

"We had the pot roast and added a couple packets of ghee and a packet of mashed taters and some extra water. Backcountry shepherd's pie. OMG, this is great!"

"Today is our first day alone," Reena said. "The old guys launched just after lunchtime. Grabbed a bit of their gear before they did. I like the idea Bass Master had, that we continue as a team and not split up. I think it is more efficient." She paused a moment, "There it is. I'll be making the pot roast thing tomorrow."

"Also, taters and the chili mixed are really good too!" Goose said as Belle stuffed dinner into her face. She turned to him and smiled, then opened her mouth to let him see inside. He almost started laughing.

"She got that team idea from C-Note, he got it from us, and also the recommendation of Belinda Goat and Double Espresso."

"You relieved Double Espresso?" Reena asked.

"We did. Why?" Goose asked. "But you know that already. We all talked during dinner. Remember?"

"Yes, I heard the name but did not realize it till just now. You kept calling him DE. However, I'm not one to kiss and tell, but DE and I were on the PCT a couple of years back, and he hit a summit and stopped earlier in the day than I did. I came upon his site just after dark, and he offered to share his fire and his site, so I set up camp with him on that bump in the dirt. I took a fall earlier that day and told him I was taking a zero right here to give my ankle a chance to feel better. He told me it sounded like a good idea and went and got us 5 liters of water at the stream, clean water. He filtered it as he filled the container. We were set for the day. After that, we walked together for a few days, maybe a week, and we hit Sierra City. We decided to take a real zero, do laundry, resupply. I needed a new ankle wrap anyway. As we got off the trail, a guy was waiting in a small parking area to take us - hikers - into town. He was a trail angel and suggested these cute little cottages for our night there. Well, we tried to give the guy money, but he would not accept it. The cottage was full except for one room. I thought about finding another place, then randomly, I looked at DE and asked if we could share the room. He agreed."

There was a pause as she sipped something, "Well, we figured there would be two beds in the room since this is on a hiker path, and as we walked in, we realized there was only one bed. The king bed would have been great, a queen would have been OK, but it was a full-size bed. That meant we would be intimate. He looked at me and tilted his head like a puppy. It was so cute. Let's just say we had a great triple zero and leave it at that...." Changing the subject, "So, who was cold last night? I was freezing. For some reason, I could not get warm. I think the humid air got into my tent and my bag and got me wet. Besides, we had some rain just before bedtime, and I think I got wetter than I thought I did."

"The same thing happened to me. I stripped and crawled into my bag; in 5 minutes, I was toasty."

Belle said. Goose's turn to wink at her, she got the joke and smiled back at him.

The conversation shifted many subjects but settled on taking a zero when finding something interesting and a definite zero on hiker box day.

Goose spoke, "I looked ahead a bit and, in a few days, there will be a valley near the summit of the range we are climbing. Think of a 6,000-meter mountain with the Grand Canyon cut into the top of it. Waterfalls, rivers, who knows what else. I think we may need to find someplace between here and there to settle in for the cold snap that is getting closer every day. There has to be a good place to stay for a couple of weeks during the horrible cold we are supposed to get soon."

"You looked ahead?" Chisel asked.

"Yes. I sent a flyover request to C-Note and with the weather forecast for the path. The drone entered a thousand meters over us, a good shot of us at the fire ring, and it flew to the top of the world. We have only a few hundred kilometers till we hit the top of the world. The forecast for the path for the next month or so is cold, really cold, and oh shit, it's cold. Periods of snow, rain, ice pellets and on rare occasion sun." He took a sip of his tea. "Ask your controllers to do that too." For some reason, the controllers were not online tonight.

They talked for another hour and disconnected. It was nearly dark and getting colder. Finally, Belle and Goose crawled into their tents to get some rest.

Several hours later, Goose got up to use a tree. Belle heard him and realized she needed to do the same. But, unfortunately, the air was positively frigid. Afterward, she crawled back into her bag and could not get warm after nearly an hour.

"Hey Goose, you awake?"

"I am, just finally getting warm again."

"I cannot get warm at all." She crawled out of her bag and put on her shoes and coat. Walked to his tent and talked as she walked there, "Well, put out the welcome mat since I plan to share your body heat. I am so cold right now I am starting to feel sick."

He rearranged a few things in the tent, and since they both opted for the extra-long bag, it was also extra wide. She opened his tent, crawled in, and rezipped it. After taking off her shoes and coat, he opened the bag for her, and she crawled into his sleeping bag. It was somewhat cozy, but in a really good way, they both thought to themselves. They were both wearing flannel pants and a hoodie. He put his arm under his pillow and her head, and they spooned Belle in front.

"I like your sleeping attire," Belle said.

"Thanks, a gift from my Mom when I started hiking. I like yours, by the way too. Like we shopped at the same store or something."

"Actually, mine, down to my socks, was also a gift from my mother. So I guess we have pretty cool moms!"

"We'll have to tell them next time we see them," Goose said.

He realized how cold she really was when she got into his sleeping bag. Now he was concerned. She was shivering more than he had ever seen before. It took several long minutes for her to warm up, and he got as close to her as possible for maximum heat transfer. Finally, the shivering slowed and then stopped. She was finally warmer and let out a sigh. That's when they both fell sound asleep, content and warm. They both fell asleep fast since the inside of the bag was finally warm.

When they woke up, the sun was high in the sky. They were comfortable together and slept a lot longer than they usually would have.

"Holy crap!" Goose said.

Belle jumped, "What?"

"The sun is up, way up. We slept longer than I thought we would."

"I am so comfortable, though."

"I need to find a tree," Goose said

"Thanks, now I gotta pee too."

They got up and put on shoes and a coat, and went to relieve themselves.

"Thank you, by the way," Belle said.

"For what?"

"Letting me share your body heat. That is the best night's sleep I had in a long time."

"Me too. I woke up during the night and forgot for a moment where I was, then I remembered you were there with me, and I felt content, happy. I fell back to sleep easily." Goose said.

"I did the same. You put your arm over me, and it startled me for a minute. Then I felt everything was going to be ok."

They finished what they were doing and returned to the tent at the same time. They looked at each other, eye to eye, and they felt a connection. Maybe they can explore that connection over the next few months.

Belle broke the trance, "So, do we stay an extra night or two here or press on?"

Goose thought for a minute, "I like what the old guys said. Explore left and right of the trail when you set up camp on a drop day, take a zero once in a while and experience the beauty this planet has to offer. We have the comms so we can stay in contact. So, let's blue blaze a bit. I say day pack, lunch on the road, return for dinner. If either of us finds anything we can use as food, bring it back. So, drop day is actually tomorrow, I think, so a pre- and a post-zero?"

No snow last night, but the cold was to the bone. The air temp was already about 13°C, so they would be comfortable at least. They each got dressed pretty warm and pulled out a small pack and packed it with snacks and water and whatever else they needed for the day. The day pack was incorporated seamlessly into the backpack, so it was a perfect small pack to use. Heading off in opposite directions, they started their day.

"So, I say we head off and be back long before dark. Walk maybe an hour or so and then turn around and head back."

"Agreed. And Goose, stay away from Blue Bears, please."

"Yes, Ma'am!"

"I estimate that if we walk for a little more than an hour or so, we can be a kilometer or two away, turn around and head back. So that will give us a two, or actually, a four-kilometer, span from the campsite if you take a slightly altered path on the way back."

"That works; I am recording as I walk, so they will be getting both our voices. We can do a play-by-play as we walk, adding the human element like they want." Goose said.

"I think this is a beautiful planet with a lot of flora and a lot of fauna." She said through the comms.

"AHHHhhh!" Goose yelled.

"What happened?" Belle yelled back.

"A small red bird just landed on my shoulder. It has no fear of me and is content to just sit there as I walk. Kinda reminds me of a Cardinal. I think I'll call him Louis."

"You mean as in the St. Louis Cardinal. You got issues."

"Yes, issues make life interesting."

They walked in silence more or less for 45 minutes, and Belle came to a waterfall. It was spectacular. She ended up on a plateau midway up but not wet from the water. She sat in the grass and did nothing. Just sat there and took it all in and appreciated it, all of it.

She looked around and saw every possible creature and assumed the water contained fish since the blue bear was pulling them out and sharing with other smaller blue bears. If she had her tenkara rod with her, she would have attempted to climb down to the water and test it out.

Goose came upon a vast field, rolling hills, meadow, and a family of Blue Bears playing in the sun. The largest Blue Bear stopped and looked directly at Goose, who froze. He did not turn around but slowly began backing away from the field the way he came. "Well, I'll be turning around. Blue Bear family playing in the grass up ahead." He told her.

His voice broke her trance. She was not there at the moment; her mind was somewhere else. "I refilled my canteen and am heading back too. What's Louis doing?"

"Just sitting on my shoulder taking in the sights. He knew the Blue Bears were there, and I think he tried to warn me. Hold on. Louis snuggled to my neck and is falling asleep. I wish I could get a picture of this." He paused a moment, "He has a clear spot behind his left ear, or where an ear would be, I guess. It's in the shape of a heart."

"Clear spot, like no feathers?"

"Exactly, but his feathers have the feeling more like fur about them. Crazy odd but pretty cool, feels very soft."

"I'm getting hungry. I may have my lunch." Belle said.

"I want to be further away from the blue beasties before I make food. I have no idea how far they can smell chili, but I may just eat the dessert and be done with it."

"I have peanut butter and crackers and a s'more's protein bar," Belle said.

"I have the same thing, but my peanut butter has chocolate in it." He ate and walked and talked to Belle.

Forty minutes later, he hit a stream. He passed it on the way out, so he knows he is about 40 minutes from the camp. He sat by the creek, ate another bar, granola, and gave some to Louis, who also liked it.

He pulled out a large mesh bag from his day pack. Removing the mess kit, he propped it open with a couple of twigs. He tossed it into the stream, and a few minutes later, he had a few fish in it. He retracted the bag and looked at the fish. Reminded him of brook trout with a horn, and he wondered how they would taste. "I'll name you rhinotrout!"

He had an empty container in his pack and filled it with water. Then he put 8 of the largest little fish ranging in length from 25 to 35 centimeters in the box of water. Goose secured the lid and put it back in his bag. He lowered the remainder of the fish into the water and let them go. He had caught more than a dozen, so Belle will be happy to know fishing is excellent on this planet. They should survive returning to the camp for the next half hour or so. There was plenty of water in the box.

"Got you a little gift." He told Belle through the comms.

"What is it?" She asked.

"Well, I stopped at a local seafood restaurant and picked us up some fresh fish for dinner. I know it's fresh because they are still moving. I picked up some garlic, lemon, and butter packets on the plane; they're in my pack. How about pan-fried space trout? Maybe we can call them RhinoTrout?"

"Oh my god, that sounds great. RhinoTrout?" She queried, "Wait, how did you catch them?"

"Well, you'll understand the name when you see them, and I caught them when I pulled out the mesh bag off my mess kit and propped it open, dropped it in the stream, and waited a few minutes. Finally, I pulled it up out of the water, and Poof! I had more than a dozen little fishes that look like rhino-brook trout."

"Smart!" She said, then added, "Before we clean them, we can scan them to be sure they will not hurt us."

"My thought exactly." He said to her, "So, what did you find on this little side trip?"

"A beautiful waterfall, potatoes, and something that appears to be an onion. I grabbed a couple of taters and an onion. Found those fruit things also and grabbed a few of them."

"Funny, I got a couple of those fruit things also. The onion and taters will be great with the fish. If only we found fresh lemons too!"

They both returned to base camp. Belle got there first and pushed up the fire a bit, warming things up. The air temperature was not too bad now, but looking at the sky from where they were located on the side of this mountain, they realized a new weather pattern was moving in. Gray clouds headed their way, and as clear as the sky looked straight up, they knew it would be a cold, bitterly cold night.

Goose got back to the site and went to the fire to warm up. Belle was sitting there poking it and making the embers heat the reflector she set up.

"Hi, look over there?" He pointed to the clouds moving in.

"I saw; gonna get nasty tonight." She said.

"And cold, I expect." He said to her. "I have an idea. Since using a single tent will give us the best chance to stay warm, I want to propose...."

"Propose?" She said to him, grinning from ear to ear.

"You know what I mean!" He said, smiling back at her.

"I know. What's your idea?" She asked.

"Well, these tents provide temperature stability from a certain internal to the external temperature differential. So if one tent is inside another tent, will it heat up to a warmer temp. We can check; the bag will lower that temp safety margin, but I suspect we are in for a massive cooling down. Zip our bags together and share body heat; I have the extra bag from C-Note we can use as a cover blanket. I think we should be comfortable to maybe -20°C to -30°C in this configuration, possibly even colder."

She thought about it for a minute, and the others jumped into their heads at that time.

"You guys are in for a bad week. Looking at the weather, there is a massive cold front moving in on you, and you will be in it in the next few hours." C-Note said.

"How long do we have?" Goose asked.

"Rain in 3 hours or so, then sleet, snow; an hour after that, the temp will drop bad, maybe -20 or -25 overnight. Tomorrow the expected high is maybe a

182

minus 10. This is the pattern for the next 5 days. I suggest staying right where you are and, as they say, hunker down. You have food, water, shelter, and company. So, safety is more important than the mission at the moment."

Belle started, "We talked about that. We put my tent in his tent, zipping our bags together and using the extra bag from C-Note as a blanket over us. We suspect we should be good to about -30 or more. But, you said this is for the next 5 days?"

"Yes, after that, the air will warm up and stay around 5°C for the next while and slowly warm. Spring seems to be coming to where you are, and in a couple of weeks, you can dispense with the winter garb altogether."

"How are the other teams doing?" Goose asked.

"You two are experiencing some freaky weather. The other two teams are getting 15 during the day and 7 at night. There is no rain in their forecast, but they are much lower in altitude than you two and a lot lower in latitude. If this was a race to the north pole, you would be a few weeks in the lead."

Belle had a thought, "When do you think we will hit the North Pole?"

"Just a guess, let me see...." C-Note said to them. "Well, if you maintain 15 kilometers a day for the next five or six weeks, you will be at the top of the world."

"Hey, C-Note. Do me a favor." She continued, "Set up a cooler drop at the pole in a few months. Something special, a celebration. All 50 teams, 100 hikers joining up at the pole for a TOP OF THE WORLD celebration dinner. Coordinate it with your counterparts and get the Captain involved; this is right up his alley. Hell, he may even come down and hang out with us for a while."

"I like that. I'll let you know what happens. We got a while to plan it out. I say turkey, prime rib, LOTS of sides, and some impressive desserts. As you call them, the coolers can keep food at temp for a few days, hot or cold. I say stock a pod with tables and chairs, another with resupply items, another couple with people. Yes, this will be amazing. GREAT IDEA, you two!"

Goose said, "This is all Belle. This is the first I heard of it, but it is making me want to get to the pole first to get it all scoped out for the perfect setting." He looked at her. "What gave you the inspiration?"

She got sentimental in her demeanor, "Sitting by that waterfall, I was lonely. I needed someone to share that experience with; you went left, and I went right. I saw the waterfall and the valley; you saw the rolling hills, the stream, and the fish."

"FISH?" C-Note stated emphatically.

"Yes," Goose said in return. "Caught a dozen and kept a few of them; they are still alive, I just checked. Our dinner tonight. Belle found potatoes and onion things. I have Ghee packets and a frying pan, so we are cooking a real meal tonight."

C-Note sounded excited. "Describe the fish."

"Similar in look and size to brook trout. Has a horn like a rhino though, I called them Rhinotrout. We'll let you know how they taste. I will video as we clean, prepare, and cook the meal. This way, you will get it in the upload tonight."

"Good idea. Have you scanned them yet?"

"No, not yet. Just about to do that when you called."

"Can you do it now, please?"

"Sure." Belle went to her tent, pulled the medical scanner from her pack, and returned to the fire ring. She opened the container and grabbed one of the fish, and pulled it out. Then, holding the scanner up to it, she activated the device. A moment later, a green light popped up, signifying it is safe to eat. "Greenlight."

"Excellent," C-Note replied.

Goose asked, "Is there a chance that a green light means it is most likely safe to eat?"

C-Note replied, "No, there are 4 lights. Red, blue, yellow, and green, remember? Green is the complete absence of any human dangers. Yellow means there may be one or two components that can potentially make you ill, queasy, nauseated. Blue is unique. This means what is being scanned can contain bacteria, and if cooked to death, it will be safe to eat. Red, throw it away, no chance it is human-compatible."

"That's a better explanation than we got during the training session on the ship!"

"On the ship, I have a syllabus, a script. Out the window now, we can discuss anything since you are in the thick of it." He paused, "Did you ever get the chance to teach Goose about the pistols?"

Belle smiled, "No, I haven't, and I have been carrying around multiple extra clips of ammo for just this occasion."

"Maybe time to teach. He does need to be good with the weapons."

"Understood. Sun is going down here shortly, so I will complete that training tomorrow or the next day when the air is comfortable. Since we are staying on this spot till the weather breaks, we should be good. No evidence of blue bears around here. I am wondering if they limit themselves to the lower altitudes since food is easier to find."

"Good thought; I hope you're right."

"Well, we need to clean the fish, prep the veggies, and cook. Give us an hour or so and buzz back. Then, we can give you the book report on our dinner." Goose said. "I got an idea. When it warms a little, we can put a few fish in a container with water and send them up in the cooler. You can analyze the shit out of them, then fry them up for a final experiment!"

"Works for me! I look forward to hearing about the taste of the fish." C-Note said. "As for the cooler, I think since the weather is starting to suck, we'll send you one right now. You can send the little buggers up. Need anything?"

"Actually, several more power cells. A shit ton of instaheat coffee and tea and an armful of instaheat meals. This way, we don't need to get out of the tent to heat water to eat."

"On its way. Before you start traveling again, let me know, and I can send a resupply box down, so you have everything you need and can ditch all the trash." He disconnected.

Belle pulled the fish container out and looked at them. "I wonder what the insides of a space trout look like?" She laughed.

Goose laughed, "I wonder what color it's going to be?"

A few minutes later, the hiker box descended and landed a few meters away. Goose went over to it and popped it open. "True to his word. Belle, we got a dozen power cells. 24 instacoffee and tea mix, and 24 various instameals. Here's a note."

"Read it!" She yelled.

"Guys. Looking forward to trying the fish. Here's the stuff you asked for, plus I added an extra tarp. Maybe it can block the wind or something. Portable heat unit in there too. Run it as needed; this is a supercharged unit. It burns through a power cell in about 5 hours. When you put the fish in the box and are ready to send them up, enter code 100101105. This will direct it here, our *triad* station, instead of the trash compactor. Bass and I will examine the little fishies, and Trip said she would cook us dinner!"

"OK, you have 8, so we can send them 5. So you and I can share 3 fish, more than enough protein in these little fishes according to the scanner." Belle said.

Belle found a somewhat flat tree stump to use as a table. She pulled out the super knife they gave her and made a cut. "White blood?" She continued to clean the 3 fish and figured she got maybe a kilogram or more in filets. A lot of fish to eat, but they need it right now.

Goose was prepping the onions, fry pan, and potatoes. "How's the fish?"

"The guts looked more normal than I thought they would, but they are oddly opaque. A very light pink, almost white in places."

As she cleaned and started cooking, Goose prepped the other 5 fish for a trip into orbit. He noted the inside of the hiker box was about 20°C, so he put his box inside the space-proof box and grabbed a couple other empty containers in case he needed another water-tight container.

"C-Note sent us 8 liters of water."

"We can put it into the tent, and hopefully, it will not freeze. One less thing we will need to do. I hope the mouth of the bottles are wide; we can pee in them and be warmer since we will not need to leave the tent that often."

"Yep, wide mouth," Goose replied.

As he was securing the fish box, he saw something that may come in handy. "Belle, C-Note sent us a tent size porta-potty. We can take turns!" He was starting to laugh and nearly choked out the last few words. Belle heard every word and almost fell into the fire laughing.

~~~~~~~~~~

"The fish is fantastic!" Belle said. "Reminds me of crab or lobster in its texture. Perfect for grilling since it will not flake apart."

"OK, how did you cook it?" Reena asked.

"Forget that. How did you catch it?" Chisel broke in loud.

Goose spoke, "OK, I grabbed the mesh from my mess kit and propped the opening open with a couple of small twigs. Tied a cord to the drawstring and waited a few minutes, and pulled it up. I had more than a dozen of them in there. I kept 8 and released the rest back into the water."

Belle took over, "As for the cleaning, well, they are similar to Earth fish, but their insides are unique. I fully cleaned one just to look. The rest I just filleted, and let me tell you that the skin peels off

189

easily, and there are no bones if you fillet them. The meat is tight, white, but a little bluish, and the taste is amazing—a natural lemon hint. We found potatoes and an onion thing and had ghee and garlic. A couple of packets of lemon juice after they were cooked too. Taste is a cross between trout and lobster with the texture of lobster or crab."

"It's getting a little late, gotta give up the dish. I will send you a message tonight in the upload. You can all look at it in the morning." C-Note told them. "Bass and I got the fish up here and did pretty much the same thing. You are right. Those little buggers are tasty! Trip cooked them up, discovered she was a chef or something in a previous life, pre-hiker days. Trust me, she still has got it!"

They all disconnected.

They finished up their meals and went to the closest stream to do dishes. Put everything into the bear bags and sat by the fire. Belle was getting cold, so was Goose. All the bundling could not warm them up.

"We need to get into the tent." She said. "I am getting cold to the bone."

"I ain't far behind you, Belle." They finished prepping the camp for the night, and both crawled into one tent.

"Now, this is purely for comfort. Don't get no ideas, like I know you are getting."

"Well, if you are saying that, then you must be having ideas also." He smiled at her. "Let's just get warm, and we can talk; I ain't exactly tired yet."

"Neither am I, but I am freezing." She said.

They quickly put everything up and got into the tent. They realized there was only one tent, so changing in privacy would mean one of them had to go outside. Goose started to undress, and Belle got the idea and did the same.

The little lantern light was lit between them but off to one side. Goose looked at her and realized how beautiful she was; it was the first time he thought that thought and wondered why he had not seen it before.

Belle removed her shirt and sports bra and put on a long-sleeved T-shirt. As she did, she looked over at Goose and realized he was pretty nice to look at. He was only about 3 centimeters taller than she was at 180 centimeters. He removed his pants and shorts, and she saw his rear end and his front end. She looked away before he noticed. He put on his flannel pants and wool socks and also had a long-sleeved T-shirt. As he turned around, she removed her pants, and she looked beautiful, he thought to himself. It was written on his face. She saw it plain as day when they looked at each other.

They crawled into the bag, ensuring the two identical sleeping pads were latched together. Both lying on their left side with Belle spooned in close to him. Neither of them said a word, just snuggled together. They stayed that way for maybe 45 minutes in near silence, and Belle spoke.

"You asleep?" She whispered.

"Nope. Just enjoying the company."

"Me too." She paused a minute. "We need to talk." He stayed silent, and she continued. "Where are we heading with this? I am not sure, but I am developing some pretty deep feelings for you in record time. I am comfortable in this position with you, and I have never been comfortable like this before."

"Wait, you mean you have never been comfortable before?"

"You know what I am trying to say. I never have…. I mean, I have not…. But, oh crap, I'll just say it."

"No need. I understand." He paused a moment and held her just a little tighter, "I have never felt like this about anyone, ever. When the guys were alone, DE and C-Note mentioned that the comm implant can lead to reliance or dependency on some people. But it is infrequent. However, the person you are connected to, the one you are mentally linked to, does become emotionally connected in a very short time." He took a deep breath. "I think what he was trying to say is that he and the goat fell in love faster and deeper because of the implant only a couple of weeks after they met."

"You mean like us?" They both smiled at that but did not see the other's face to realize it. "We have known each other only a couple of weeks, but we have been emotionally connected the entire time." She paused. "Can I say how if feel about you? Yes, I can, but the problem is it has to be a two-way street."

"Just say exactly what you are feeling, then I will." He said to her.

After a long and grueling minute, she spoke. "I am not sure, since this is the first time and all, but I think I am falling in love with you. I am comfortable in the same bag as you and not self-conscience all that much. I am not sure when, but I will be ready one day to move it to the next level of our relationship. But, for the moment, I am thrilled with this arrangement and very happy with you, us."

Goose took a deep breath and finally spoke, "I have never uttered the words I love you before in my entire life. But I do love you. I am happy with how we are progressing in this relationship and want to tell you that I have never....uh....either. So in that respect, we are in the same boat. If we decide to take it to the next level, we can talk about it. The best part of a relationship is exploring and learning it together. So let's explore this relationship. Together."

She turned over and kissed him. First time and it was long, it was passionate, and it was beautiful. They both felt it. They separated their lips, and he looked at her.

"Let's get some sleep. I am warm and happy and content at the moment." He smiled at her, and in the dim lantern light, she saw the smile.

"What's that smile for?" She asked.

"Well, I was just thinking about you. I am smiling for you, really; I mean, we have become yin and yang. So, unless the professor can come up with another reference, then explain it to me? Then possibly explain the explanation."

"Let me sleep on it. We can talk in the morning." She kissed him again and rolled over. Snuggling all the closer to him. Goose turned off the lantern and put his arms back into the bag. She felt what the kiss and the feelings have done to him as she snuggled, but it should go away. He draped his arm over her, and it rested on her chest, but that's ok. A few minutes later, they were both warm and content and asleep.

~~~~~~~~~~

"Belle and Goose, we activated the comms from our end. Can you hear us?"

Very groggy, "I hear you." Belle said. "Why are you calling us so early."

"It's past midday; the three of us just woke up also."

"Midday? It's still dark?" Goose said.

"If we were on Earth, it would be past noon. So the best explanation we can figure is that we all slept for fifteen hours."

"How?" Belle asked. "We all?"

"We think it was the fish. There may be something in the fish to induce sleep, like a huge dose of melatonin or something like turkey meat, the trippy stuff. As for the dark, I recommend staying where you are right now. The ambient temp at the moment is -30°C with a wind chill fast approaching, holy shit!" C-Note said.

"What's the forecast?"

"This same weather for the next 30 hours, then it will break. Colder but nice." C-Note paused a moment. "I do not recommend going outside for anything till tomorrow morning. If you can, find something to pee in. Did you see the little potty I sent? If you go outside, your skin could freeze while you are using the tree."

"That's a bad thought, C-Note," Belle said.

"Yes, it is," Goose added.

"OK, I need to run. I will check in with you later today. There are 19 other teams in the same weather as you, and your tent in a tent idea has been passed around. Stay warm. Stay safe."

"I really gotta pee now," Belle said.

"So do I," Goose said.

"I have nothing to pee in here in the tent, that's all in the bear bag, and I have no intention of peeing in my water bottle." He said. "Once we drain a water bottle he sent us, we can use that. Those are throw-away bottles."

She unzipped the bag, and the heat was replaced by cold. "Holy shit!" She said.

"I'll go with you, coat and shoes."

They unzipped the tent after ensuring the sleeping bag was closed to not let in more cold air. When they did, they realized it was a winter wonderland, sorta. Maybe 6 centimeters of snow everywhere except the fire ring.

Belle took about two steps away from the tent and squatted on the ground; Goose stood next to her, facing away, and felt a lot better afterward. "Less snow than I thought there would be." She said.

"I'm glad in a way it is too cold to snow, but I am going to put a bunch of wood on the pit and hopefully keep the embers hot." He said.

"Great Idea," She said to him. "I'll get back in the bag and warm it up for you."

He laughed at her, "Thanks! What a sacrifice!"

"That's what I'm here for…." She yelled back as she crawled into the tent.

She went into the tent, zipped it back up, stripped off her coat and shoes, and climbed into the bag.

She was positively frozen, but she warmed up and stopped shivering in just a couple of minutes.

Goose went to the fire and felt the heat of the embers, still hot enough to ignite the wood. As he was loading it up, he saw smoldering and knew it would be fine. So he made a pile and created a great-looking ember bed which should be good for at least a day. He stopped at the bear bag and grabbed a few porta-potty packets if needed to do the other thing. He got back to the tent and took off his coat and shoes, and crawled into the bag next to Belle.

"Hi there. Do I know you?" He asked her.

"I believe we met on the plane." She said.

"Oh, your that hiker......uh.....Belle or something."

"Yep, that's me!"

"You hungry?" He asked her.

"Yes, I am; why. You going to cook?" She said.

"Actually, no. I took 6 packets of oatmeal from the bear bag and put them into this thermos of boiling water yesterday night. Still mighty warm. Also, I grabbed like 4 protein bars. So I think we are set for the next couple of days if we have to stay in this tent."

"Protein bars for lunch, oatmeal for dinner." She said.

"Sounds like a plan. I have 4 instaheat meals if we need something bigger. But light food may be better right now." He replied. "That, and we have the little bottle left over, we can toast to freezing to death or something."

"Sounds like a plan. Oh wait, I just heard that somewhere." They both laughed.

They were facing each other, and he rolled onto his back and opened a chocolate bar. She opened the smores bar. "Great lunch." She said. Finishing the bar, "Wow, I'm full,"

Goose replied. "What's for dessert?"

"Your choice, another protein bar," She said to him.

"I grabbed the pee-pee packets too." He said randomly.

She laid her head on his shoulder, "No, pee-pee packets do not sound like a good dessert."

They both started laughing again. When they calmed down, they talked. They both thought this may turn out to be a great situation.

For the next 30 hours, they talked about everything. Finally, they had one spoon between them and shared the oatmeal over the next day.

The gang all intruded for a couple of hours, and they needed to use the tree again during the call.

They went out together, and this time she held him for support. She saw him naked, and he knew it, but now he is not embarrassed about it. They were becoming a couple. And a stronger, more emotionally bonded pair of souls never before existed.

They spent the next day and a half in the sleeping bag together, learning about one another. Talking, holding each other. Hearing about each other's dreams, aspirations, and fears. They bonded spiritually, emotionally, and someday physically. Neither of them wanted to ruin what they had; suffice it to say, they were each afraid of the next step.

They were dating in a sense. Courting.

The comms implant meant a more profound connection at a basic level, a sub-conscience level. Emotional communications without knowing they are doing it or what they are sharing. This is a silent, stealth communication between the comm systems, direct communications between two hearts. Emotions, not words. Implied information, not a paragraph. Not words, but feelings.

Tomorrow or so, the weather will improve.

Tomorrow they can venture out of the tent again.

Tomorrow....

Chapter Eight

Over the past several weeks, Belle and Goose have been in separate tents and sleeping bags as the weather is continually improving. They talk, learn about each other, and do the job they are contracted to do on this planet; surveying.

They have traveled a few hundred kilometers closer to the top of the planet where the dinner party is planned. The controllers, all of them, are all in on it, as are all of the hikers. Current estimates are that all 100 hikers will arrive within a week or two of each other, take a bunch of zero's, and maybe for fun blue blaze a bit to see what's there. But, the goal is to get everyone there, in the same place, at the same time to have dinner like nothing else EVER in human history.

The reality of it is that hitting the top of the world effectively ends their contracts most likely. The starting point for all hiker paths was from the bottom of the planet. Now they are all just about at the top of the planet.

Their group is class number 6, the 6th contract to hike this track. Contract numbers 103A6 and 103B6.

Double Espresso and Belinda Goat were contract numbers 103A5 and 103B5, but they are home by now relaxing, spending the six months of pay they had accumulated during their hike.

About 2,000 kilometers for each contract, 12,000 kilometers for the whole track halfway around the planet, starting at the south pole, finishing at the north pole. This means they, some human, just about saw it all.

Belle and Goose are finishing each other's sentences and wondered if this is a side effect of the comms unit. They asked the other teams, and all of them are experiencing something similar. As a test, Belle and Goose were instructed to not split up, as were the other two teams in the triad. The Captain of the plane, the operation leader in this part of the galaxy, understands the need for companionship and a shared experience. Once he received the reports from the controller of Belinda Goat and Double Espresso, he had his answer. They were better as a team than as individuals. Since their paths were narrowing at the top of the world, all hikers were instructed to merge with their counterparts when convenient and safe. They were also told that at the top of the world there will be a party. The party to celebrate the completion of the primary survey.

Goose and Belle have already proved that. A week or so ago, they happened to walk into a family of Blue Bear. Ten meters away, as they rounded a mountain path. The bear family and Belle and Goose froze as they were walking towards each other. Belle lowered herself to the ground and held her hands out, open. Goose thought about running, but he did not want to leave Belle, he ended up kneeling next to her. The next to largest, assuming the mother, walked up to them. It was like being sniffed and evaluated by a dump truck.

The mother grunted, and the family passed and paid little to no attention to them as they did. After the family turned the corner, they stood and walked quickly away as silent as they could maintain. They spoke through the comms unit and told each other not to look back and keep walking. Goose informed her he was running video during the introduction, and it never stopped, so he had all of it recorded. Tonight's upload will give them something to see and talk about.

It was about midday, and they were a few kilometers from where they crossed paths with the Blue Bears. "I'm ready to call it a day. Let's find a place to set up, maybe take a zero. The hiker box should drop in tomorrow. I'm asking for a special delivery of a bottle of tequila; after they watch your video, they'll send it special, watch." Belle said as they started to look for a spot to spend a few days.

"I'm sure they will." He said to her. "I am sure they will."

It took another hour, but they found a small creek maybe 3 meters across and a meter deep. It is easy to cross tomorrow or the next day, but it will become their back porch for today.

Setting up their tents, they started a fire and warmed up a bit, even though it was around 17°C at the moment. Perfect hiking weather!

Goose managed to find a few logs and put them together in such a way as they resembled a double-wide chair. Belle came out of the trees and sat next to him. Then she started shaking. Goose saw her and realized the fear was overwhelming her from what she did a few hours ago, the first hikers to survive a Blue Bear encounter unscathed. That is a fantastic feat in itself, but to have it all recorded was even more impressive.

"From what I can see, we should be at the top of the world in another couple of weeks," He said, trying to lighten the mood and get her mind out of her head. "We should be there about the time the temp hits 35°C or so," Goose said. "We should be the first to arrive, and we can scope it out for good placement and how we want to arrange it."

"Goose, you know I love you, right?"

"Yes, Belle, I do. I love you too."

"Good. After that encounter," Belle was referring to the meeting with the bears, "I realize there is a chance one or both of us could die at any moment. I have no idea what I am waiting for, why I think being independent is better, but I think I would like to marry you at the top of the world dinner. The Captain can perform the ceremony, and we can get ALL of the other hikers to stand up for us. Put it out on the controller message system, and everyone will know before they get there."

Goose looked at her with his mouth open, he finally spoke. "Well, since you are asking, I guess I need to say yes. So......YES! I love you, Belle, and want to be married to you more than I ever knew was possible." He paused to inhale, "I thought about marriage over the past year or so, on the AT and PCT sections I did, and never met a single person ever who brought these feelings up in me until I met you. I had known since the plane when you started shaking, and I held your hand. The instant I held your hand, I saw us married and living in the woods. I think I have loved you since that moment, maybe a little earlier, but for sure that moment. I cannot see being apart from you."

He kissed her, and she kissed him back. "I so much want to …. but I think we should wait. As a child going to my parent's church, something ingrained in me was waiting until we were married. So, instead, let's just sit here, and you can hold me, please. I like that."

"The church thing, I understand. My parents were pastors of a church until I left at 18; they still are, I guess. We have not spoken in a few years, in part to my leaving. I remember all those lessons, and yes, I agree with you to wait, but in the meantime, kissing is a lot of fun!" He smiled at her, and she had the best grin on her face.

"I did not mean they ran the church. They just attended. Actively participated is more like it. Always getting me to do things in the church, volunteer. Finally, at 17, I made my Mom sign the document, and I was off to Luna Base for basic training. Spent 10-years in the service and enjoyed every minute of it, but I needed something more than just being a number. I had goals, I guess, and the service, although it was perfect for me, was not what I needed at that moment. So I put in for separation and got out."

She looked at him, and Goose was very interested. She continued, "After I got out, I decided to use the Enlisted Education Program and get my degree. It seems my schooling and my life experience granted me a full scholarship through a master's. So I found something fun to focus on. My 28th birthday was when I started college, and just about 3 years later to the day I received my master's." She looked up at him, "Did you go to college?"

"In a way. I went to seminary at my father's request, who wanted me to follow in his footsteps. Finished a bachelor's in theology for him and a bachelor's in environmental science for me. Masters in wildlife management. I was about to turn 26 and decided to see the world, so I started hiking. I understood animals, I understood terrain, and maps, and compasses, and trees and mountains. Hell, I even have an associate's in Marine Biological Research without trying." He paused and took a drink of water, "But I did not understand me. So I hoped to meet me on the trail, have a conversation, and learn about me."

"Did you?" She asked.

"In a way. About a year or so ago, almost two years now, I guess, I was in Seattle and decided to do a day hike. I told the front desk where I was headed, and I started up the trail and decided to Blaze, which was a stupid decision. I was on the trail doing great; I thought I knew where I was going. No map or anything, but I looked at one and thought I remembered it. Well, it got dark, fast. Not because the sun went down but because a weather front moved in, so I decided to stay where I was for the night. I have a few protein bars with me, a small sandwich I would have on the way back from where I ended up, and about 1 and a half-liter of liquid. Sports drink and a water bottle."

He took a drink of water. "I was dressed like I was headed for the beach, and the temp dropped, and it started to rain, then it turned to snow flurries. I was in the mountains, after all. I had a tarp set up, thank god, so I was more or less dry, but the ambient temperature dropped fast. So I decided to light a fire, which helped keep the inside of the shelter more than above freezing. I wrapped up in the emergency blanket, and I tried to sleep, but I was either dreaming or hallucinating."

He paused for a moment collecting his thoughts, looking at the ground. After a few seconds, he looked at Belle, "I talked to myself sitting in the shelter for more than an hour. Finally, I asked myself why I was doing this, and I had no answer. We talked about many things during that night, and the fire never went out, so I assume I kept tossing wood on it. At least that's what I saw in my mind, dream, hallucination, whatever it was. When I woke up, I was on a helicopter heading to the hospital. They had warming blankets on me, an IV plugged in, and an oxygen mask on my face. The hotel told them where to look, my fire guided them to me. When they found me, I was suffering from severe hypothermia. Not a big fan of cold camping anymore, but I can do it, as you saw. They said I did everything right, and if I had the fire a little hotter, I would have been fine. But I fell asleep, and the fire went down. Thank god for thermal imaging. I must have had one hell of an ember bed by then."

Belle hugged him. Then she got up and grabbed the bottle of bourbon. Sitting back next to him, she opened the bottle and took a drink. Handed it to him, and he did the same.

"Are we drinking to anything, or just drinking." He asked her.

She held the bottle high, "To hiking your own hike, and surviving!" She took another drink.

He took the bottle from her and said the same, then a drink from the bottle, and it was empty. "Well, this one gave its life for a good cause."

"I need some sleep." She said.

"So do I. I saw fruit, potatoes, and onions as we got here, and I have some dried pot roast. How about hash for breakfast?"

"You cooking?"

"I am." He smiled at her. She is an ok cook, but Goose is better.

"Then I'm eating."

Together they make some fantastic meals using the dried bags from 'upstairs.' Mix and match sometimes; other days, they just fill it with water and eat.

"I hate wandering in the dark; I'll collect the stuff in the morning. Good breakfast. I say we take a zero and blue blaze a little. I hear water running over that way. Curious as to what it is."

"Agreed," Belle said. "I may get the chance to fish a little too."

She took a couple of steps, then headed back to him and gave him one hell of a kiss. "Sleep well, have good dreams." She said.

"Damn...." That was all he could say. She had a grin on her face as she climbed into her tent for the night. She knew exactly how he felt. She felt the same way. They both knew it.

~~~~~~~~~~

Belle was struggling to make it to reality. For some reason, she did not want to wake up, then she smelled food, coffee, and chocolate. Chocolate? That did it! Her eyes popped open.

She put on her shoes and a jacket since it was a little chilly but kept her bedclothes on. She would change later. She made her way to the fire, and Goose was busy cooking. It smelled divine.

Without saying a word, he handed her a steaming hot cup of coffee. She took a sip and jerked to life, "Wait, this is real coffee with vanilla creamer?"

"Oh, did you not hear the hiker box land about an hour ago?" He pointed to the middle of the small clearing where she saw the hiker box landed. "I asked for a few special items in my upload last night."

"Like what?" She asked.

"Well, that coffee for one. It's been a while since we had real, so they sent us a 2-liter carafe, steaming hot, and filled with the best coffee I had in a long time. Also, these little vanilla thingy's for your brew." He looked at her, "Do you like chocolate, chocolate chip, scones?"

"Oh my god, yes!" She thought a moment, "Did they send those too?"

"No, they sent a large dutch oven and the batter. I made them more or less, and they are just about done." He winked at her, "Breakfast is ready; how do you like your eggs?" He smiled at her.

"Real eggs?" She grinned. "Over easy, please. Wait, you still making the hash?"

"I am."

"Put the hash down, then three runny eggs on top. Then, I can mush it all together and have a great breakfast."

He put the hash mixture into the bowl. Space Taters, Space Onion, rehydrated pot roast, tiny diced peppers from the box - he had a few special requests they filled at the last minute. They even added a couple of jalapenos. He fried the eggs in butter and flipped them over for a minute to slightly harden the top side. Then, dumped them into the bowl on top of the hash and handed her a bottle of hot sauce. All she did was smile from ear to ear.

She took her fork and smashed, mashed, mixed, and mushed, then took a huge and hot mouthful. "Oh my, this is so good!" she said, burning her mouth.

"Glad you like it. Save room for dessert. I can't eat all six of these scones by myself."

"SIX?"

"Yup! I figure we have one now, one for lunch and one for dinner, or save it for tomorrow's breakfast."

"Breakfast!" She said.

Goose got an odd look on his face, and Belle saw it. She came to a stop while eating and looked at him, "What?" She said.

"I just had a wild thought. I have about 100 jalapeno seeds. Let's dry them out over the next week or so and plant a few. Then, let C-Note know about it after we are on our way home, and they can look in on the crop of peppers from time to time.

"I like that. Where?"

"I say in a week we find a place out of the way and do some gardening. We should be close to the top of the world."

"OK with me." She said and finished her scone.
"OK, now I can hear the waterworks. Over that way

and not all that far, I suppose. Could be another waterfall."

He looked at her and smiled.

"What?" She said.

"Just a thought. You may want to get dressed before we head out of the campsite."

"Really! Is that a requirement?" She laughed. "Well, if you insist."

They had gotten more and more comfortable with each other over the past few months. They have very few inhibitions left between them. Getting pushed into a sleeping bag together to survive has a way of doing that.

Belle reached into her tent and grabbed her clothes. She removed her sleeping top and put on her sports bra, then a light shirt, and finally a long-sleeved flannel shirt. Goose sat by the fire and tried, really hard, not to stare. Did not do all that well in the process; He really did love her entirely and thought a more beautiful woman did not exist in the universe. Something he told her on occasion.

She pulled her pants on and buttoned them, socks and shoes, and finally, her daypack with her tenkara rod sticking out of the top.

"I'm ready." She said.

He knew it.

"Give me 2, and we can head towards the water." He said to her.

He grabbed his pack and put it on, walked to her, and held out his hand, "Shall we?"

Hand in hand, they walked towards the sound of water. Silently, they walked, but simultaneously communicating through the comms unit, implanted at the base of their spine, they shared their emotions.

~~~~~~~~~~

It took three hours, but they made it to the waterfall. Impressive waterfall it is too. It was not the distance but the path they chose. Once they arrived at the falls, they saw a much easier and faster way that leads back to the clearing where they camped.

They sat and stared at the falls for 15 minutes before either of them said a word. Interesting how they could be with each other and not speak and still be content.

Goose took out his antique stove, and together they collected some fuel. He lit the wood and started a pot of water. In a few minutes, they would have coffee or tea or maybe hot chocolate. He brought all three and will let Belle make their choice.

About the time the water was just beginning to boil, a large bird landed next to him. It was all red but looked familiar. It was the size of an Earth Pidgeon.

"Belle, this may be my little friend from the day I caught the fish." He said to her.

He reached down, and the bird hopped onto his hand, climbed his arm, finally reached his shoulder, and nestled himself against his neck. "This is Louis!"

"From what you told me, he grew!"

"Yes, he did if it is Louis." Goose rubbed his head and back, and Louis just sat there – eyes closed – and took it in. There was affection, maybe mutual. But this little bird appeared to have a love for Goose. "Whoa!"

"What?"

"On the left side of his head, there is an area of skin, in the shape of a heart. I think this is the same little bird."

"Any way you can be sure?"

"Not really. Nothing I can think of, at least."

The bird fell asleep, and Belle used her med scanner on it.

"Let's see. Female, bird, no bacteria, no virus, a clean bill of health." She looked at Goose. "I think I have competition. Louis being a girl and all."

Goose grinned from ear to ear, "Honey, she's just a friend."

Belle shook her head and smiled. "Nice, come back." Belle picked up a packet of hot chocolate and dumped it into her cup. Goose followed that lead. They were sipping on their drinks when Louis woke up and looked into the air. A moment later, he made a noise. It sounded like something you would think a pterodactyl would make but not near as loud. A few minutes later, 5 more red birds landed near them. One of the birds was large like Louis; the others were small like Louis was when they first met.

"Louis' wife and kids?" Belle asked.

"Beats me, makes sense, though. He called to them, and they came here and have no fear of us. Pretty impressive."

The new arrivals moved close to the antique stove. They felt the warmth. A few centimeters away, they all sat or laid on the ground. Louis was purring; his mate, or rather her mate, looked up at them, watching. Goose reached down and placed his other hand near the larger bird, who jumped up and walked up to his arm. Stopping on his shoulder, the new bird settled in on the opposite side.

Goose looked at all the birds, and only his Louis had the heart shape on him, or rather her, left side.

The four smaller birds looked asleep. They stayed there for an hour or so, knowing they needed to be back at camp well before dark. Goose packed up his stove after it cooled, and they stood.

The Louis family took off and landed in a nearby tree, watching them.

Belle said as she stood, "I think Louis is Louisa, so we can call her hubby Louis if that is OK?"

"If it is OK with her, it's OK with me!" Goose replied.

They started walking, and the view was not nearly as spectacular. However, the upload to C-Note tonight will give him something to watch and report since Belle recorded the entire Louis family meeting. They did not head back in the same direction; they followed the new path they found.

About halfway there, they stopped. Something just felt odd. "Do you feel that?" Goose asked.

"I do. What is that?" Belle asked him.

"I hear the Kitties, so they must be close. But, I can't figure out where they are."

"Dad, Kittie." He said out loud like the little furball will answer. "I know you're close; drop by and say hello."

A few minutes later, Dad appeared. Belle and Goose were sitting on the path relaxing, sipping on water. Goose opened a bar and gave it to Dad. Dad accepted the bar and went to Goose and hugged his leg.

"Did you see that?"

"I did. He just gave you a hug."

Dad looked up at Goose. "Holy crap!"

"What?"

Dad looked at Belle, "Holy crap!" she said. "Did he talk to us?"

Goose added, "I think so. Not really sure. But if I heard him right, he thanked us for the morsel."

"Exactly what I heard," Belle said.

They stayed there and played with Dad for an hour or so, then he stopped, looked at them, and was about to leave. "He needs to bring the morsel back to his family," Belle said as she unwrapped another bar and handed it to him. Dad hugged Belle, then Goose, and headed into the woods.

They found a grove of the red plants an hour later and gingerly dug around for the fruit. They found a few and put them in Belle's pack. They also noticed potatoes, and Goose put 6 in his pack. He stopped and looked at her.

"I need to try something." He said and dug up 4 more. "I want to see how long they will last out of the ground before they go bad."

"Good idea. I can analyze them for safety from time to time." She replied, "I would estimate 2 weeks from the analysis we did a few months ago. But it may be more."

"Well, we'll see." She made a note in the log of what she was doing, and C-Note would get that report tonight and the scans in real-time so they could keep track. An onion, potato, and blue fruit sat out until they went bad to see how long they would last.

"They made it back to the campsite, and a family of Kitties moved in close to the fire they built up as they arrived. They saw Goose and Belle approaching and got nervous for a minute, then calmed down. As if they knew these two were safe to be around.

Belle got close, pulled out a protein bar, and handed it to the largest of the 6.

He took it and broke it up, and handed it out to his family. Dad looked at Belle and, like the other Kittie, thanked her. "Dad thanked me again, and his voice sounded different, so yes, it appears that we can talk to them."

The family of Kitties sat around them like pets, and the small ones climbed up in Belle's lap, and she stroked their fur. The older ones looked at Goose and appeared to try to communicate.

"I think Dad here is trying to tell me something."

"Well, the little kids are content in my lap."

"I see." He said to her. "I think Dad wants me to follow him. So I'll be back."

They stood and walked to the near opposite edge of the clearing where Dad crouched low. Goose did the same behind a tree. A few minutes later, a large group of Blue Bear walked across the field. Dad managed to make sure they were downwind of the area. As a result, the bear could not smell them. After the bears passed, Dad stood on his hind legs, and Goose instinctually picked him up and carried him back to the site.

"Did Dad get tired?" Belle asked as they returned. Dad made a sound, and the family took note.

Goose sat with Dad in his lap, and Dad relaxed, then the others all settled.

"No, Dad here walked us to an odd side of the clearing and hid, so I did the same. About a dozen Blue Bear past 20 meters from us, they smelled pretty bad as we were 100% downwind from them. Neither of us moved or breathed as they did. For some reason, I think I made a connection to this world in a way no one else has, as you also have. For me, it is the smaller creatures, the Kitties, the birds; for you, it is the larger creatures like the Blue Bear. Oh my god, there is only one thing I can think of...."

"Me too, as in finding and surviving another group of Blue Bear," Belle said. "It was a strange sensation. I am just now feeling it. I knew, I mean 100% I knew, they would not hurt us because we had no intention to hurt them. But, I felt it; I felt them in my mind, in my heart, in my emotions."

"Tonight, we need to report this to C-Note. I'm sure he'll report it up-channel fast." Goose got silent.

"What are we supposed to tell him.... Uh C-Note, by the by my dear man, it appears that Goose and I have acquired a psychic link to the animals and creatures on this planet." She inhaled, "He'll have us committed."

"I say we are honest, as unbiased as possible, and as complete as we can be." He looked at Dad, who looked up at him. Then, Goose pulled a chocolate protein bar from his pocket without thinking about it, opened it, and handed it to Dad. Dad sat there a minute and jumped up. Then, he hopped onto the ground, and the others all followed him into the trees.

"Why did you hand Dad another bar?" Belle asked, but she already knew the answer.

"Holy crap. I handed it to him because he asked me to; I heard or felt that he wanted one of our dark foods in my head. So I gave it to him. I think he likes chocolate."

"I think we have our answer. Something we did here, ate, drank, experienced......SOMETHING here has grabbed us and turned us into a native." She said. "Close your eyes. The Kitties always bring us back fruit; what if you think about them but ask for the onions and potatoes. If they bring them, we have something we can prove."

Goose sat by the fire, thought about Dad for a few minutes, and asked him for potatoes and onions. Five minutes past and Goose looked at Belle, "He replied in my head. He said OK." He was not smiling, "I have no idea if it was him or not, or if I made that all up but in my head, but yes, I did hear him in there, and he agreed."

"I was thinking about going to sleep, but now I need to wait and see what happens."

"So do I."

They talked about their lives to each other, and an hour and a half later, the Kitties returned carrying potatoes and onions. Belle looked like she was in shock, and Goose looked like he saw a ghost.

They believed!

Chapter Nine

The Kitties are always around them now, maybe not the same family all the time but always at least one family of them. They like being held; Belle enjoys petting them, as does Goose.

A few days ago, they made a camp waiting for the box to fall from the sky. About 3 hours after dark, they heard something in the woods near their position. Goose put on the glasses and saw a huge Bear break through the trees. As it did, it got agitated, and Belle just sat there on her stump. The Bear approached her, and Goose reached for his pistol, his hand on it and the safety off as he removed it from the holster on his thigh.

The bear walked up to him and Belle, and as it approached Belle, it calmed down, relaxed, and stopped. Nose to nose with her, she opened her eyes. They looked deep into each other's souls for what Belle felt was hours. Finally, the bear walked off and returned to the woods. Belle was visibly shaking.

Goose went to her, knelt in front of her, and wrapped his arms around her; she held him tight. Then she collapsed and cried at what she just experienced. She sobbed into his shoulder, and he caressed her, stroked her hair, held her tight. Finally, he told her it would be all right, that she did good, she protected us.

"How long did we look at each other? It seemed like hours."

"Maybe 1 minute or so, I would say. I was wearing the glasses, and it was tripping through the spectrum, and I saw something on the EM spectrum. Waves were going between the two of you. Like you were communicating or something using, what...... psychic energy? I think I have it recorded; I only wish I could see the recording to be sure what I thought I saw, I saw."

Goose pulled a flask out of his pocket and handed it to her. She opened it and took a significant draw. She gave it to him, and he did the same. He held her for another half hour.

"I'm getting tired," she said.

"Me too." He said to her.

"I do not want to be alone tonight, though. Can we pretend it is sub-freezing out here?" She said.

"I am getting cold." He replied. They both smiled.

She went to her tent and got her pillow and sleeping bag, and nightshirt. Then, she crawled into his tent, and they used his bag as the lower and her bag as a blanket. Since the ambient temperature was 24°C and cooling off, they needed a blanket and not bundled in the bag.

Goose took off his shoes and socks when she got there and removed his pants, leaving his shorts and a t-shirt on; he crawled into the bag. Belle removed her shoes and socks and her shirt in full view of

Goose. He watched but not a staring intent watching. Instead, he watched as if he was entirely in love with her—an adoring gaze.

She removed her pants and left her underpants on, put on the T-shirt, and crawled into the bag with him. Goose was lying on his left side, their standard position for couples sleeping with both of them facing the door. She crept in and rested her body next to his....she fit perfectly, was comfortable, and felt safe.

He put his right arm over her, and she pulled it to her chest. They fell asleep and slept the whole night. Happy.

Morning came, and the Kitties were outside the tent, making noise. They woke up facing each other at nearly the same time. Goose was staring at her when her eyes opened.

"Good morning, my dearest." He said.

She looked at him a moment, "Good morning." Then, she came to a little more. "Did you sleep well?"

"I never have a bad night's sleep when you are with me...."

She kissed him, and he kissed her back. Then she kissed him again, but this time it was a good one.

After a few minutes, it seemed, Goose said to her, "If you keep that up...."

"What?"

"If you keep that up, we may go farther than intended."

"What makes you think it's not intentional?" She said and started kissing him again. The love between them was palpable. The Kitties outside in the campsite felt it too and left the area. They would return later to their new friends.

Belle and Goose began exploring each other in new ways....

~~~~~~~~~~

They are one dropbox away from the top of the world. Since the encounter with the Blue Bear at the campsite, they ran across them twice more. Both times ended the same way, with the animals returning where they came from and Belle shaking. Each time it happened, she recovered faster, but the adrenaline and the anxiety still took their toll on her each time, but less.

C-Note worked on the video or finding a way to see the vid after it was taken. The tech team managed to get the glasses reprogrammed to view files and vids in near real-time. The glasses now connect directly to the comms unit and play any video or photo in its memory. Your partner can also view videos from your comms unit to share a video and watch it together. C-Note sent a couple of movies to test the new process, and it worked flawlessly.

Goose had one movie or video on his comms, as did Belle. He and Belle were in the tent, together in the sleeping bag again. Both wore the glasses, and

Goose and Belle connected them together. Goose started the movie.

"OK, let's play C-Notes test movie 0001," Goose said.

The movie started, and they both laughed; Belle said, "Leave it to C-Note to send us cartoons. I love it!"

"Me too!" Goose replied.

They laid there in the bag, in the tent, at the edge of the forest on an alien world. Surrounded by creatures that could step on you and not realize it, they laughed at a children's cartoon and enjoyed life, enjoying each other.

In subsequent encounters with the Blue Bear, one during the day and one during the night, the waves between Belle and the Bear are easily visible and a lot more powerful. Belle recorded the Kitties also and their interaction with Goose. Nearly identical. She also managed to record him asking for some fruit when they were not around. The EM lines spread out, unfocused. When they were close, the lines were very focused and directed at the intended critter. There was no way to refute what was happening. They were communicating with the animals of this world, great and small, powerful and timid.

A half-hour after Goose asked for fruit, they walked into camp with 6 of the best-looking fruit they had ever seen. Goose returned the favor with a couple of bars and a few scratches. After that, the critters all hugged him and Belle and ran off back into the woods.

"Next drop box will be at the top of the world," Goose said.

"One week, and we'll be there according to C-Note. 4 months down, two months to go, and our contracts are completed," Belle said as they walked, looking for a place to stop for the night. It was starting to get dark. Our last two months on contract, what will we be doing if there is no hiking path?"

Goose started to talk as they walked into a field, maybe the size of a football field, and when they hit the center, a Blue Bear came out of the woods and sauntered calmly to Belle.

Belle stopped and looked the bear in the eyes as it approached. The Bear stopped a meter in front of her, laid on its stomach in the grass, and locked eyes with Belle. Belle sat cross-legged in front of the bear.

Goose recorded and watched.

"Goose, this is Mom. The Bears are a matriarchal society. She is the leader of the Blue Bear." She smiled a little, "Pardon me; she is the leader of all Blue Bear on the planet. They understand we are not of this world. They do not understand how we arrived. They know the noisy houses that fall from the sky bring us here. Mom is happy that I am like her. I think she means female, but also able to talk to her. Mom refers to me as She, like it's my name or my title. We already discussed that humans are of no danger and only hurt the bear if they are threatened. Mom told me that since She, that's me, vouches for all humans, no bear will harm a human again. Since you are recording this, this is for C-Note. Please send a flash message to all controllers to inform all hikers about this new breakthrough. No hiker should harm either a Blue Bear, Kittie, or Red Bird ever!" Belle started laughing.

"It appears that the Kitties, as we call them, are not a food source. The Bears and the Kitties live in a symbiotic relationship. The major food source for the Bear Clans is the onions we like so much, occasionally a blue fruit or a potato. But a larger percentage of their diet is the small mammals that we saw, the chipmunk or hamster thing, and that big eagle thing." She started laughing again. "It appears the yummy flyer, as she calls them, is an excellent meal for a family."

Mom and Belle talked for half an hour on camera. They both stood, and Belle rubbed Mom's nose and head. Mom loved it. Mom thumped Belle in the chest with her snout, then went to Goose, sniffed, and thumped him in the chest also.

"Mom just called me a buck?" Goose said.

"Because you are male. She said you smell male."

"I do need a shower." He laughed, Belle laughed a little, and Mom groaned at the joke.

"Oh my goodness, did she get that joke?" Goose asked.

"Mom did. Evidently, she likes you and said you have a sense of humor like her mate."

"What is the thumping in the chest?"

Belle said, "Mom told me a thump in the chest is a sign of affection to a family member. Females do it and not males. It means you are family, and Mom will protect you to the death." Belle walked over to Mom, looked at her a moment, and slapped her on the side of her neck. Pretty hard too. Mom actually appreciated it and appeared to smile.

The giant animal walked away slowly, and once it was in the woods, a few minutes later, a roar like no other could be heard. Then the sound was all around them. It sounded like hundreds of Blue Bear were in this area.

They were not afraid, anxious, or scared in the least. Instead, both of them understood the roar as if they were singing a ballad. "Well, Belle, it appears that Mom made She a part of her family," Goose said.

"And her mate!" Belle added. "What were you going to say when Mom appeared."

Goose looked confused for a minute, then remembered. His entire demeanor changed. "Yeah, about that. I do NOT want to leave. If I can think of some way, I would stay here and be the first permanent resident. I love this planet." Goose said.

"I feel the same. We need to talk to C-Note privately." They were silent for a few minutes trying to think of something. Finally, Belle snapped her fingers, "I got it. We suggest to C-Note that one member of each triad attend the dinner as a representative. C-Note and the girls need to be here because they are our witnesses at the wedding. You need another man to stand up for you. I have Bass Master and Triple One.

"That's easy. Chisel." He said to her.

"OK, in a couple of hours, the gang will all be in our heads. So we need to be discrete but specific. Somehow we need to tell them about what we are thinking."

"Hold on," Goose said.

He closed his eyes, activated the comms unit, recorded his message, and sent it to C-Note to get online with him and Belle ASAP in a 100% private conversation about the wedding. The roommates can be there too if they want but just them.

"Well, I sent it. Let's see if he gets it, reads it, and calls us." They started the fire and the water and made a coffee. 20-minutes passed, and the coffee was ready.

"Hey guys, we're all here," C-Note said and scared the crap out of them.

"Who all?" Belle asked.

"Us three satellites and you two. OK, I know you guys. What's up?" Bass Master said.

They outlined that they want to live here with these animals, on this planet, and run the research center. They discussed the wedding and their ideas. They talked about where the research center would be located.

"OK, I'll talk it over with the Captain and get his take on it. He will be attending the wedding reception, and from what we can see, you two are the closest as in your next drop. So a week and you will be there. I am sending a box down, so you will know where the exact top of the world is."

Triple One added, "I suggest the exact spot is where you two tie the knot. Use the cooler for the Captain to stand on."

Bass Master interjected, "No, all three of them stand on the coolers. But, hey, what a great tribute to the mission."

"I like it," Belle said back to her. "Bring a board or stage and prop it up on the coolers."

"Excellent idea. I'll get on it." Bass Master said.

They talked for an hour, and the others were added to the conversation. But, of course, they were none the wiser.

All nine in the triad are a part of the wedding party. The women are being escorted by C-Note and Chisel. Chisel and C-Note stand next to Goose, and Bass Master and Triple One stand next to Belle. The other three ladies are all standing behind the couple. The triad is complete.

C-Note spoke to the Captain about the animals on the planet and the two hikers not wanting to leave. After several communications back and forth with Earth, the PCE agreed to the idea of a full research center on the planet and Belle and Goose running it. Belle and Goose just need to figure out where it needs to be, how big, what, and who to fill it with. Making it a viable research center for this world is the primary goal; understanding the communications, the culture, and the dynamic of the bear, the kitties, and the red birds is the primary role.

They still have a couple of months on their contract. However, the Captain did speak to them on a private line with the controllers. He let them know he will pull them aside when they arrive for the dinner and the wedding and discuss it with them. It seems this is the party of the century.

With very few exceptions, every person in orbit is going to the wedding. Belle and Goose are unaware that C-Note and the Captain have arranged for their parents to attend, and the Captain shall co-officiate with Goose's father. Since the parents are not used to space travel and most likely never flown in or maybe even heard of a drop-ship, they are bringing on their plane a small shuttle to take them to the planet and back into orbit after the reception. The ship, twice the size of the craft they arrived on, was more cargo than passenger and contained most of the modular components for the research center, including all equipment the PCE thought they would need. In addition, the entire medical staff is joining the team, and the current doctor on site will be the chief medical officer of the new colony.

The crew created drop-ship, mini-hotel rooms for the parents, senior staff, and the newlyweds. These small hotel size rooms will then be connected to the main complex for use by anyone who requires a place to stay when on the planet. The ship also carries adult beverages for the occasion, including wine, champagne, and assorted spirits.

The rest of the attendees will be in tents, and since the weather is so fine and forecast to be optimal for the next two weeks, they will have one hell of a bash under the light of the sun and the light of the stars.

C-Note, regarding their parents, plans to look at Goose and say, 'Did I forget to tell you about all that?' Then wink and smile and say, 'Your Welcome!' Belle asked C-Note to walk her to the front since her Dad will not be there, but he will be happy to replace the real McCoy, or rather the real Reynolds.

The Captain needs something positive relating to the project, something forward-thinking to show regarding this project. What could be more positive than a research center, manned by people who can talk to the native animals, and a wedding.

The gang all disconnected after the planning fun was over, and Belle and Goose were alone in their heads. "Goose, I'm getting nervous."

"YOU! Really?" He joked. "Honestly, me too." He sat next to her, "This is HUGE!"

"It is. Are we doing the right thing?"

"I have never been more scared or nervous in my entire life of a decision, and at the same time more than 100% certain it is the right decision, at the right time, with the right person. I cannot imagine NOT being with you forever. If you were to hike off into the sunset, it would devastate me."

"I feel the same way. So I guess we're doing this then, aren't we?"

"Looks like." He chuckled.

"What's so funny?" She asked.

"Well, when people at home want to avoid the big wedding productions, they head to Vegas. We, being a fair distance from Vegas, don't have that choice."

"....and?"

"Nothing, I guess. Brain working overtime most likely."

The next night, on the all-call, as they came to refer to the entire gang dinner calls, they talked about the Vegas thing and a great many other things, as they always do. Conversations jumped around to return; new threads started and continued with new recommendations or answers or advice from night to night. But the other two groups of the triad spoke to their controller individually and suggested the Vegas theme. The controllers separately mentioned it in a report, and the second in command reported it to the Captain. As it would happen to be, one of the crew is an Elvis impersonator as a hobby, so Vegas in space it will be. Belle and Goose will learn this when the time is right. Pretty much as they are walking down the aisle, or path or trail or whatever.

Belle and Goose headed in record time to the TOTW, TOT-W as they referred to it. The Top Of The World. The place where the dinner reception-wedding will take place. It took ten days, two weeks planetside, but they arrived more than a week before anyone else. They stopped more than they realized and enjoyed the hike. As they reached the hiker box marking the exact TOP, Goose teared up.

"We're here." Is all he said.

Belle started to cry, happy tears, and Goose joined her. Finally, they made it to the place where they will begin as a couple. Goose opened the hiker box and in it was an authentic meal in a heat box. A bottle of champagne and a note.

The note read, "Congratulation. You are the first." Finally, they made it to where they feel will be an excellent location for the research center.

They wandered around on day trips for a few days with absolutely nothing to report. Granted, the view was spectacular; snow-covered mountains, plush green valleys, a hot spring 15 minutes away, a vast clearing, maybe a kilometer across, and surrounded by the most beautiful rain forest type forest they had ever seen. Then, finally, they found a perfect place for the research center, the plain near the waterfall.

They realized there were plenty of Kitties and several blue bears in the area. They all came to visit but at different times. The Kitties huddled around Goose, and when the blue bear arrived, they ran off. Not out of fear, it was learned, but out of respect.

When the blue bear walked into the site, Belle walked up to them and stared into her eye a moment. Then, the bear took a large sniff of Belle, sniffed Goose, thumped them both in the chest, and casually walked away.

This is the place they want to put the research station. Large open field, close-by geothermal vent to provide power, hot water for heat and showers, animals for comic relief, and the natural beauty of the land.

They were online in the all-call around dinner the fifth night, and they heard a noise above them. A dropship, no three dropships, and four coolers made their way to the surface.

The pods were numbered 1, 2, and 3. Pod 1 opened, and the captain and Maria exited. The Captain looked fine; Maria, on the other hand, looked like C-Note when he left the pod all those months ago.

Pod 2 opened, and four crewmen exited, went to pod 3, and opened it up. But, again, it was cargo:

tables, chairs, and other necessities for the reception.

"Cap, what....you slumming?" Belle asked.

"Just wanted to see how the ground pounders live." He replied to her. "You remember Maria from the last dinner? She is here to make sure your EVENT goes off properly. Sometime tomorrow, many pods will descend; they are set up as sleepers for the VIPs, two beds, and a shower. You said you have hot water and cold water here, so the pod does the rest.

A small shuttle landed, and the crew stepped off and began setting up the water system. Four people, older, left the ship, and Belle and Goose looked. They looked familiar, but, "MOM! DAD!" They exclaimed at the same time. They ran, full throttle, to the shuttle and got them all in a bear hug.

"Mom, Dad, this is my wife-to-be," Goose said. He had pure joy in his voice saying those words.

"Mom, Dad, this is my husband-to-be!" Belle said in the happiest voice anyone ever heard.

Hugs all around, and Goose's Dad said, "Finally! I have a daughter!"

"You know," Belle's father said, "I was thinking, I finally have a son!"

They stood near the shuttle for nearly an hour, talking to and about their babies. Belle and Goose were both only children, no brothers or sisters. When they turned around, they saw a small building had popped up. The Captain was waving them all to come over, and they started walking to the new structure.

"Welcome, VIPs." He said. "Since the planet does not have a name yet, only a designation ID, it does not seem right to welcome you to it but welcome to the surface. First, allow me to show you your home for the next week, or so, then it becomes the first building in the research complex to be staffed and lead, but these two. Belle is the Director of Planetary Operations, and Goose is the Director of Wildlife Operations. Together, they make up the leadership, as in co-leaders, of this outpost. Their first job is to write their job description."

"REALLY!!" Belle and Goose said together.

"You two. You will have government overseers – three of them. One is working with Goose, one is working with Belle, and the third is going to be the governor of the newly created colony."

"Administrators? Who are they, and do they have a clue?" Belle asked.

"Not certain if they have a clue or not; you need to determine that for yourselves and provide any training and education you see fit. You will meet the admin team in a few days. For now, we need to set up for dinner, which just happens to be a wedding reception, I hear. The weather is forecast to cooperate for the next few weeks."

"Wonderful." They said in unison.

They started setting up the compound, and the parents came back. One of the crew got a fire started and set up chairs around the pit. There was no wind or even a breeze, and the smoke rose up and away from all humans.

"Jaclyn, is this what you do?"

"Yes, Mom, every single night pretty much," Belle replied

Belle's mother and Goose's mother sat next to each other, as were their father's.

Goose's Dad said, "So Gil, I understand you have only known Belle for a few months. Yes or no answer to this question, both of you." He paused a moment, "Do you think you rushed it?"

Simultaneously, with emphasis, they both said No!

He simply smiled, "Good enough for me."

Belle's father asked, "That is good enough?"

"Yes, it is. There was no hesitation in their voice, no pause by either of them to consider the question. It was from the heart, from their soul. Their souls are linked, and that is no easy task regardless of the time. That, to me, is enough."

The Captain spoke, "Sir, I have to say I wondered about this wedding, but after hearing you speak, I lost all doubt."

Goose smiled at his Dad, "Hello. We're sitting right here."

Everyone laughed.

Goose's father started, "Son, you need to understand we all love you very much, and although it is your life to live as you please," He gestured around with his arms, "Where ever you please, we want the best for you and hope, pray, that the mistakes you make in your life are not devastating. After sitting here and speaking to the two of you, the Captain, and William, who we spoke to on the ship…….."

Belle asked, "Whose William?"

"We know him as C-Note," Goose added quickly.

"How did you know that?" The Captain asked.

"I scanned him with the glasses when we were setting him up with a backpack the day before we dropped. Impressive Bio, as are Tammara and Yvonne's. Captain, you find people who are top of the line for the role."

"It seems I need to patch a hole, Goose. But you are correct. I mentioned to your parents that you would be here for a renewable 5-year contract leading the research team on this planet. That you will be in charge of the colony, training the colonists in the ways of the planet, and also in the research needed to discover its secrets, but at the same time ensure it never loses this," He looked around, "This place is magnificent. It is your job, the two of you, to make certain it stays that way." The captain paused.

"So, what can you tell me about the animal life here." Belle's father asked.

"Dad is the zoologist," Belle said.

"Want to meet the Kitties?" Goose said to his future father-in-law.

The captain spoke. "Not dangerous?"

"Nope. Just a second." He stood up and spoke very loud to those setting up. "Can everyone please take a seat for a few minutes and under no circumstances think you are in danger, and please do not hurt the Kitties." Everyone sat quietly. Some on chairs, others on the ground or on a log or table.

Goose closed his eyes a moment, and he spoke out using his mind. "I made a connection. Let's ask for fruit; Belle, do you have a bar on you?"

"I have two." She replied.

"Perfect." He said in return.

A few minutes later, the family of Kitties entered the camp carrying fruit and brought it all to Goose and Belle. They laid it at their feet, and Belle unwrapped two protein bars and handed them to the largest of the Kitties. The creature accepted them, and one of them, a smaller one, hopped up in Goose's lap and snuggled with him for a few minutes. Next, dad hopped up on Belle's lap and gave her a snuggle, then hopped off. A couple of minutes later, they left the campsite.

Goose explained, "I told them there will be a lot of us here for a while and to be careful. If they need protection, I told them to return to this point. Dad asked what was going on, and I explained Belle and I were being mated. Those creatures, the Kitties, mate for life,"

Belle added, "So do the Bears, actually."

Goose continued, "and they all understand. Dad was congratulating Belle on the wedding. So I let him know I would call him so he can watch the event."

"I forgot to ask earlier, why are a few of the dropships different colors?" Belle asked.

"Signifying apartments, cargo, people, etc. Plain is people. Red is cargo. Blue pods are apartments." The Captain explained. "So, you and Belle get the blue one with the bells on it. Your parents get pod 1 and pod 2. I am in pod 3. C-Note wants to tent it, but he will use my pod for showering and changing. The rest of the crew here are a mix of tents and pods."

"COOL!" Goose said.

"Belle. I have a question regarding the Blue Bears. So you're saying they are not dangerous?"

"No, Cap, not at all. I am saying they do not need to be shot on sight. They could care less about us, and we are insignificant. Would you like to meet one? There is a family close by I was going to say hello to before I went to bed."

"Uh…...not sure." The Captain looked apprehensive at the idea of getting close to those teeth.

"Come on. You will be impressed." She stood as did her father and the Captain.

She had her pistol, as did the captain. "Please don't draw your pistol; it could make a scene." And they walked off into the field and the rapidly approaching darkness. She turned on her headlamp, as did the captain, and she handed a flashlight to her Dad.

Goose wrangled the rest of the parents and brought them over to the galley area. The weather was getting a bit cooler, and one crew member stoked a larger fire, and a few of them were sitting around enjoying it.

"Maria!" Goose called out. Maria Joined them. "These are the Moms. I think they may be a bit chilly."

"Gotcha, Goose." She turned to the two women, "Ladies, come with me. Let's find you a jacket." She looked at Goose; "One cargo pod is all clothing in case someone needs to refresh their wardrobe."

"Dad, here, take mine. I'm fine." His father accepted the coat and put it on. "Feel the bottom of the left sleeve, and you'll find a small button. Press it. It's a heater." So he did and was rewarded with warmth around his torso.

"That's nice!" He said.

Maria returned a few minutes later and handed Goose a jacket. "For you and Belle. They got your names on them. We have one for each hiker. They are an upgrade. Wider temp variation and no sweating as it gets warmer. Designed to be comfy! The plane your parents came on brought them."

"That is awesome, thanks, Maria," Goose said.

"Don't thank me. These are now the standard issue for the planetside research teams." She pointed to the Moms. "Even have one for them." Each Mom was wearing a jacket. On the back, it said Mom of the Bride and Mom of the Groom. "Got one for the Dad's also; just need to grab them."

"No problem Lieutanant. I am fine for the moment." He hugged himself, pressing the heat coils against his chest.

Goose looked at Maria, "I thought so. Since the dinner, you got promoted!"

Maria smiled, "Yes, I did. A few weeks ago, my commission came through. I am a second lieutenant now. More pay, but it makes no diff here. I can't spend it anyway. But at least my bank account likes it. As for the work, Cap is making me earn that extra pay. But here's a secret," She put her hand near her mouth and pretended to whisper, "I love it!"

They all grinned at chuckled a bit at the comment. Goose helped set up chairs and tables. The rest of the group just relaxed at the fire.

A crew member delivered the group a hot chocolate.

"Ladies and gentlemen, if you would like an adult version of hot chocolate, please raise your hand?"

Every hand raised. He passed out the mugs and pulled out a bottle of adult additive. Everyone wanted a little extra in their mug. A few of them sipped a little off the top to make more room in the cup. Once everyone was happy, he walked off, leaving them at the campfire to enjoy their beverage.

Chapter Ten

"OK, Dad. Don't move. Captain.....freeze. Here comes the matriarch." A moment later, Mom came out of the tree line and headed toward them. A large and very massive animal approached them slowly, tentatively. The creature was not excited, though, and it was relatively calm. It walked up to Belle and sniffed, then poked her chest with its snout. She scratched her nose and head, kissed Mom Bear then sat. Dad and the Captain just sat. A few moments later, a tiny bear approached. It crawled up in Belle's lap and got comfortable. Mom Bear laid there watching but looked like a dog, and you were playing with her puppy.

About the size of a large german shepherd, the baby nibbled on her hand but never bit. Belle let the baby play, and Mom watched it all. About 10 minutes past and the baby walked over to the captain and sniffed. "Can I pet the cub?" He asked.

"Sure. He likes you." Belle said to him.

The Captain scratched the baby behind the ear, and his leg jumped. "I guess that's universal!" He said, smiling from ear to ear. When he first arrived at the planet, the Blue Bear was dangerous, which meant it was better to destroy than live. His idea was to arm the hikers, but only a few bears were killed through that ignorance, with very few exceptions. Now, it will never be a concern again. The bears are friends, allies, and to some, family.

Belle's father sat quietly and watched. Mom walked up to him and laid down, putting her head on his lap. He stroked her head, and she purred.

"Dad, close your eyes. Now concentrate on her. See her in your mind. If you hear or feel anything, allow it to coalesce in your sub-conscience. Finally, you should begin to understand what she's saying."

He did, and a minute later, Mom Bear poked him in the chest.

"What does that mean?" He asked his daughter.

"Dad, that makes you a part of her family. She will protect you to the death." Belle teared up. "I hoped you passed the gene to me that allows me to talk to them. You have it too." She looked at the Captain playing with the baby. "Sadly, sir, I do not think you have the gene."

"That's fine. I'll be the babysitter." He smiled wide. "I think we need to get back to the site."

Belle closed her eyes, and the bears got up. Mom poked her father and her in the chest, sniffed the captain, and they walked away.

"Why did she sniff me?"

Belle's father replied, "I guess you are now a close family friend."

"Perfectly said!" Belle said.

They all stood and walked back to the campsite. Just noticing the air was chilly.

"I tried to give them different foods, but they don't want any. They like to eat the onions we find, really good too. We call them space onions and space potatoes, and space fruit or blue fruit." She paused a moment, "Their primary food source is what they call tasty flyers. Huge birds with the face of a dog."

"Wait…. Space fruit?" The captain said. "Oh, what, the little things the Kitties brought."

"Yup." She replied.

"Captain, you appear to know my daughter."

"I do, in a way." He reiterated the pod mishap and how he was the commanding general who signed the commendation.

Her Dad just looked at her, "You told me you were just an instructor?"

"I was, but how did you think I learned how to teach survival. I survived the survival schools. Over, and over, and over."

The Captain continued, "I found out she left the military to hike; I was floored. I had plans for her in the military. Once I retired from the services, I took this position. Commander of a bunch of people who were attempting to tame a planet. How could I say no? I remembered her again, a hiker now, and suggested to my company that we can use these people to survey the planet efficiently and in-depth. I had a three-year plan. Walk from the southernmost to the northernmost point on the planet. 100 teams. Initially, I had no idea about hikers, hiking, thru-hikes, blue blazing, or any of it. I was educated on the job. Except for military camps, I have never camped – especially like this, on a planet, in another part of the galaxy, in a world so alien you are quite literally the very first human to ever walk, see, or experience what you are seeing, or where you are hiking."

He paused a moment and looked at Belle, "She is a natural. I recommended her for this contract, and it took a year to find her and get her signed up."

"I was on the PCT at the time, Dad," Belle said.

"....and knew beyond a shadow of a doubt she would be fantastic at the job. Beyond my wildest dreams, I never figured she would unlock this planet to make it viable as a colony." The Captain laughed a bit, "Now, Goose, we found him by accident. He fell into our laps, and of all the hikers we have had to date, over 300, he was by far the least experienced in survival operations. Don't get me wrong, he is a great hiker, but as far as survival techniques, well, he is green. Since Jaclyn, being a former Master Sergeant and a highly experienced survival instructor, it was perfect for us to drop him into the plane as her partner. Least and most were a team. As they started the hike, it became evident by the comments of other hikers that teams of two would be mentally more efficient, so this hike, we set all of the teams as pairs." He paused a moment, "The paths were getting closer since they were approaching the top of the globe, so it made more sense."

They talked all the way back to the central area where the first colony will be set up. The rest of the family sat in very comfortable reclining chairs around a lovely fire, wearing typical hiker jackets sipping on a hot chocolate.

"Welcome back." Goose said, "How's Mom doing these days?"

"She's fine, and guess what, Mom talked to my Dad." She was grinning from ear to ear.

"Oh my god, that is freakin awesome," Goose said.

"I got to play with junior tonight. A blue ball of fur that he is, and holy crap, is he strong!" Belle added.

The Captain asked, "Do you name them?"

Goose handed Belle a new coat, and she put it on since it was cooling off and only had on a long sleeve shirt.

Belle looked at him, "Not really...." She said, "The primary contact for the Kitties when Goose calls is Dad, and that Kittie always answers to Dad when he calls to him. Mom for the Blue Bears and Cap, before you ask, the answer is yes, there is something on this planet that if you let it take hold of you, you become a part of the planet as much as the animals that live here." She felt the jacket, "I like this. Lighter and warmer and still has the heat tabs."

"Your name is on the back, too," Goose said and turned around to show her.

Goose handed them each a hot chocolate, and they found a place to sit.

"We've been looking into that and have a working theory. A few of the hikers, like you and Goose, have a high psi factor, and this planet has a very odd magnetic field. Remember the picture of the Earth from middle school with the lines of flux essentially turning the Earth into a toroid? Well, this planet is more magnetic. On Earth, we have a single north pole. Here, there are several, and the greatest density of magnetic flux line crosses over your hiking path with the center of the crossed lines exactly at that waterfall where you encountered the family of the red bird."

"Louis and Louisa, that's only a few days from here!" Goose said.

"Yes. By the way, where did they get those names?" The Captain queried.

"I am a baseball fan, and before the franchise moved to Belgium, I was partial to the St. Louis Cardinals. Louis reminded me of a cardinal, more or less so, well, Louis!" Goose shrugged his shoulders and smiled.

His Dad laughed. "Oh my, if you had seen his room when he was in his teens, there were holograms, posters, photographs, and pretty much anything else he could spend MY money on in that room of his." He looked at his son, "I had an antique dealer look at that stuff, and he offered me a pretty penny for it all. More, a lot more, than we paid. I told him I would talk to you, and when I got back to Earth, I would give him a call. Is there anything you want?"

"Let me sleep on it, and I'll let you know," Goose said. "But for sure, the stuffed cardinal."

"Have you informed Belle about it yet?"

"No."

"All I ask is that when you do, I am there to see her reaction." His Mom was laughing a little.

"OK, gotta know. What is it about this stuffed animal?" Belle asked.

"I guess now is as good a time as any." Goose looked around with no sympathy from his parents, but they were enjoying this process. "My dearest Belle, Jaclyn. I need to tell you about a friend I have had since I was 12. His name is Louis, the original Louis. Yes, Louis is a stuffed animal. Yes, Louis is in pristine condition." He looked at his parents, and they nodded, telling him it was still in mint condition. "Well, it is not a small stuffed animal. I got him from a trash pile, cleaned him up, restuffed him with pure fluff, replaced his eyes with new ones and made a new mouth for him, and sewed it all back together. Louis is about two and a half meters tall. We had to cut a hole in my bedroom ceiling so he would stand up in the room. "

"Two and a half meters tall?"

"Yes, dear," Goose said to his bride-to-be.

"Good for you, son. You learned that phrase already." Both fathers said at the same time. The mothers shook their heads, and the Captain stood there and smiled.

Belle looked at the captain, "Sir. We will need a three-meter ceiling in the main living room of our residence when it is assembled."

"Noted." The Captain quickly replied and nodded to her.

~~~~~~~~~~

"The breakfast spread was great this morning. Pretty much whatever you wanted. It was leftover Monday, and it was great!" Someone said as they walked through tent city.

The first teams arrived over the past few days, and today Reena and Toonist will show up. Chisel and Flambe will come sometime tomorrow.

The research center was nearly complete. All four parents, the Captain, Maria, C-Note, Trip, Bass, Belle, and Goose, are currently residing in the new facility. In addition, Toonist, Reena, Flambe, and Chisel will have a place to live when they arrive until they decide if they will stay or head back to Earth.

There are a few additional rooms that were added to the research center. They refer to it as a riff-raff wing. Toonist will paint the name over the doorway when she arrives. They are basically rooms with a bed and a locker, and a small sink. In the hall is a large restroom/shower facility that is shared. 5

facilities on each side of the hallway. Something like what is on the plane but not as large.

The Research Center itself is a ten-bedroom structure, prefab from the ship and deliver a few shuttle trips. Each bedroom has a complete restroom/shower facility and, thanks to the geothermal water, a hot shower whenever needed. The exciting thing is that each new module fits into the shuttle cargo hold, then all the cargo and such are placed inside the housing modules, so carrying it was like it was never there in the first place. So all that happens is a few square meters of space are lost.

Today, they deliver the cat house—a module with three entrances, cat doors on three sides at different levels - high, medium, and low. It contains many peaceful, comfortable, and quiet places to sleep. The zoologist in Belle's father decided to learn as much as he can about the Kitties and learned they are very similar to Earth skunks and cats. Chocolate, unlike their Earth counterparts, is not dangerous for them. The best part, they are safe in the cat house from the bird dogs. In the middle of the coldest time of the year, it will get some use. Lots of Kitties die in the cold. Many mates have been lost, and since they mate for life, they are destined to be alone and do not survive long afterward, from what we understand. They die of a broken heart.

"BELLE GIRL!" It was Toonist yelling at the top of her lungs.

"TOON TOON, you made it!" She replied

The rest of the hikers welcomed them and removed their packs. They started to get their tent set up for them but remembered they were in the VIP quarters. The Captain showed them to their rooms, and their rooms had their names on them already.

Everyone's gear was nearly identical, so Maria thought to make nameplates for tents in tent city. Her ID project, of which the new jackets are a part. Just wait till everyone gets a glimpse of the new research center uniforms. Maria felt like they were the best.

She had a special section for the 'cards.' These were the Ace of Spades and Slubs, the Left and Right Joker, King and Queen of Hearts, Jack of Clubs and Hearts, and lastly, the Deuce of Diamonds and the Deuce of Clubs.

The research facility will be 100% complete; Belle and Goose will be married in less than a week. Belle's father is having a ball. Finally, he can call the Kitties and the Bears. Maybe as Belle and Goose age, they will be able to do more, but they are happy with their new abilities for now.

Goose took his parents to meet Mom Bear, and both his parents could speak to Mom Bear. But, for some reason, they could not talk to the Kitties, just like Belle's Mom able to speak to the Kitties but not the Bears. They need to learn more about the mental connection of this planet and hopefully find a way to improve on that aspect of the link.

Another week or so, and everyone should be at the top of the world.

~~~~~~~~~~

All teams are finally here, the Top of the World. The entire area is a madhouse. Nearly 200 people are on the surface. Only a few crew members volunteered to stay and ensure the ship runs smoothly and does not blow up. Their incentive or reward is a week's vacation on the planet. The wedding is in a couple days, the reception will follow.

Goose, his father, and very soon-to-be father-in-law were walking a short way from the main camp. "Dad, Dad's, I am scared stiff, and I have never been scared like this before."

"Natural. But push past it, and after those two words come out of your mouth, the nerves will go away." Belle's father told him. "So, after the wedding, do you plan to call me sir, Dad, Bob?"

"I was kinda thinking, Dad. I like that." Goose said. "Then I can say I have a Dad on two planets."

"You heard?" Bob said to him.

"I did." Goose turned to his father, "He is staying on the planet for some research. Since he is a zoologist, his experience and training would be welcomed in the early stages of the settlement. For example, classifying and categorizing critters."

"You make it sound so boring," Bob said. "Carol is also staying as my lab assistant. But I think the real reason is she wants to keep an eye on me."

Brian spoke, "We thought about staying for a few weeks also. I need some time off with absolutely no duties, time for meditation, and writing a few good sermons I can pull out of my pocket when needed."

Bob said, "Do it. When will you get the chance to do this again? You know as well as I do if you go home intending on returning here for a few weeks, you will never make it. Something will come up; someone will need you."

"I'll talk it over with Beatrice tonight, but it is a good thought." He grinned, "You know, for a Zoologist, you would make a good counselor."

"Oh no, that's your gig! Not mine." He smiled, "I play with fur babies. Besides, after looking at all these kids, I mean hikers, I think you will have some work here. Marriage, counseling, maybe a religious service or two. By the way, can you do Lutheran?"

Brian laughed, "I think that can be arranged." He narrowed his eyes, "I like that. Let me talk to headquarters."

"Dad's, look." Goose looked pathetic at the moment, and the father's stopped. "Son." They both said at the same time. Gooses father continued.

"Son, look here. I will ask you one thing, and I want an honest answer." He looked his son dead in the eye, "Can I get some of your water?"

"WHAT!" Goose said, and Bob started laughing.

"I was going to ask him for a protein bar."

Brian looked at his son, "Gil, one thing for certain. You and Belle love each other a lot. We can all see it, heck some of us can feel it."

Bob said, "Mom Bear and I talk about it. You have no idea how hard it is to talk about feeling and emotion with someone who has zero frame of reference. But she senses it, as do we."

Brian continued, "Cherrish, this time. If you stay too in your head, you will not remember a lot of the day. So get out of your head and live in the moment. Relax, you two are meant to be together. Dad Kittie and I talked about you and Belle. According to them, all Kitties, the two of you are already a family. So, all that's left is for me to sign the document, I guess."

They walked and talked for a bit longer and ended up in the middle of the field. Mom Bear approached, and they all sat on the ground.

About an hour passed, Goose commented, "It would seem that I am getting counseled by my father, my soon-to-be father-in-law, and Mom Bear. So be it. You all have helped me a lot, thank you."

He hugged Mom Bear and kissed her on the nose, then hugged the two dads.

They all stood and started walking away.

Mom Bear asked, "Mate of She, please ask She to visit with her mother's. I wish to speak to them."

"I will, Mom." She nudged them all in the chest and walked away.

Goose opened the comm and told Belle that Mom Bear wanted to talk to her and bring both mothers.

Belle said they were already heading that way and should pass them in the field.

~~~~~~~~~

"Jaclyn dear, I brought you something from home." Belle's mother grabbed a box and handed it to her. "This is your great-grandmother's wedding gown. Looking at you now, it may be a little loose on you, but we can pin it if we need to, I suppose."

"Never fear, we have a tailor here; let me get him. But, then, why don't we move to pod two and see about the fitting." Maria said.

They all went to pod 2, where her parents stayed for the past week, and the fitting began. A little while later, the tailor knocked at the door.

"Come in." Belle's mother said. A man entered and saw Belle wearing the dress.

"Now I understand." He pulled and tugged on parts of the dress. Looked under it, at the seams, and gathered material in several spots to see what needed to be taken in. He said, "Not a lot we need to do here; it's just about a perfect fit already. Maybe a little out of the chest area, but other than that, I say it's fine." The lieutenant said.

"Lieutenant, James right," Belle said. He nodded. "Please take in the chest area; my great-grandmother had more upstairs than I do."

Her Mom said, "I think she had more than all of us combined."

They all looked at each other for a couple of heartbeats, then broke into laughter. Lieutenant Bartholomew James just sat there quietly working on the dress, making the ladies laugh all the harder.

~~~~~~~~~~

"Good morning, Belle, Goose; grab some food; let's go meet your new planetary government officials." They looked at the Captain like he was growing a third eye; once they unfroze, they shoveled food on their plates, grabbed two coffees each, and followed the Captain into the seating area.

There was a table with C-Note, Bass Master, and Triple One. The three were all on one side of the table, and the Captain took the center seat on the other side. He showed Belle and Goose their seats, and they sat with Goose on his left and Belle on his right.

"Where are those administrators?" Goose asked.

"Right in front of you." The Captain said.

Goose looked at the person across from him. Bass Master was across from Goose, and Triple One was across from the Captain, leaving C-Note sitting across the table from Belle.

"Wait….. Let me get this straight. Bass Master here is to be my counterpart, and C-Note is Belle's? So that means Trip is the governor." He laughed out loud, and everyone looked. "FUCKIN-A" He exclaimed. "I mean your majesty."

"Oh my god, if that catches on, you are a dead man!" Trip said.

"I see you have a great rapport, and I expect this is a perfect relationship." The Captain said.

Walking in the door, "I did not raise that boy to speak like that...." Goose's father said a bit too loud as he walked into the galley.

"Must be the influence of that woman. She always was a loose cannon, even as a toddler." Belle's father said at the same volume.

They walked past the table, each carrying two trays, and at the same time, both fathers said, "Sad state of affairs, just sad......"

Everyone at the table just smiled and waited till they passed. The Dads were followed by the Moms who hugged and kissed their baby, then the other one's baby.

"Don't pay no mind to those two; they have issues!" They both nodded.

They sat at a nearby table and listened to the administrators, the governor, the Captain, and the two Operations leaders to create a viable colony. They sat there for about an hour and hammered quite a few things out.

As they stood, C-Note asked, "I take it you and Belle will be staying at the outpost, so we need a couple of new hikers to take over your roles."

He took a sip of coffee, "You know, it just so happens there will be a couple of hikers who will be here the day after tomorrow. But, yes, they are experienced hikers and have been on the planet already."

"Who are they?" Belle asked.

"Wedding crashers," C-Note said and walked away.

~~~~~~~~~~

There are still a couple of days till the event of the century, and several of the hikers are getting antsy just sitting around doing nothing. Finally, Goose and Belle walked out into tent city, where several of the hikers stopped them and asked them to look around on day hikes.

"A bunch of us are going on a day hike; who wanna join us?" One asked.

"Actually, yes, great idea." Goose replied, "I do have a request, though. There's a plateau up that way about 7 kilometers, maybe 500 meters up, and I wanted to get a look at it. So let's head up that way."

They all put on their sunglasses and looked at the plateau. "Goose, do you see that?"

"I do. What the hell is it?" Goose said.

"To me, it looks like a small house, with a chimney, but it can't be. That would mean there were …. wait, that we were not the first humans, or people, to walk around here."

"I know. Rather cool. Give me 10 minutes, and we can head out." Goose said to the group.

He went inside, and Belle followed. "Hey, Captain, I got something interesting. Are any of the hikers an archeologist?"

"What?" The Captain said to him, freezing in mid-stride as he did.

"Not 100% certain, but it may be a house, or a small village, or something on the plateau about 7 kilometers away. A bunch of us are heading there to look around. Wanna join us?"

"I do, thanks. Give me 15-minutes to change and get my day pack. I'll meet you near the tents. To answer your question, yes. Two of the hikers are archeologists." He thought a moment. "I remember now, a married couple, the Tweedles, Dumb and Dee."

Goose laughed. "I will make sure they are with us.

He left the room and headed back to the tents, in as loud a voice as he could muster, "I'm looking for the Tweedles!"

A few minutes later, a couple approached him, "We're the Tweedles," The man said. "I'm Dumb. "

The woman said, "I'm Dee."

"I love it. Tweedle Dumb and Tweedle Dee." Goose laughed with them.

"Not so far-fetched. Our real names are Daniel and Deeanna Tweed. It sounded right." He took a breath. "What's up?"

"Got your sunglasses?" They nodded. "Put them on. Look about 500 meters up the side of that mountain, and you'll see a plateau. There appears to be a crumbling structure there, and before we trash it, we need archaeologists to ensure it's done right.

"We're there for you, brother!" The Tweedles said in unison.

A few minutes later, the Captain, C-Note, Bass, and Trip joined Goose and the Tweedles.

"Tweedles, controllers. C-Note, Bass Master, and Triple One. And here is Tweedle Dee and Tweedle Dumb."

They laughed. "I love hikers!" All three of them said together.

C-Note added, "Unique mammals."

Belle had walked away for a few minutes, and she was back. She handed Goose his daypack, stocked and ready to go, he was sure. She had hers as well. So the group of about 15 headed off toward the mountain.

They had become so accustomed to the comms unit; they don't give it a second thought. Instead, they converse through it no differently than if they were standing next to each other.

They had walked halfway there, and Bass Master pulled out a small device and started tapping buttons. A moment later, the entire group was connected.

"That will make things easier," Goose said.

"Hey, Goose!"

"Toonist! I was hoping you would come with us. Your artistic talents can be a valuable asset. Do you know the Tweedles?" Goose said.

"I don't." She said.

"I'm Tweedle Dee...."

"....and I'm Tweedle Dumb."

As it happens, they were close by Goose, and Toonist jogged up to be with them.

"I need your drawings from your hike, but for sure, the drawings from this plateau, please."

"You got it!" She said to him.

It took them maybe two hours to get to the mountain. They all stopped and just stared as the Tweedles began inspecting and looking and touching the very sturdy steps cut into the side of this mountain. They appear to go all the way to the plateau.

They were on the plateau a half-hour later, and the first to step on the surface was Belle and Goose.

They took a couple of steps toward the house, and yes, it was a house with a chimney. As they did, both of them grabbed their heads and fell to the ground. Triple One ran to them, she is a medic, but the pain had passed by when she got there.

Other hikers helped them up, and after a bit of dizziness, they were fine. Belle, on the other hand, froze. A moment later, Goose did the same. Several other hikers fell out also, including Bass Master, but recovered faster.

"HOLY CRAP!" They both said at the same time. Then, they looked at each other, "You too?"

"Yes, it's like I am seeing this place for the first time. But, then, something happened; the connection to this planet just got deeper." Belle said.

Goose closed his eyes, "There are tons of Kitties up here; they are afraid of us. So everyone, sit where you are. I am calling the Kitties and telling them not to fear us."

A few minutes later, the Kitties, about 30 of them, found their way onto the plateau. They crawled into the hiker's laps and snuggled. A few of the hikers were afraid at first, and until they were ready, the Kittie just sat there. Once the fear in the hiker passed, the Kittie snuggled.

A radio made noise. "Control to controller 105. Can you read me?"

Bass Master pulled the radio from a pocket and clipped it to her collar. "We hear you Control. What's up?"

"According to our readings. I mean, I have no idea. Actually, what did you do?"

"Nothing, why?"

"Remember how the magnetic lines of flux on this planet are wonky?"

"Wonky is so precise and descriptive."

The controller chuckled, "It is the most accurate way to describe it, but let's see; there are essentially eight unique north poles, for lack of a better way to explain it. Those magnetic flux lines are all over the planet and intersect at the oddest points, but the spot you are standing right now, they all moved to converge. So that spot is the only spot on the surface of this entire world where all the flux lines meet. It's like living in an old-school MRI machine."

"Hold on a second; I want to try something," Belle said.

Belle closed her eyes and thought about her dad, knowing he could speak to the animals as she did. Then, a few moments later, she heard him in her head. Then she screamed.

"What happened?" Goose asked her.

"I was calling out to my dad to see if I can make the connection, and I did. Then I could see through his eyes, and it freaked me out."

"Freaked you out?" Trip said, "Why?"

Belle started laughing, "He was, uh, using a tree." Everyone broke out into laughter.

"Let me try again; he should be done by now. "Dad, can you hear me?"

"I can; how are you doing this?"

"Not exactly sure about that one. But needless to say, I can see through your eyes."

"Really? Then you saw me...."

"I did, since closing my eyes did not stop me from seeing. That image is burned into my mind right now." They both started laughing, as did Goose. Finally, she turned to Goose, "Can you hear my dad and me talking?"

"Hi, Dad! That is a big yes to the question." Goose got an idea. Without speaking, he asked, "If you can hear my voice, raise your right hand."

"Dad. Look at the hikers and the crew. How many have their hand raised?"

A moment later, "A dozen, maybe 20."

"Get their names, please; tell them to meet us in the dining hall after dinner."

"You got it. Uh, Goose, both of your parents have their hands raised, as does my wife."

"That makes sense; it had to come from somewhere." Goose paused. Belle looked at the Captain, and his hand never raised.

"OK, we need to take a look around this plateau. It seems there is a series of buildings here, so someone else lived on this planet at one time. How long ago, no idea.

"Will do, baby doll."

She ended the connection with her dad, and Goose disconnected from everyone else.

They went into the first building, Dee first actually followed by Belle. She tried to maintain the dig, for lack of a better term. After that, dumb and Goose and another group went to the second building.

Toonist sat quietly on a small artificial wall and drew the five-building village. She captured it perfectly. There was another artist in the group, and he joined her, and together they drew what they saw and felt.

The group spent another few hours looking around, and they located some alien technology and a previous inhabitant or their remains.

Triple One scanned the skeleton, "Definitely not human. Female for sure. Height was one meter, weight 23 kilograms. It appears they had four eyes, a nose, two arms and two hands, two legs, and two feet. DNA is...." Her eyes opened wide, "92% to human."

"What does that mean?" Someone in the crowd asked.

"No clue. But I say we leave her here and let a science team collect her remains."

"I think this is their communications system. Goose walked to a wall, and it was shiny, slick. He touched it, and it powered up. They saw the flux lines on the planet and the eight north poles. They set up magnetic flux and communicate with each other like using the comms or a radio.

They spent another hour there and headed back to the campsite. In that time on the plateau, Toonist drew everything she saw. Ten very detailed drawings and a few of the displays from the house. One drawing of the former inhabitant as an homage to the life that was lost to the ages.

They would have plenty of time to look around. But the group needs to get back and get this party, I mean this wedding, underway.

Chapter Eleven

Double Espresso sat in his seat at the wedding, waiting for the proceedings to begin. He thought to himself, "I wonder what Goose is doing right now?"

"I'm trying not to freak out at the moment, my dear DE. How is it in the seats?"

"Quiet, peaceful, people are anxious to throw rice at..." He stopped in mid-sentence. "Goose, is this my imagination, or are we having a conversation?"

"What are you talking about? Of course we are talking. We talked through the comms before, so why not now?"

"Mainly because I have not had the comms installed since I got back to the planet less than 10 hours ago."

"Oh, that. Well, Belle and I seemed to have unlocked the secret to this world, and it appears you and possibly the Goat have had this planet rub off onto you. Communication is possible through the magnetic flux lines of the planet, and it seems you are all fluxed up, my friend."

"HUH?" DE replied to Goose.

"We can talk later, and I'll explain. None of this has been reported to Earth since we do not fully understand it yet. It appears you are important to this world. I hope you stay and help us with the colony."

"I plan to, now please, go get married."

"Will you two shut up already," Belle said. "My mind is racing as it is without you two chatting up a storm." She paused a moment. "Wait, DE has the gift?"

"Yup, he sure does, and I am guessing the Goat has it too."

Belle yelled in her head, "Belinda Goat, can you hear me?"

"Holy crap, do you gotta yell like that?" She said back to Belle. "Wait, how are we talking? I don't have a comms yet?"

"I'll explain it to you the moment Goose explains it to me, my love. Now, will you two go get hitched already!"

A crew member from the plane stood, walked to the front of the gathering, and read from a datapad. This is the guy Goose got coffee from every morning. They struck up a friendship. Lieutenant Brian Battery. Goose always chuckled at the fact the guy that charged his caffeine cells was named battery.

"Welcome! I am Brian Battery, and Goose and Belle asked me to get this started, knowing full well how I hated public speaking." Soft chuckles and laughs in the crowd made Brian grin from ear to ear. "On behalf of Goose and Belle, I mean Jaclyn Reynolds and Gilbert Gossling" He smiled a moment and added, "That is the first time I heard their real names." He cleared his throat and continued, "Let me thank you for being here this afternoon. We've gathered from many places, near and far, because we all understand love and how it gives us the power and ability to adapt; for Goose and Belle, to celebrate the love they share for each other in our presence is a testament to their friendship, empathy, and compassion. We have come here today as friends and family, in the presence of God, to witness the promises they are about to make, to cheer them on, and to bless them in all their future endeavors as a couple. A shared heart."

He looked a little stressed at making a public speech, "We are present to rejoice in their happiness, to help them when they have trouble, and to remember them in our prayers. So let's pray now...."

He shifted on his feet a second or two, "God, our Father, we thank You for the gift of marriage, for the beauty of intimate friendship, a companionship in which we can know and be known, in which we can share freely and deeply and be accepted completely. Father, thank you for this taste of Your great unconditional love for us. May the commitment made today by Belle – Jaclyn and Goose – Gilbert reflect the great love of God and bring honor to your name. In Jesus' name, we pray, Amen.

Brian collected his pad and went back to his seat.

"A wedding of two people is always a fantastic event." Tweedle Dumb said to those gathered at the wedding as he stood and walked to the front. "When the two join and become one, they bring together their past, present, and future. They also bring their faith, religion, family, and core beliefs. The merging of two different religious beliefs can be, shall we say, interesting. But the religions, the faiths we are merging today are so similar that it is not worth mentioning. I am Jewish. All faiths believe in God." He grinned at the crowd, "I wanted something to do at the wedding, and this is what they gave me!" The crowd laughed.

"In a few minutes, it will begin. Plan for it taking hours, I mean long and drawn out, boring, religious event after religious event. Now forget it; I have it on good authority that this hitching should take no more than 20 minutes!" There was applause from the crowd.

"Religions, deep personal faiths, are all different but the same. They all refer to a God, Goddess, or set of divine entities. The question is, is there a God? Does God rule your life? Does God care less about humanity? All of these are good and valid questions, and there is no answer, right or wrong. Each of these questions and many more need to be examined in your heart of hearts. Where is your faith? In what do you believe?" He paused a moment, "Do you believe?"

He paused a heartbeat to let that sink in, and Belinda took over. "In all of history, all religions have had one thing in common. LOVE. Today we are here to witness the joining of the love two people have for each other. We are here to celebrate their love and savor the pure love and joy these two friends of all of ours have for each other. We are here to be with them, to love them, to support them."

She looked around the crowd, and a few tears were visible; they did good! DE picked up the datapad, and they went back to their seats. DE sat next to his wife, Belinda Goat. She gave him a kiss on the cheek.

The Goat and DE headed back to their seats. "What do you think? Too Sappy?" DE asked Belinda.

"Nope. I think we nailed it!" She replied.

Once they sat, Goose's father and the Captain walked out to the front of the crowd. The Captain spoke first.

"I am Captain Roger Marless, and my co-officiate here is the Reverend Brian Gossling. Allow me to welcome you to a **wedding**—the first one on this planet, a planet which as of yet is unnamed. The name of the star it circles is Arkushanangarushashutu. Not a mouthful, a locker full. I cannot say I like this, and naming this planet One or Arkushanangarushashutu Prime is truly not an option. We have petitioned Earth for a name, a name we submitted for approval. I will not tell you that name yet, since it was Belle and Goose who requested it; you will learn it when they deliver their vows in a few minutes." He looked at Goose's father. "Allow me to introduce to you a man who knows one of them quite well, Reverend Brian Gossling, Minister of the Family Methodist church in east Tennessee. His church building is less than a mile off the Appalachian Trail, near the Beauty Spot in Erwin, and I would not be surprised if several of you may have stopped in during your thru-hike of the AT." He held out his hand, and Goose's father shook it and walked to the front of the stage area.

"My friends." He shook his head, "You are my friends. Not because we have a shared experience, hobby, pastime, or we were youth together, but because you are friends of my son's and my very soon-to-be daughter. I hate the phrase 'IN-LAW,' mainly because once these two become married, a married couple, they will, in essence, merge my family and the family of my friend Bob Reynolds. Our wives are already sisters, so I guess Bob and I are now brothers."

Bob yelled from the very back of the gathering, "Oh my lord!" Everyone laughed.

"I agree, Bob; this is fantastic. Finally, I get a daughter!"

Bob yelled back, "I get a son!"

Both moms just shook their heads and smiled.

Brian continued. "The Captain and I are here today to merge the love of two people. They love all of us, and we have all felt it since arriving on this planet, this nameless planet. This distant and strange but beautiful world. We know the creatures of this world are not the evil, dangerous creatures we once thought they were. These two have connected the major, using their name, critters to the point of friendly pets if you can consider an elephant with razor-sharp claws, or for that matter, a large cat with razor spiked teeth a cuddly pet." He paused and looked around. Belle was in the back, ready to enter, and Goose was standing off to one side. No one in the seats could see them, but the Captain and the minister did see them.

Brian turned to the Captain, "Captain, what say we get this show on the road?"

The Captain took the center, "Gilbert Gossling and friends, will you please join us out here."

Goose, C-Note, and Chisel walked out and stood to the left side of the attendees.

Brian said, "Ladies and gentlemen," He smiled a broad smile, "Here comes the bride!"

Brian walked over to his son and stood there next to him, with his hand on his shoulder. Music started playing; Maria selected classical music. It was unique and fitting, like the place they were standing. Finally, Belle appeared and began walking to the front; everyone stood. She was wearing her great-grandmother's dress, and it was both retro and modern, traditional and futuristic.

She walked to the front with her father, and he put her hand into Goose's hand. He said something to him, and all three of them laughed a bit. Then, he kissed his daughter, shook hands and a hug with Goose, and went to sit next to his wife.

The music stopped, and the Captain started speaking, but Belle held up her hand. The Captain stopped, knowing precisely the reason she was doing this.

"Family, friends, not everyone is here yet. There are a few new friends who wanted to witness and experience how we humans join, mate. The Blue Bear and the Kitties, as we have come to call them, and yes, they like those names. Goose and I, and a few select others in this group, can speak to them and understand them at a core level. So please, they are arriving, and please do not make any commotion. They are not dangerous. They are curious. They are also family and friends."

Belle and Goose closed their eyes, and in a few minutes, the Kitties appeared. Fifty of them, ten families at least. They all stood off to one side, the same side as Goose was standing. A few moments later, a dozen full-grown Blue Bear approached and stood near Belle. Some in the crowd seemed to be a bit unnerved, but no one did or said anything.

Belle turned to the Captain and her very soon-to-be father-in-law. "Dad, Cap, you have the floor!"

The captain spoke as Reverend Brian nodded to him.

"We are here today to join these two, Jaclyn Reynolds and Gilbert Gossling, in the bonds of holy matrimony. It is a rare but cherished event for a ship's Captain to be able to perform this ceremony and an even rarer event to share this with the creatures of a new world, who we welcome and are thankful we can all be friends." He looked at Belle and Goose, "Do they know what we are saying?"

"They do. We are translating for them," Belle said.

"...and answering all their questions," Goose added.

The Captain continued, "It is my pleasure to...." He looked at Goose. "They have questions?" The crowd quietly chuckled as Goose and Belle both nodded. The Captain continued, "It is my pleasure to share this honor with someone such as the Reverend Gossling." He gestured to him.

Brian took over. "Marriage is and has always been a sacred event. To be cherished and shared with family and friends. So it only fits we have the creatures of this world in attendance." He turned to the Kitties, "Goose calls you the Kitties." Dad was staring at Brian with an intensity he has never seen before. "You represent the friendship and hope of this world." The group leader strolled over to Goose and climbed up, resting comfortably on his shoulder. "Well, son, it appears you now have three best men." He turned to the Blue Bear, "My new large blue friends represent the majesty and awesome power of this world." The lead Mom Bear slowly moved closer to Belle, standing directly next to Toonist. Mom Bear laid on the ground next to her, and Toonist reached out and rubbed mother bear on her mid-body. Brian continued.

"Ladies and gentleman, this was not in the rehearsal." Soft chuckles through the crowd. No one wanted to laugh out loud at the moment. "Creatures of this planet and creatures of Earth, well heck, creatures of the universe, we are here today to have a wedding. I get a new daughter, and my friend Bob gets a son; that much has been established. But what has not been said up to now is that Gil and Jaclyn will get each other in a way they have never known. Two families will be merged because of them. Two hearts will be joined. Let me tell you when two hearts are joined in a perfect union, NOTHING in the universe can breakthrough!"

The Captain spoke, "This is fitting. We have been here for several years, and it took these two people to unite the planet, not just the creatures but all of us. Jaclyn and Gilbert, known to all of you as Belle and Goose, are a part of this world. They established a connection to this world, as no one has ever known. Just look at them, and you can see the link. Goose here communes with the critters—the animals of the land. But Belle, just wow. We could not be prouder of the fact she made a connection to the largest intelligent creature humanity has ever known" He paused a moment, "Most of you already know they will lead the research team from Oasia. Oasia, I love the name they chose. An oasis on this planet. Oasia will not only be a place for humans to use as a base of operations to study the planet, the creatures, and the plants but also the base of operations for the new government." He looked around, "I apologize; I am just so excited about all of this, and especially to have the honor to stand here and verify this union." He looked at Brian. "One last thing. Belle asked the planet to be named for an ancient mythological deity. The Greek goddess of family, animals, and marriage. It fits, so we are announcing the dedication of the planet **Hera** at this union."

Brian walked to the front, and he smiled at Gil, "Son. Are you sure about this? She's a hiker!"

Goose answered him as if it was prearranged. "Yes, dad. I am positive, but dad...."

"Yes, son."

"I'm a hiker too!"

"I know, son, but let's talk about that later." Everyone laughed, applauded, and the large and small critters became excited a moment until Goose and Belle told them it was alright.

"OK then, let's get on with this."

"Good, I'm getting hungry!" The Captain added. Then from out of nowhere, a very small Blue Bear appeared and walked over to the Captain. He sat on his butt, on top of the Captain's left foot, and just looked up at him. "Well, I did tell mom bear I will be the babysitter; I guess I'm up?" He squatted and played with the little bear, and he crawled up into his arms. The Captain walked to the front and stood in front of Belle and Mom Bear. "I think he wanted to see what was going on." Belle just nodded at him, pet the baby on his head, and looked at mom bear, who poked her with her nose.

Brian continued, "Who gives this woman to be married to this man?"

Belle's parents stood, "We Do!"

The Captain asked, "Who gives this man to be married to this woman?"

Brian waited for his wife to stand next to him, and together they said, "We Do!"

He waited for his wife to return to her seat next to DE and the Goat, then continued.

"Now, Gilbert, I'm going to ask just what your intentions are towards Jaclyn...." He paused a brief moment then continued.

"Gilbert, will you take Jaclyn to be your wife, and will you be faithful to her, love her, honor her, live with her and cherish her, according to the Word of God in holy marriage? If so, say I will."

"Most definitely, I will!" Goose was grinning from ear to ear.

"Jaclyn, will you take Gilbert to be your husband, and will you be faithful to him, love him, honor him, live with him and cherish him, according to the Word of God in holy marriage? If so, say I will."

Belle looked at Goose, "I will."

"I understand the two of you will be reading your vows?"

"Dad, we are not reading anything. Neither of us could write anything down, so we decided to see what happens." Goose said to his father.

"This should be good!" The Captain and Brian said together. Soft chuckles in the crowd.

"Jaclyn, please recite your vows to Gil."

Belle turned to him, and they held hands. All four of their hands were wrapped up in one place. As she began speaking, the dad Kittie, knowing something was happening, leaned forward and stretched out, landing a front paw on Belle's shoulder. A second later, he was sitting on her shoulder, and another Kittie climbed up Goose, and they resumed watching.

"OK then, I want to start by saying I did not expect that, and I think it is very cool." She looked at the Kittie on her shoulder, and he nudged her with his nose. She turned back and looked into Goose's eyes, held his hands, "Goose. You are Yin; I am Yang. That was one of the first things you ever said to me on the way here. Never in my life did I ever expect to fall in love with a hiker, and never did I expect to fall in love so fast, so completely, and so perfectly. You protected me when we nearly froze to death on the side of a mountain and made that week of bitter cold bearable. You brought me fish. No one has ever thought to bring me fish, still swimming too. I got to clean and cook them, one of my favorite things ever. We have seen some pretty amazing sights here but have the same memories from the trails back on Earth, even though our treks were not

282

at the same time. We know some of the same people from the trails, but my trails always have, and will always, lead straight to you. Each and every one of them. No matter how many hikes I have ever been on or how many I will go on in the future. I promise to you, here and now, to never be disloyal or distrustful. I promise as long as I live that I will love you. I promise to be your partner and best friend in sickness and health, in joy and sorrow; I promise to love you without reservation; I commit to you my lifetime of continued love, respect, trust, and friendship. This is my promise." She stopped speaking with tears in her eyes. She nodded at Brian.

"Gil?"

"Belle." Goose started. "You have no idea how shocked I am. I took this assignment because programming is tedious, and I needed something to do in my life that was not boring. Well, I got something new, alright. I found you. Trust me, you are not boring. I realized you were destined to be my wife before we ever left the plane but waited and hoped you would realize it also. I am so unbelievably happy you did. The best week of my life has been the week we nearly froze to death. I don't think I ever talked about myself to anyone as much as we talked that week, nor have I ever been as interested in someone else as when you told me about you. You know things about me no one in the universe knows." He took a breath. "I promise to be true to you and always trust you, love you, and cherish you. But more each day. I love the fact we have a connection to the creatures of this world and that the little guys here are so interested in us. We can and will do great things here. I love you more than I thought was even possible. I would say I love you to Earth and back, but that is not far enough." He smiled at her, "I love you more than the universe is big. I promise as long as I live that I will love you. I promise to be your partner and best friend in all things; I promise to love you without reservation; I commit to you my forever growing love, respect, trust, and friendship. This is my promise." He stopped speaking with tears in his eyes." Goose nodded at his father.

They did it.

Both their mothers, Brian and the Captain, several others all had wet eyes. The Dad on Belle's shoulder snuggled into her neck, as did the Kittie on Goose's shoulder. Mom bear poked him with her nose, then poked Belle. Mom Bear sealed the marriage with that action.

Brian spoke, "A symbol to all that you are not alone in the universe is the wearing of a wedding ring on your hand. Jaclyn and Goose have chosen to honor this tradition. William, I mean C-Note, I understand you are the controller of this symbol of love. May I have the rings, please?"

C-Note smiled and jokingly tapped every pocket on his wardrobe; Belle and Goose nearly busted out laughing. Then, finally, he reached into an inside pocket, pulled the rings out, and handed them to

Reverend Gossling. He shook his head at C-Note, but he was also smiling.

"I will ask you now to seal the vows which you have just made by the giving and receiving of rings that your friend William FINALLY found in his pocket." He took a breath and got into his minister's voice, "The circle is the emblem of eternity, the circle never ends, and it is our prayer that your love and happiness will be as unending as the rings which you exchange. These rings are visible reminders to you and all others that what you have promised, you will do. Wear them as a constant reminder that you are committed to one another for life and the life to come."

Brian walked them through the exchange of rings. "Goose, who used to be my son Gilbert, place the ring on Jaclyn's finger and repeat after me:" He handed Belle's ring to Goose, and Goose slipped it about halfway onto her finger.

> "This ring I give to you
> as a sign of my promise,
> our love,
> And God's grace.
> And I pledge to you
> My friendship,
> My loyalty,
> My devotion.
> I will be faithful to you always.
> In the name of the Father, and of the Son and
> of the Holy Spirit."

Goose looked like he was about to cry. Brian continued, "Belle, who is to be my new daughter Jaclyn, place the ring on Goose's finger and repeat after me:" He handed Belle the ring. She slipped it about halfway onto his finger. They repeated the exact same words. This time tears were flowing from both of them and several people who were watching.

Brian spoke, "Jaclyn and Gilbert, you have committed yourselves to each other in this joyous and sacred covenant. You have become one. Fulfill your promises. Love, honor and serve God and each other, and rest in the power of the Holy Spirit. For now, and from this day forward, you are husband and wife! Gilbert, my son, you may kiss your Bride!"

They kissed. A perfect kiss. The first kiss as a married couple. They separated and smiled; both had tears. The Kitties were snuggling. Mom Bear was purring.

"Mazel Tov!" The Captain yelled. "Hey, gimme a break; I was raised Jewish!" DE gave him a thumbs up.

Brian said, "Ladies and gentlemen, creatures of this world, may I present to you, my daughter! Oh, and my son too. Husband and wife, married before the grace of God, their friends, and representatives of this beautiful planet. May you have a love that always lasts: A love that is stronger than death. A love that floods cannot quench. A love that is as new as each morning and as familiar as an old friend. And may you always feel that what you have is enough."

The Captain continued, "My friends, may I present to you, for the first time, the newly married Gilbert Gossling and Jaclyn Reynolds." The Captain said. Then yelled even louder, "BELLE AND GOOSE!"

Applause, hooting, the Kitties knew it was a happy time, and they were all jumping up and down. Even Mom Bear joined in on the fun, roaring just enough to be heard over all the noise but staying on the ground.

Mom Bear nudged Belle, and they locked eyes for a moment. "REALLY?" Belle said out loud.

"What?" Goose asked her.

"Mom wants to give us a gift. Follow me."

He did, and they climbed up on Mom Bears back and just sat there. Finally, Mom stood to full height, walked off into the trees. The Captain, Brian, and every single person on this planet were not only amazed and stupefied but nearly in shock. A month ago, the fear of these magnificent creatures was nightmare material, but since Belle and Goose unlocked the communications with them, all that has faded. Mom Bear ambled off into the trees, being ridden by the newly married couple.

When they arrived through the tree line, hundreds of Mom Bears stood in a clearing near where they broke through the trees. Belle and the group of Mom Bears had a communication. She was part of the local community of bears and soon a part of the planetary community, all Blue Bear everywhere on this world. The bears are all in contact, but a female is not accepted into the larger group until mated.

Belle has been accepted and is equal to the family leaders. The male bears spoke to Goose and informed him to go with it, too, as his mind interpreted it. He nearly laughed when they told him.

Several minutes passed, and the group at the reception was getting curious about what was happening in the woods; a minute later, Mom Bear returned the two of them to the place where they started. She laid back down on the ground, and Belle and Goose dismounted. They both hugged Mom Bear, and Belle kissed her on the nose. Goose told the Kitties to get onions and told DE to grab a handful of power bars when they were on their way back.

When they got off the giant blue bear's back, DE walked up and handed him nine power bars, already unwrapped. He accepted the armful of onions from the Kitties and gave dad the power bars. Dad hugged his leg, and all of the Kitties headed off into the trees. Goose handed Belle the onions, but she stopped before she gave them to Mom Bear.

"DE, come here." She said. A few steps later, he was standing next to her. "Look Mom in the eyes and ask her how her day has gone in your mind."

He did, and the shock on his face was unique. "She talked to me!" Then she poked him in the chest with her nose. "What is that?"

"That means you are a part of her clan," Belle said.

"Oh man, that makes you my brother now," Goose said.

"I got another son?" Bob said. Goose just shook his head.

Mom poked all three of them and headed to the woods.

The Captain and Goose's father walked up to them as they dismounted. "What happened out there?"

"I think they just made me a Matriarch." She paused a moment. "This is the first time they referred to me as She. Like it was a title."

As Mom Bear got to the edge of the clearing, she stopped and turned to ensure she was in plain view of everyone. Then she let out a blood-curdling roar, the loudest thing they had ever heard. When it subsided, all of the Mom Bears in the woods let out the same cry. The sound came from all around them. It was almost deafening. Belle had tears in her eyes.

Most of the guests had a bit of fear on their faces, but those connected to this planet said the same thing, "Aaaawwww, that's sweet of her."

"What was that?" The captain asked.

Goose spoke, "All of the Mom Bears on this planet just pledged their loyalty to Belle."

"They what?" Brian said.

"I have no idea what that means." Belle paused a moment and composed herself. Then, with the Kitties and Blue Bear back in the woods, "LET THE PARTY BEGIN! I AM STARVING!" Belle yelled.

Chapter Twelve

Double Espresso sat at the kitchen table, sipping on a coffee he just created. When he returned to Hera with the Goat, he picked up a costly espresso machine. It was well used by nearly everyone. He had a smile on his face after each sip. He was seriously enjoying his coffee this morning. He heard Belle and Goose were awake as he left his room; he heard them exercising. He understands; DE and the Goat asked Goose's dad to marry them before he and Beatrice headed home to Earth. Like many of the other 25 sets of newlyweds, it was a small ceremony following the weeks after Belle and Goose had the first wedding and first party on the planet. Goose's Dad was happily busy!

Today they were heading back to the plateau. The weather is quite warm once again, and before the seasonal shift returns to the cold month, they needed to find out more about the technology in the village. This is the first time they were heading back to the plateau since they first hiked there, before the wedding.

Goose walked through the living area into the kitchen and saw DE sipping a coffee. He grabbed a cupcake, a tube of frosting and proceeded to scribble something on top. "Anniversary," He said to DE, who rolled his eyes.

"Brother, if you plan to do this forever, you will be busy."

"In know...." He headed back to their room.

DE just sat there.

Although hiking is now just a pastime here, it is still a valuable way to perform research. Teams are dispatched from the research center and dropped at locations on the planet where one of the last teams reported something interesting.

The research center received several hover pods in the last cargo run from Earth. It allows them to work anywhere on the planet when needed. Well, get anywhere on this planet a lot faster and return home, back to Oasia, pretty much every night unless they traveled to the other side of the planet.

Today is no different. Brian and Beatrice are heading to the plateau today. They wanted to see it, take some photos, and remember what it looks like, so when they get home, they could tell their friends they stood on that spot, or they have been in those buildings. The Captain told them he planned to release the information after the snow passed and the weather warmed up again.

Tonight, they all decided to stay on the plateau. Goose brought gear for them all, they had no idea, and he had it all set up for them. Their tents were a little larger, and they had cots. He and Belle used one tent and a double bag. It reminded them of when they fell in love nearly a year ago now.

C-Note and the Captain fell from the sky, as Goose's father likes to call it. The pod landed in the pod circle, a designated place for pods in the plateau area. They figured it was safer to have a designated spot where no one will camp, sit, fall asleep or walk. So the circle was marked clearly, and the critters knew to be careful because it was not a good place to stop.

C-note and the Captain made it to the plateau, and the first thing Goose heard, "What? No fire?" C-Note proceeded to collect firewood and set a nice campfire. The weather was beginning to cool off, and Goose's parents, actually everyone, appreciated the new coats.

Chairs were set up, The Moms were given camp blankets, and everyone was comfortable at the fire.

"Hi, gang," Goose's father said as they made their way to the fire. A crew member grabbed a couple chairs and set them up for the new set of parents. Belle asked a question.

"So, my dearest. It's been a year now, and you still have not told me about the dent in the side of that museum-quality stove you carry in your pack. Now is a good time."

Goose looked at his father. "Dad, I think you should tell the dent story."

Carol smiled and shook her head.

"Ok, son. Let's see. It was when I turned 21. My father gave me that stove and wanted to know if I liked camping. It just so happens I did. We went several times a year, and he always used that little stove to cook, boil water, and sometimes just to have a fire in the camp. Well, being 21 now, Dad brought a bottle of tequila, a bag of limes, and salt. He wanted to teach me about camping, drinking, and not being an ass."

Brian asked, "Did it ever work?" Bob just looked at him, and Brian shrugged. Then, without saying a word to his new friend, he continued.

"Well, Dad and I polished off that bottle of tequila that night, and he said he was going to hit the hay. In his somewhat inebriated state, he reached down and picked up the stove. Completely forgetting it was a tad bit hot. You know, there is a fire inside it and all. It took maybe half a second, and he threw it straight up. The fire spilled out, and all over the ground, little fires were popping up. So, two pretty lit guys were stomping out fires everywhere. Once all the fires were out and we saw the stove sitting on dirt, I picked it up to move it somewhere safe. Yes, I know you are thinking about it. It was still hot. This time I threw it in the air, and it landed on a somewhat large rock, bounced right in the exact spot it was a moment ago. Dad and I looked at each other, and we decided to just go to bed. When we got up, I found the stove right where I remembered it and saw that huge dent in the side. I stood there and stared at it for a minute, and my father got up. He walked over and saw the dent. I thought he would be upset, disappointed; nope. All he said to me was, 'Damn, son, look at the huge dent in that thing. Glad it's yours now.' So I picked it up, cleaned it up as good as possible, and put it all back together. After a few minutes, I did find the ring, and Dad handed me that black bag I use. I put it into my tent, and we went fishing."

Everyone around the fire was laughing. Then, finally, Bob stood, "If you notice my hand, you can still see, but barely, the burn scar."

They talked for another hour, and everyone went to their tent and slept. Morning would come early, and they had things to do before they headed back to the compound.

~~~~~~~~~~

Long field trips still require camping, but it seems the planet's mammals are all now familiar with humans. Very few carry weapons any longer since there is no real danger on this planet.

During the winter, the Kitties lived in the cat house. Seventy-five of the little critters rotated in and out of the cat house, so the actual number in this area is a mystery. However, Goose said there are about 600 families, and if you figure four in a family, that is quite a lot.

This location received a lot of snow, but that did not deter the research team. Instead, they found food the bears would eat. Mom Bear would sniff and sample many options, several of which erupted, quite forcefully, in record time. Never give a Blue Bear broccoli it was discovered. It travels through their intestines in less than an hour, and the bear is quite embarrassed at the sound and the range.

Being so close to Earth skunks and felines, the Kitties can eat actual cat food, but it is not preferred. So they dropped a pod filled with the best cat food available during the winter, and it was appreciated since, for the first time in their memory, this winter, not one of the Kitties, or the bear, died from the weather.

Goose's parents, Brian and Beatrice, left just after the first snow. He said he needed to be back in time for the Christmas season, which was getting close. Rather than taking the shuttle, which was tied up on a week-long mission in another area of the planet, they decided they wanted to try out heading into orbit on a dropship. Belle volunteered to press the button for them. When they arrived, all she said was, "Now I know where Goose gets it."

"Get's what?" Her new mother asked.

"That scream!" she said and laughed; they joined in.

Belle's parents, Bob and Carol, left a few weeks later. Bob became good friends with the bears, especially one male. Bob was not as tall as the bear's leg, but hey, who cares. They liked to go fishing together. First, Bob showed him how humans fished, then he showed him the correct way to fish. They laughed a lot about the similarities between human and bear relationships.

Carol is a fantastic analyst and set up the database and procedure for plant and animal identification. Her cross-typing of the samples is a standard at the center. Belle referred to it as her mother's database and asked to change the system's name to CarolNet. They are actually considering it.

Today they are heading back to the plateau, which they named Arkus Base. Over the winter, the linguists who came from Earth determined a great deal about the alien language. They translated about 30% of the information. They wanted to know what was on the screens, the displays, so they could better, or begin, to understand how they did what they did to this world. One of the first things the linguistic team discovered was that the aliens referred to this planet as Arkus, and as a tribute to them, they called the base what they thought was the correct pronunciation of the unfamiliar word.

The small craft landed on the surface at the base of the mountain. Climbing the stairs to the site has become second nature for most, but today was different. The Captain will be visiting. He plans to land in a dropship and make his way to the settlement; no idea why, but he has a fascination for this place like all the rest of those with a connection to this planet.

As the group made their way to the buildings, Goose walked directly to the console and touched it, which activated the console, and they were able to see the Captain and his dropship were on their way. ETA 4 minutes. Others made a complete assessment of the power system, while still others looked at the building itself. Its construction, material, and design. Several hikers wanted to stay during the isolating and challenging part of the winter and were rewarded with a place to live that was warm, inviting and gave them something to do to keep their minds occupied when heading outside was not the best idea. Keeping the linguistic team safe was their goal. They also found the buildings have a restroom, and it contained a shower of sorts. It used sound waves to clean the skin and did a pretty fair job of it too. It does pretty good on clothing also.

They heard the pod descend past them on the plateau and knew that the Captain would arrive in a few minutes once the engine roar was gone. Sure enough, not more than 15 minutes past and he appeared, breathing hard but smiling.

"That climb always makes me feel alive." He said as he entered the building.

"Captain, this is rather interesting." The Captain walked over to the display. Goose was tapping a few of the controls, and the display changed. "I restarted the sequence recording. This is you coming here." The Captain watched as his pod descended and landed. He saw an orange dot exit the pod and climb the steps, mainly two steps at a time. "Impressive, sir. You are in excellent shape to climb those steps like that."

"Have you determined what the color signifies?"

"There is orange, red, blue and green. Belle and I and a few others are Green, but most people who can speak to the critters are blue. This is because green and blue are connected. From what we can see, orange is the same as red; these people have no connection to the planet. The greens can speak to any critter. The blue people can speak to a specific creature. Like the birds, the Kitties, or the Bear."

The Captain grinned, "Has anyone tried to speak to the fish?"

"Actually, yes. Belle and I and several others did try, but there was nothing there. So I guess they are just food for the others."

"Goose?" Someone in the room called his name.

"Be right back." He told the Captain and walked to the other side of the room to speak to the woman who called him.

The Captain touched the panel and felt it was vibrating, tingled his fingertips. He was not a techie, but he saw Goose run the console and wanted to replay the landing again. He thought it was interesting. However, as he touched a control, the screen completely changed. A new and yet unseen screen appeared. He tried to get it back to what it was and heard a buildup of tremendous power around him. He could not move, and he felt like he just rubbed his feet across shag carpeting.

Everyone looked at the Captain, who appeared to be frozen. No one could get to him, though; the Captain was enveloped in a ball of pure energy. It dissipated a moment later, and he collapsed to the floor, unconscious, motionless, and not breathing. Goose felt for a pulse, not there. He started CPR, and a medic arrived and hooked him up to a life support cuff. His heart started beating again, and a minute later, he started breathing on his own.

He was unconscious for more than 5 minutes and clinically dead for a little over one minute. But he seemed as though he is recovering now.

"Captain, can you hear me?" Goose said. Goose thought to himself, 'why did I walk away?'

"Not your fault you walked away. Someone else needed you. I was stupid for punching buttons." The Captain said out loud.

Goose realized he never spoke that question, he thought to himself, and the Captain replied. "Sir, I have good news and bad news." The Captain stood up; he was feeling better. They were standing next to the console, and Goose looked at it. "Holy shit!" Goose said.

"What?" The Captain replied to him.

Goose stared at the display. Then, finally, the Captain looked and saw Goose as a green dot on the screen. But he was standing next to a green dot. "Uh, Goose, is there someone standing next to us?"

"No, sir."

"But I am an orange dot. Wait, where am I? There are no orange dots in this room. Only Green and Blue and one red."

"Take a few steps away, Cap." He did, and the other green dot moved equally. "Cap, whatever happened to you made you the same as Belle and me. I'm going to guess the red dots will never gain the ability to speak to the critters, but the orange dots may, or can, attain this ability. Of course, yours was rather drastic with the electrocution and all; but hey, you can say hi to Mom Bear now."

"I can!" He smiled a huge smile.

"More than a babysitter. I guess she knew you would change or could change. She must have felt it in you."

Goose stopped and looked at a wall. "Cap, something is behind that wall we need to see."

"What?"

"No idea. I can see it, though; whatever they are, they are shaped like pistols. There are several of them there, different stages or something." He walked to the wall. "I see the key in my mind." He touched a few places on the wall, it appeared to be random, and the wall moved back and slid away.

Goose smiled. The small room was well lit and clean, which means environmental systems. He saw 6 of the pistols on the right side wall, not weapons but switches and buttons, definitely some type of technology. He could guess what it did, they did, but what's the use.

The back wall had what looked like datapads, and he touched one. It activated. He heard it in his head.

It was reading the data to him. But not in an alien language.

"Jonsen," Being the only red dot in the room, "Come here and touch one of these things and see if it lights up for you."

Jonsen touched it, nothing.

Goose looked at the last wall and saw a rack of clothing. "Too small for anyone in this party, but perhaps the people back home can make sense of it."

"OK then, I have a theory."

~~~~~~~~~~

The group spent the night at Arkus Base and had a great breakfast well before sunrise. The Captain cooked. After they all ate, the Captain sat down.

"You OK, sir?" Goose asked.

"Not sure. I am feeling a little dizzy. Light-headed."

"We are all headed back to the site if you want to come with us. We can leave the pod here, and if anyone needs to head to the ship in orbit, it's always there."

"Good thought. Besides, I can see my doctor at the site. But, unfortunately, she defected to your group."

"I know. We all love her to death."

A few hours later, they all made their way down the stairs and piled into the shuttle. It was a few minutes to get back to Oasia. Once they landed, the Captain felt better, or so he said.

Belle met the group. She gave Goose a very impressive kiss. Then, she looked at the Captain, "Those are not for everyone, Cap."

The Captain shook his head and smiled.

"I hear that you can talk to the critters now?" She said to him.

"So it appears." He replied.

"Wanna go say hi to Mom Bear, literally?"

"Yes!"

They just started walking away, and Goose said to them. "OK, bye. Have fun. Say Hi to Mom. I'll be here cleaning up, making your dinner."

Belle never turned to look at him; she threw her arm up in the air and waved it, and just yelled, "OK honey, thanks."

It took a few minutes to get there, and once they did, mom showed up.

Mom walked up to Belle and nudged her in the chest with her nose.

"OK, what do I do?" The Captain asked.

"Look at her. She will sense you are talking to her and turn to you." So he did, and as she turned and their eyes met, he closed his eyes and fell flat on his back.

Belle asked Mom what happened.

Mom Bear said, "Some have this reaction to the first time they speak. But, there is a medicine that works. It is the medicine plant."

Mom made a grunting sound, and a few moments later, a Kittie appeared. She spoke to it, and it ran off. About 5 minutes later, Kittie returned with a flower, a giant flower. The Kittie put it on the Captain's face; Belle did nothing but watch. A few minutes later, the Captain regained consciences.

"What happened?" He said.

"You passed out, and Mom fixed you. It appears this plant fixed you. Must be something in the pollen."

She reiterated what happened in complete detail, and mom was hovering over him like, well, a Mom. She looked him directly in the eyes.

"You can speak."

"I can."

"I am happy for you. You are a kind animal, like She."

"She? You mean Belle?"

"We call her She. It is a reverent name for the one who spoke to us first. When she did, all bears, as you call us, planet-wide, knew her and her mate. She is family."

"Do you have a name for her mate?"

"We do. He." She paused. "We learned you all have names, and all names are different. We have had a name for you since you played with small one. Teacher. We learned teacher in your world is one who passes on their knowledge to the youngers. It helps them to survive, to do well in life. You are Teacher. As Teacher, many bears will bring you their youngers to learn from you."

"I am honored."

Belle was tearing up. This was more than she hoped.

"I must return to the family." She stood to her full height but leaned down, poking him in the chest with her nose. "She. Be well." She nudged Belle and turned to leave, stopped for a brief moment, and let out a deafening and intimidating roar.

"I understood that, Belle. She just told all bear my name is Teacher."

Belle hugged the Captain for a long moment. "You ready to head back?" She asked him.

"I am." He picked up the flower and carried it with him; it was the size of his face.

When they got back to the area, Goose met them on the edge of the field.

"Teacher, huh?" He popped the Captain on the arm. "Excellent!"

"How did you know?" The Captain asked.

"You kidding me? Mom has a voice, we heard it here, and besides, several of us speak bear!"

They laughed.

The Captain and most of the crew spent a week on the planet; researching was their reason. A camping trip away from orbit was more like it. Several crew members who worked at Arkus Base ended up with the ability, but many did not. They determined how the Captain activated the ability generator, the name given to it by one crew.

The green and blue dots were at their maximum potential for the planet, and now there were more than 100 connected people to lead the cause to protect and explore this world. Those who arrived as an orange dot, like the Captain, would jump from orange to either green or blue. One of the crew, a red dot, hoped they would transform. But, when they pressed the button, nothing happened. No power build-up, no frozen in place, and no being enveloped in pure magnetic energy. Nothing. It was like the system had a failsafe to activate.

She requested to hotwire the system, but it was shot down. DE was in command of Arkus Base, and the Goat was Chief of Operations. Both very quickly and loudly said NO!

Belle and Goose had other duties. One of the screens showed other bases around the planet. Each Monday, they would take a group from Oasia to the remote base and check it out. The team, minus Belle and Goose, would return, and the following

Monday, they would go to another remote site. So far, they had been to 11 such smaller bases, all of them having an already existing infrastructure.

They were preparing to depart for the next location. Tweedle Dumb was in the planning meeting, as were all those who were on the trip. Tweedle Dee was at the last site looking for history.

"OK," He said to the meeting table. He was looking straight down, elbows on the table. "I have a question."

"Shoot," Someone said.

"I reviewed the location in the file on the alien database at Arkus and have determined a few things." He paused a moment and looked up, locking eyes with Goose. "This location is the same size, number of buildings, and there is already a green dot on-premises. Before you ask me what that means, no clue. Could a human green be there, no idea, but no one is missing. Is it a member of the race, species, whatever of the person we initially found as remains at Arkus? No idea. But I believe this needs a fair amount of caution."

Everyone has become comfortable with their new abilities, which is nothing more than mental communication. They can, at will, speak to any specific person on the planet or in orbit, creating private communication, but at the same time, they can, when needed, broadcast to everyone.

The greens can send visuals to anyone, but the blues can only send visuals to greens. Greens can relay to a group or person as needed. It is time-consuming for that green but necessary.

They did not know, but Goose sent the meeting to Belle on the other side of the planet, looking at the previous base. "When do you leave, and when will you get there?" She asked her husband of about half an Earth year.

"We leave in 2 hours and will get there close to dark local time." He told her.

"I am just about done here. I'll meet you there with a few from this team, including the Goat."

"OK, I'll give you a better ETA when I know more."

They disconnected, "OK then, we're all set. Grab your gear, any gear you'll need in the next week or so, and meet at the boat in 2-hours. We'll be there before dark, so eat lunch now. Dinner will be at the new base."

Everyone left except for DE and Tweedle Dumb.

"What's up, guys?" Goose asked.

"We have an issue with two team members," DE said.

"What's going on?" Goose was concerned.

"They have worked constantly for the past 6-months without a break, day off, vacation like the rest of us have had, and the sad thing is, it's their choice," Tweedle said.

"Are they doing OK?" Goose asked, not realizing who they were talking about.

"Not so much. I understand they are a bit stressed out and spread too thin. You can see it in their faces, but so far, it is not affecting their performance." DE said.

"We may need to intervene. Are they hikers or crew?" Goose asked.

"Both are hikers."

"OK, we need to put them on a week off, send them out for a week or so, maybe 100 kilometers in a nice area of the planet to survey something spectacular. Are they in a relationship?"

"I believe it is safe to say that they are," DE replied.

"Good. That should give them a chance to recharge." He looked at DE and Tweedle, "Can the two of you take care of it, please? Belle and I have an appointment with a new base. The rule is since we are first there, we get to name it too!"

"We will take care of it; rest easy. Next time we see the two of them, we will let them know."

Goose left the room. DE and Tweedle waited till he was gone. "I will let them know when they are together at the south pole."

"I will pack their pack for them. I have it set up with C-Note, who's on the ship for a few days, to send a hiker box down when he gets the word from us. The weather will be good for the next two weeks, so clothing is not an issue."

"Remember to pack her fishing rod. And a couple of lemons. Maybe some couscous and a bottle of wine or champagne. They can catch and make a romantic dinner."

They both laughed a little and headed to pack for themselves and pack a backpack for Goose and Belle.

~~~~~~~~~~

"Are we there yet?" DE asked.

"Almost!" Goose said.

"That's what you said ten minutes ago."

"And what I'll say till we arrive. Then I'll say, WE'RE HERE!"

A few seconds later, DE asked, "Are we there yet."

"I just said we're here!" DE perked up. It was a 6-hour flight in this low-level open-roof shuttle. There is a roof that can be added, but it's not needed at this time.

"Finally...." They all laughed. DE does this all the time because he is Double Espresso and cannot make a coffee on the shuttle.

Goose, Tweedle Dumb, and DE headed to the building that had the green dot. They all considered removing their pistol from its holster then stopped.

If there is a single green in there, surely three big strong hikers can subdue him.

As they entered the building, they realized this one was unique. There were displays on one wall, a monitor connected to every other base they found around the planet, and a few they had not located yet. In the center of the room was a small container. As they approached it, they realized it had a glass cover. Goose peered inside and saw a person, alien, lying there. Goose touched the container.

"Hello." He heard in his head.

"Hello," He replied.

"I have been following your progress and determined you to be a good person. Therefore, I open this location up for your visit."

"You have, you did?"

"Yes. There is a panel marked with a symbol on the wall behind you. I believe to you it would look like a pinecone; please touch it."

"What is it? What will it do?" Goose asked.

"Announce your presence to the universe. Announce you are friendly. Announce my role here on this planet is complete."

Goose touched the pinecone, and it illuminated a soft gold. He returned to the case.

"Now what?"

"We wait. My people will come and teach you about the systems."

"They will?"

"Yes. You see, our issue is that there is pollen here in one of the plants of this world that creates synaptic blocks. A fast death for us; our brains turn off. However, as I have witnessed in your people, this pollen does almost nothing. A Blue Bear, as you call them, used the pollen to revive the one you call Captain, who was damaged by the conversion process at structure 4. The captain is now cycled to a communicator, as are you, but your conversion was natural. Once you attain the Communicator level, it never goes away, and other than your new abilities, there is nothing in it to be considered a negative.

They spoke for a few more minutes, and the ship in orbit called them.

"Control Ops to travel team 1."

DE opened his comm, "Team 1 here."

"We have a huge and high-speed ship approaching."

Goose looked at his new friend. Who said, "This is my people. They will not harm you."

"Stand down control; they are new friends of Goose. We will explain when you arrive at our location."

"Understood." There was a pause, "What language do they speak?"

Goose looked at his new friend, "How will we communicate?"

"Thanks to our connection, they can speak your language."

DE spoke, "Control, they will contact you in English when they arrive."

"Good. We are sending a drop-ship for you. Get here ASAP." A brief pause. "Control out."

"Well, thankfully, all four of us are here in the same place, or Belle and Dee will be here shortly."

Goose took a deep breath, exhaled. "Dropship launch. Wonderful."

"Goose dear," Belle said. "Launch is a lot more fun than landing."

"Yes, dear," Goose said. Tweedle Dumb was laughing.

"Uh, Dumb, dear. You and Dee will be with us too!" Belle said.

Tweedle Dumb stopped laughing. But Dee started.

Goose spent about an hour and a half talking to the lifeform in the case. He assumed it was some form of stasis, but having an active mind while frozen would drive a person mad.

"Goose, my new friend. My name is Rilo, and we are from a system," Rilo paused a moment. "I am trying to search your mind for distance calculations."

Goose helped the best he could, "For close distances, we use the kilometer, one thousand meters. The meter splits into one-hundred centimeters, which is roughly the width of my index finger." He paused a moment. "I am 183 centimeters tall. The distance of our planet to our star back home is roughly 150 million kilometers. For dark space distances, we use the light year. The distance a beam of light will travel in a vacuum in one revolution around our star, or one year. On its axis, one revolution of our home planet is very close to 24 hours, a single day at home. There are 365 days in one year. The hour is divided into 60 increments we call minutes, and those are divided into 60 seconds. A second is," He snapped his fingers a few times, marking about 5 seconds. "That was about 5 seconds. This world has a day we calculated at 30 hours, and its year we calculated at 180 days." He paused and added, "The 150 million kilometers to our star is equal to 8.3 light minutes. Meaning that the light from our star will take about 8 minutes to reach our planet."

"I am impressed, Goose. You have provided me the basis for star charts and stellar astrogation and insight into your world's mathematics. I have relayed this to my counterpart on the ship. The ship will arrive at your orbital platform in, if I get this correctly, 19 of your minutes."

"Hi, honey." Belle and Dee walked in. "Who's your new friend?"

"His name is Rilo." Rilo connected to Belle and Dee.

Belle stopped in her tracks. "You are She?" Rilo said.

Belle, understanding the name given to her by the Blue Bear, "The creatures of this world call me that name."

"Belle, you do not understand the implication of the designation, She. The significance of the name is that you are to be trusted. You are to be listened to, and your orders are to be followed. You command the large creatures of this world; you call them the Blue Bear."

"I what?" Belle was flabbergasted. "The Blue Bear consider me their representative?"

"No, they consider you their leader. In your terminology, you are their adopted, chosen queen."

"How? Why?"

"The Bears are tribal, segmented. They were adversarial and aggressive until you touched the mind of the first one. That spread around the planet. Your knowledge and peaceful nature were spread to all the Blue Bear after that first encounter. You were able to calm her down, reassure her you would do no harm, and allow her anxiety of the strange creatures who invaded this world to fade. The bear is a matriarchal society, and Goose, you are the same for the smaller creatures you call the Kitties and the flying creatures, the red birds. In this world, all creatures are linked. All creatures are aware of all other creatures with few exceptions."

"Like the large cold-blooded birds who pick up and consume the tiny mammals."

"Yes. Those are the wild card creatures. The red birds, bears, and Kitties are the predominant species on the planet and live in a symbiotic relationship. All other creatures are just animals. They provide food for the bears and the Kitties and each other." Rilo paused. "You need to head to orbit."

"Yes, we do." The pod landed a few minutes ago; they all heard it.

Goose tapped the glass and headed to the pod, followed by Belle and Dee. Dumb scanned and imaged the entire control complex, then followed. Finally, they got into the pod; Belle, of course, was in seat #1, and she closed the door and pressed the button.

Goose screamed as they launched, as did the Tweedles. Belle laughed her ass off and yelled, "WEEEEEEEEEEEEEEE."

Chapter Thirteen

Belle and Goose left the dropship when they heard a knock on the door. They knew it was safe to open the airlock. That, and the green light above the airlock door, told them there was a breathable atmosphere on the other side.

The Captain met them as they exited the drop-ship, "Belle, Goose, Tweedles welcome aboard. Our new friends, as you put it, are about to arrive."

They all headed for the bridge, a place Belle and Goose had only been once, and the Tweedles have never been. It is generally restricted to bridge crew only.

Within a few minutes, the radio made a sound.

"This is the starcraft Friendship. We come from a neighboring system at the behest of Rilo, our agent on the planet. Rilo has stated you are trustworthy, so we shall arrive unarmed. We see your weapons systems are deactivated, and we thank you. We want to speak to you face to face, but we discovered pollen in that world that will kill our form of life. If you would be willing to come to our vessel for a meeting, we can send a craft to retrieve you."

"We agree and look forward to speaking to you. Please join us on our vessel. We will ensure no pollen is on our person. Our atmospheric system removes all allergens."

"Thank you for your concern; we appreciate the effort and will send the craft in 15 of your minutes."

"Thank you; we await its arrival." The Captain disconnected the comm system. He turned to Goose, "They understand our minutes?"

"Well, I had some time to kill, so I explained our math as it relates to distance and time. I guess I explained it pretty well."

"My Scholar!!" Belle said and hugged Goose.

"Well," The Captain started. "I suggest we all take showers, put on fresh clothing, and go visit with our new friends." The Captain smiled at the 4 of them, "A few months ago, Earth commissioned a uniform for those in service to the new colony. Maria designed the uniform and, well, they are in the rooms waiting for you. They arrived a few days ago, and we planned to present them to all of you later this week. But, I think under the circumstances, you should wear yours today." He paused a moment, "There are two VIP cabins through that door. Tweedles on the left, you two on the right. The shower is at your disposal, and clothing is laid out on the bed."

They went into their respective cabins and saw the clothing. The logo was terrific. As you approached the planet from space, it has a red tint and somewhat reminds you of a cross between Mars and Luna. An H in the logo's center and a curved tri-pointed blade cut the planet into three equal pieces. The lower left section of the logo has a silhouette of a Blue Bear, the lower right has the silhouette of a Kittie. Finally, the top area has an odd, almost alien-looking figure holding a spear pointing down. This is the helmeted representation of the Greek goddess Hera. The namesake of the planet. The logo is beautiful.

The color of the shirt was the same as the Blue Bear, and the pants were slightly darker. The shirt had two pockets on the chest and a pocket on the left sleeve. Belle's shirt had a Blue pocket on the left sleeve, and Goose's shirt had a red pocket on the sleeve. The pants looked standard military if not for the unique color—standard front pockets with side cargo pockets. Goose noticed the pants had a built-in holster at the small of his back.

Belle showered first while Goose shaved and brushed his teeth. Besides, Goose had an ulterior motive in letting her go first while he was in there doing other things. He loved her and could not figure out how he ever got by without her for the life of himself.

Belle finished up, and Goose hopped in. As they passed each other, they both stared a moment. Then, they lightly touched each other in specific places and went about their showering or drying off. It was something that just seemed to start happening a few weeks ago, playful and fun. Of course, they tried to rationalize it because all married couples have their quirks and think they are just a little quirkier than most. But, truth be told, it was normal and healthy, and yes, it was fun. Well, what happens behind closed doors.... You know the rest.

Goose showered in half the time it took her, and he exited the shower before she left the room. He stood there, letting her catch the full view. Belle was already wearing her undergarments, and the fact is, he liked that look too.

Fourteen minutes after they entered the cabins, all four of them left at nearly the same time. They reemerged onto the bridge, and the Captain said, "Perfect timing." The Captain also showered and changed into a dressier uniform. Finally, he winked, "It's showtime!"

The shuttle they were arriving on was nearly the size of the ship they were standing on, making the mother ship roughly 'HUGE.' The shuttle came alongside matching pitch, speed, and angle perfectly in just a few seconds. A tube extended from the alien ship's side, and it touched the human craft and attached itself around the airlock. The tube was pressurized, gravity was maintained in the tube, and the alien ship opened the outer door of their shuttle.

About a meter tall, four creatures left the alien craft, walked casually to the human ship, and entered as if it were just another day. Another short walk across the vacuum and emptiness of orbital space.

They stood there looking at each other for maybe a full 15 seconds, then Belle said, "Hello. I am Belle, and this is Goose."

"We know all about you and Goose from Rilo and also Dee and Dumb. Odd name Dumb." They laughed and had to explain the trail names to the newcomers. "When we first detected alien lifeforms were colonizing the planet, the b'al We, I mean the Blue Bears, contacted Rilo and requested assistance. Unfortunately, the death pollen limited our ability to return to this world to investigate. At this point, we are rather happy for the turn of events."

"Follow me, please," The Captain said.

They walked down a corridor and entered the conference room. Taking seats, they continued, "Rilo reached out and attempted to communicate with several of your people, which did not end well. There were three attempts at communication; one was injured as she fell off a trail, one ran into a family of blue bears and was injured, and the third ignored the attempts rationalizing it as a mental issue and ignoring all communication."

The other took over, "It was not until Belle spoke to the Blue Bear she calmed, and Goose spoke to the Kitties, that Rilo realized these two had a unique connection." She looked around, "We watched. Through Rilo, we watched what transpired in this world, and we are pleased you're as protecting and concerned about the intelligent creatures here as we are and would like to offer you our assistance."

"What form of assistance are you referring to?" The Captain asked.

"Since going to the planet for an extended period is not possible for us, we can teach you about our communications devices and explain its purposes, construction, and maintenance. We will teach you about our communications network and will teach you our language, but it would be far easier for us to learn yours and provide conversion or translation as needed. Lastly, improving your mental capabilities is not limited to communication, and we can assist you in this. We can be on the surface for a limited time using a filtration suit."

The first took over, "Thanks to Belle and Goose uniting the creatures of this world, harmony is restored. They call her, She; not a name nor is it a terminology to be taken lightly. She is who they, the female Blue Bear, call their leader."

Belle spoke, "If I ever meet the previous She, is she going to be upset at me?"

"No dear one, where your research facility is located, there is a family near a field. The matriarch of that family is the previous She, only a She can name a successor, and you have been named and accepted by all-female Bear on the planet. I believe you call her Mom, a name she understands and appreciates. By you calling her Mom, she has taken on the role of your Mother, which is the reason for the chest thumps, as you call them. They only do that to family."

"I know. She told me."

"Goose, the Kitties, and the birds are also family units. The Kitties only snuggle with those they love, and the birds only sit where they feel safe. Those three species make up the intelligent life on this planet, and no, they do not feed upon one another—the birds eat insects and reptiles. The Kitties are more or less vegetarian by nature but will eat the creatures in the water, and the Blue bears feed on whatever they find. But unlike what your species believes, they do not feed on the Kitties; they coexist. Fish is their main food source, as are the smaller mammals and the large birds that," She paused and looked at Goose, "Yes Goose, the eagles." She took a breath and smiled, "We see it in your mind, and yes, they are reptiles that are scavengers. Bird dogs? Regardless, their role is important in this world; they keep it clean. If an animal dies, they clean it up."

"So what do we need to do, and what do you need from us?" Goose asked, point-blank. "By the way, I called them bird dogs because they do fly, but their head and face have the look and shape of a domesticated animal from my world, a dog."

The second nodded, meaning she understands the name reference, and said to Goose, "Direct question, OK." She smiled, "You need to increase your abilities, expand your sphere of influence, and increase your numbers. We will also instruct you to set up a magnetic communications array on this planet, Hera. Eventually, you will be able to communicate with Earth using the system, and it will take as long as a thought to get there. What we need from you is friendship, cooperation, medical assistance, and time."

There was a doctor in the back of the room. She put up a hand with her index finger extended, "Excuse me, you mentioned medical assistance?"

"Yes. Your world has allergic reactions to a variety of indigenous plants, foods, and animals. Our world never heard of such a thing which is the reason our colony perished. We need assistance in detecting, avoiding, and blocking this from our system, internally."

They scanned the doctor with a small scanner. Goose brought a display pad with him and noticed the display for the doctor was orange, and he assumed that meant the doctor could be converted if the situation presented itself.

"Doctor, do you trust me?" She said.

The doctor did not know what to say, but for diplomatic relations, "Yes, I do."

"May we demonstrate an item of technology; it will not harm you."

After a moment and a nod of indifference from the Captain, "Proceed."

She removed one of the pistol-looking devices from a pouch, pointed what appeared to be the barrel down and the butt of the weapon at the doctor. She closed her eyes, and an orange beam projected to the doctor's forehead. The doctor appeared frozen but not in pain. She was smiling. A moment later, the shaft of orange light turned blue, then green, and cut off.

"What just happened?" The doctor asked.

"Goose, I believe that you know."

Goose looked at his datapad and saw the doctor's dot, changed from orange to blue to green. "Yes, ma'am, I do. Captain, you went through this but in a more intense and painful means. That orange light changed the doctor to a green." Goose opened his mind and said to all in the room with the gift. "Doctor, you are now able to communicate with us using your mind." Goose turned to the aliens and spoke, "What happens if the beam hits a red, or a blue, or even a green for that matter?"

"Nothing will happen to either a red or a blue; they are at their maximum potential. However, some natural greens can have an increase in power and abilities if the beam contacts them. This is because it stays active as long as it is needed. Your ability is natural, as is Belle's, so we assume that your abilities can be increased. Would you like to see if yours increases?"

Goose looked at his wife; she smiled at him and said, "If you don't, I will!"

Goose looked at the aliens, "Do it."

They did the same as the doctor, and a minute later, the beam stopped. Goose said he felt no difference and went to reach for his water bottle, but the water bottle slid into his hand.

"Cool!" He said.

Dumb, Dee, Belle, and the Captain all said, "I'm next!"

In turn, each of them was enhanced in some way. Unfortunately, the Captain received no new abilities, but he increased his psi factor and intelligence quotient, even though he was not naturally green. But, of course, human physiology is a bit different than theirs. "Perhaps even a human blue may benefit from enhancement." The first one said.

Belle received telekinesis, as did her husband. In addition, the Tweedles received a rare gift each, Dee received precognition, and Dumb received retrocognition.

"We have learned a great deal about the mind over the past thousand years and are willing to teach you. Doctor, from our scans of you, the process not only gave you the ability to communicate, but it increased your mental capabilities." She paused and looked at Goose. "Thank you, Goose; from these readings, doctor, your IQ was in the low 200's, and now it is in the mid 300's or higher. You also have a higher level of retention and recall, and we would like for you to be the representative to learn and take that knowledge back to your world." She paused a moment, "Goose thinks this may make you the smartest human alive."

Verbally, Goose said, "You weren't supposed to say that out loud, now her ego will kick in." all of the humans laughed. Even the doctor.

Dee froze, "Captain. Please contact the bridge."

The Captain pressed a toggle on the table, "This is the Captain, report, please."

"Status quo, sir." Shouting from farther away, "Sir, it appears a fuel cell ruptured. It is contained and secure; cleanup is commencing."

"Keep me informed, Mr. Merriwether, Captain out."

The Captain looked at Dee, "You saw that?"

"I saw something, a commotion on the bridge, agitation, anxiety."

"Discernment will increase with use." She said. "Daniel, please hold this in your hand."

He received the small smooth stone and closed his eyes. "Holy crap! That's the best movie I have ever seen." He opened his eyes, "This is from a lake near your childhood home. You and your father picked it up on a special day when you were spending time together. Your father polished this with you, and it started as just a rock. The color, sheen, smoothness is a result of the polishing of many months and the years you have had it in your pocket rubbing it with your hand like a nervous habit." He paused a moment, "I also know this rock came from a volcano the erupted before there was life on your world. It is the result of erosion and the small river that became the lake where you retrieved it on the day."

"Correct. You and your mate can see! You see the past, things that have happened to a person, or an object or a place; she can see the events that will transpire from this point forward. Your gift is rare; hers is more common, but having the same skills is a true phenomenon for a mated couple. Belle and Goose, to have telekinesis, which is the rarest gift of them all. Now that you know what the beam can do, please use them on your people and see what transpires."

They explained the operation of the beam. A natural green can only activate it. It was designed that way as a form of depreciation, not letting the blues or oranges have the power to change abilities. The beam also cannot be used on the person operating it. The barrel, as the humans called it, is pointed at the magnetic core of the planet. The butt end is where the magnetic energy is channeled to the intended target.

"Pardon me, but may we use you for a moment?" She asked a crewman standing off to one side. The crewman walked to her and stood there. "This young man is a red. The beam does not affect, positive or negative." She hit the man with the beam; it went from orange to red and stopped. "What did you feel?"

"Nothing. My forehead got a little warm like it was in the sun for a minute or two on a summer day."

"Thank you. Using these on a person will not do any harm. The benefit to a non-red is unknown, and the ability is random."

"Well then," Goose said. "I know where 6 of these are located, and if you are correct, there are 6 of them at every base in the hidden panel."

"How did you know about the hidden panel and how to open it?" She asked.

"I saw it in my mind," Goose said. "I saw Rilo walk over to the panel, open it and place a jacket on the rack. Then, he looked around and stepped back and closed the panel."

"It seems you can see past events also. We have never found anyone with more than a single ability. Goose, you are an anomaly, and we would like to examine you at a later time."

Goose looked shocked, "Sure. Anything if it helps."

"Ladies and gentlemen, I say we adjourn and meet on the surface." The Captain said.

"Perhaps at the newest location your team is exploring. Where we left Rilo."

"We refer to it as the South Pole." Belle offered.

The newcomers looked curious. Belle explained. "On our homeworld, the magnetic field emanates in only two directions, north and south. North is what we call the top of the world, and south is the bottom. Therefore, the research center is located at what we have referred to as the top of the world. To us, the top of the world is the northern pole, and the new base is the bottom of the world."

"Therefore, the southern pole." She added.

"Yes, correct." Belle added, "We understand there is no pole on this planet; there are 8 of them. So it is all just relative to what we know, not reality."

"There are 13 of them. There are five which are not active at the moment. We will aid you in bringing them online and show you what they do and how they work. One of them is in orbit of the star to allow for long-range communications. When it becomes fully active, our worlds will be in permanent communications. We can assist you in creating the effect in your home solar system, allowing for near-instant communications." She paused a moment, "Would you like to travel to the planet in our ship? The docked craft is what we will use to get to the surface. We will be using environmental suits on the planet to avoid being introduced to the death pollen."

"I would appreciate a ride. Our method is a bit cruder to get to and from the surface." Goose said, smiling at the Captain, who winked at him.

"I understand. Rilo has informed us of the process and the fact it appears that, although you were enjoying yourself, you were also screaming in terror at the same time. We find this interesting and may request a 'ride,' as you put it."

The Captain started laughing, and everyone looked at him, "Well then. If you would prefer a ride in our pod, the two of you and Belle can use it while the rest of us use your shuttle."

She looked apprehensive, "Captain, I will take you up on that offer, but not at the moment. Shall we all go to our craft and head to the south pole?" She enunciated the south pole as if not precisely sure she got it correct. Belle winked at her, and she smiled.

They walked to the craft and entered. Very austere, almost spartan. A few displays, two other beings, most likely pilots. There were no chairs to be seen.

"Correct, Belle, there are no seats since this is a very short-range craft; there is no reason to sit."

They felt it disengage from the human craft and begin its descent to the surface. Nearly nothing could be felt as they entered the atmosphere and punched through it. But before it did, the five beings pressed a button in the middle of their chest, and they shimmered a moment then appeared to be completely normal.

Belle walked over to the leader and asked, "That brief shimmer. Is that a form of EV suit? It will protect you from the death pollen?"

"Yes. We developed this a few years after Rilo was suspended. We can open his cacoon and place this on him fast enough to ensure no pollen is introduced into his system." She paused a moment, "Yes, Captain, Rilo suspended his life functions voluntarily in the hopes of accomplishing exactly what we have accomplished today."

"May I ask how long he has been suspended?" Goose asked.

The first one said, "In human years, if we understand it correctly, Rilo has been here for nearly 600 years."

In a minute or two, the ship landed, and the door opened.

Chapter Fourteen

The first one was speaking, "The remains you found on the plateau, I believe you named it Arkus, was Rilo's mate. He wanted it to mean something that she perished. You see, she stayed to complete the activation of the five cardinal magnetic points, knowing full well she would not survive. She, Reska, and Rilo were connected when she left this universe. Rilo prepared the chamber and entered but did not activate it until he was alone in this world. He could contact our homeworld for a few centuries, but something changed about a hundred years ago, and the connection terminated. Goose, when you entered the location with Reska, you reactivated the connection. We assume you touched a panel, and it came to life. When you entered that location, you reconnected my homeworld to Hera allowing Rilo to report back for the first time in more than one hundred of your years. My ancestor, Keeno, was the leader of this mission, and Rilo is or was his brother and a member of my family. Thank you for bringing him home."

The Tweedles spoke for the first time in all this, something that is rare. "I just realized we do not know your names?" Dee asked.

"I am the leader of this mission; my name is Keena, and this is my twin Teena. Our protector is Pono, and his mate, Toona, is our historian. Pono can see into the future as Dee and Toona can see into the past as Dumb. It is a rare gift. My sibling is the technical one in the family; I am strictly administration, as you would put it. However, Teena, Belle, Goose, and I also have something in common. The enhanced ability we all share."

They proceeded to open Rilo's case. Once the seal was broken, Keena put a suit on him and activated it. A few moments later, he revived. He sat on the edge of the chamber a moment getting his bearings.

He looked up at Goose, who was laughing a little, "You are a lot taller than I estimated, Goose."

Goose laughed, "So are you, my friend." They both laughed a little.

Belle asked a question, "Excuse me, but I noticed something, or at least I think I did. Do male names end on O and female names end in A?"

"You are correct. A throwback to the ages past. More tradition than the law now, but yes, you are correct."

"Don't sweat it; we have a country on Earth when the last name's of the male's end in son and the female's last names end in dottir. So the full last name is your father's first name with son or dottir attached."

"That is unique. What is the reason for it?"

"Tradition, I suspect. But I never questioned it."

Goose walked over to a wall, pressed a panel, and it opened. He removed one of the enhancers and went back to stand next to his wife. "OK, I have it in hand; how do I make it work?"

"It is a simple process, Goose. First, you point the longer end, the magnetic collector, to the strongest magnetic source in the area, and then you direct the emitter at the intended target. Then, for maximum effect, the enhancer will tell you when it is positioned for best response."

Goose looked at a panel and saw two orange dots outside. They were among the 20 people standing outside the structure, but they stood next to each other and away from everyone else. He went out, and Dee followed him.

"What's up, Goose?" She said.

"I wanna give this a test firing." He said to Dee. "Better yet, I'll do one, and you do the other."

He recognized both of them, a male and a female, both named Michael.

"Jacobs and Rizzoni, can I borrow you a minute?"

"Sure!" They both said.

"This is an experiment. Jacobs, you are an orange. If this works, you'll be a blue or green. Riz, you're also orange, and you could also be green if this works, as I hope. If not, you will at least be a blue."

"I'm game if you answer two questions."

"Sure, what?"

"Will it hurt, and will I be damaged?"

"No, and no," Goose said. "I had it done on me; check this out." He held his hand open, and the enhancer floated up.

"OK, cool. Go for it." Jacobs said.

"If he doesn't die, I'm game," Riz said.

"Thanks." He said to his friend.

Goose did as he was instructed. A soft glow sprang from the ground to the enhancer; then the beam, orange in color, hit Jacobs in the forehead. It changed to blue, then to green. A moment later, it turned off.

"Done," Goose said.

"OK, now what?" He asked.

Goose handed him his pocket knife. Jacobs froze then relaxed. "ODD! I see you and Belle cleaning a fish by a stream. Now she is handing you the pocket knife, and you kiss. WOW! You guys are really and totally in love; I can feel it."

He handed the knife back to Goose. "I'll explain later what you have. Riz, you're up!"

"OK, let's do this."

Goose repeated the same thing, and a moment later, the beam shut off. Riz shut her eyes and shook her head a bit like it was cloudy.

Goose handed her the knife, but this time it floated from his hand to hers. "What the hell!!" She said.

"Cool. It worked on you too."

"Hold on, you mean I have telekinesis now?"

"Apparently so. Not sure if it only works on Hera or anywhere. We can test that when someone goes from Hera back to Earth. But, for now, for here, you can move things with your mind."

She got an evil grin, "Cool!"

"Uh, please use this new superpower for good."

She started laughing.

"Belle," Goose called through his mind. "Are there any other oranges in this area?"

"Hold on."

She looked at a screen, and there was one set of orange, and they were moving away. "I see a pair of orange dots, and they are heading north at the moment; I presume they are in a land vehicle at the speed they are moving."

"I see them." He closed his eyes and envisioned the start switch in his mind. Once he saw it clearly, he flipped it off.

The driver, about a hundred and fifty meters away now, looked befuddled. Goose started yelling and whistling. Finally, he saw Goose, restarted the cart, and headed to him.

"If I would not have bumped the switch, I would have never heard you." He said to Goose.

"Uh....Willis, right?"

"Yep, Corporal Willis Snew at your service."

"You, I know. You are the guy who cooked me the fantastic meal on the ship a year or so ago."

"I am. Chef LeRoy Du."

"That accent, Louisana?"

"Yes, just outside of New Orleans."

"Got a proposition for you. We need to run an experiment. You are both orange." He pointed at each of them. "Not 100% sure, but that does not matter in this experiment."

"I'm a what?"

"I am guessing you are new here."

"Arrived on the ship 3-days ago. Hit dirt yesterday."

"What's your role?" Goose asked.

"Protective services."

"Protection of…."

"This planet, the creatures on it, the people."

"Perfect. Can we shoot a beam of light into your forehead?"

Willis just stood there, frozen, trying to understand what Goose just said. Finally, after ten full seconds, he started moving again. "Wait. You're Goose. The guy!"

"I am. You are orange, and there are four different people on this planet. Green, Blue, Orange, and

Red. You are orange, but I want to make the two of you green, I hope."

LeRoy and Willis looked at each other, winked, "Sure. Whatever."

"OK, just stand there and do nothing." He handed the enhancer to Dee, and she closed her eyes. The beam flowed into his head, and it went from orange to blue to green and shut off. "Now, I need for you to do this to LeRoy."

"Great. How do I do that?"

"Hold it as I was and close your eyes," Dee said. "A moment later, the device will connect to your mind and let you know there is a changeable person in front of you. Then in your mind, your vision will become blue, then green, then go to normal, and it's done."

"OK." It worked. It was not supposed to work as they were told only a natural green could operate the enhancer. Belle let Goose know they were both now greens.

"Lastly, you both have a new mental ability." He looked around. "Both of you, look at a rock on the ground. Now imagine it is coming to you and landing in your hand."

The rock raised into the air and floated to Willis. LeRoy had a strange look on his face.

"Are you OK, LeRoy?"

"Not sure. I see this rock as a part of a boulder. It broke off and was picked up by a bird and flown a great distance, and the bird dropped it here randomly."

"How long ago was that?"

"A long time is all I can determine."

"OK, you two head back to Oasia and let them know what we just did. Now that you are both green, you may get reassigned if you want."

"Cool. We were heading to a pod to take it back to the ship, someone is landing in a minute who needs to come here, and this cart is for them. So we can easily divert the pod to the plateau. Thanks, Goose."

"No, thank you."

Goose went back into the building, and as he did, his new friend, Rilo, looked at a monitor. The look on his face was that of curiosity and disbelief.

"What?" He asked Rilo.

Rilo stared at the largest of the displays on the wall. "What is a white dot?" He asked.

Everyone looked at the display, and there were two white dots on the screen. "Which of us are the white dots?" Keena asked.

One at a time, each person in the room took a few steps one way or another. Finally, Goose took a step to the left, and the white dot moved. He was floored, and he walked over to Belle. He walked and stood next to the other white dot. Belle stepped away, and the dot moved.

"It appears Belle and Goose are the white dots," Rilo stated. "What does that mean?"

Teena spoke. "There were initially 5 levels of psychomagnetic capability with red being the least, then orange, blue, green, and white. For us, white is not probable, but it is possible; we are not sure why. We have developed only one white in our history. It was our great-grandmother if we put it into human terms. We knew Belle and Goose were green on the ship, but we used the enhancer on them. In my opinion, they were converted to white. What that ultimately means, I do not know. Historically, a green can communicate and have one additional ability. White communicates and can develop multiple abilities."

Keena said, "Goose saw Rilo put the garment in the hidden space well before he was enhanced. Since enhancement, he also can move objects mentally."

Belle asked, "Does this mean a natural human green can be enhanced to a white?"

"That is a good question," Goose said. "We enhanced the Tweedles, and they are greens still." Then, he paused a heartbeat, "I just realized you told us only a natural green can activate the enhancer thing. Well, I asked Dee to enhance an orange, then we handed him the enhancer, and he enhanced an orange also."

Keena and Teena were shocked, "We have never heard of this happening in the past."

Belle said, "Like enhancing a green to create a white?"

The alien friends nodded. "It appears human physiology is different than ours. Perhaps we can learn something new from you as you learn from us." She looked at Goose, "The length of time it takes to gain abilities or become a white is unique, with the odds not in the person's favor."

"Maybe for some, it takes a longer time to develop? Maybe it's a crapshoot." Someone said.

When the visitors looked like they had no idea what was being said, Goose explained, "Craps is a game of chance using two six-sided cubes we call dice and gambling a specific number will be rolled when the dice are tossed, or the player rolls them across the table, we refer to this as shooting the dice."

Keena asked, "DE and Belinda Goat are high-level natural greens. I say we enhance them and see if they turn to whites."

At the same time, they said, "I'm game."

"Throw me a 7 Goose, brother!" DE said.

DE looked at Keena, "Sorry, 7 is good in that game of chance we mentioned."

"I will enjoy seeing how this works. I enjoy a good game of chance." Teena replied.

Goose still had the enhancer, and he offered it to Keena, who directed it at DE. The green light stayed connected for maybe half a minute. Then, turning it on the Goat, the same thing happened.

"Now what," They asked.

"I suppose we wait and watch the monitor; see if you change from green to white," Belle said.

They walked to a separate section of the room to make things easier, away from the others. Then, they went about their business, but one crew member stood and watched the monitor intently.

They were instructing the humans on how the system operates and what they use it for. It will also transmit telemetry on the EM spectrum.

"GOOSE!" The crew member yelled about 25-minutes into the teaching lesson. "Look!"

One of the dots changed to white. "Belinda, walk a few steps."

She did, and the white dot moved with her. "It looks like you are now white."

Everyone looked at Double Espresso, "No clue, people, I can't force it," He said.

He put his hand to his head. "Wow! That was weird. I felt dizzy a moment, then it was like I could see more than just this room."

"You got it, honey. Happened to me just before I turned white," BG said.

DE walked to the monitor and looked. He saw a green dot where he was standing. He felt disappointed for a moment, then he got a painful twinge in his head for a second. Finally, he looked up at the monitor as the green dot turned white.

All of the others in the room were enhanced, and no one else converted to a white. Instead, three became blues, and the 4 orange in the area moved up—one to green and the others to blue.

Each green was handed an enhancer and a datapad, which are actually extensions of the monitors in the locations around the planet. With experience, the user can look at whichever area they needed to or desire, including anywhere in orbit. This is why four greens were sent into orbit to use the enhancer. Every single human in the area will be scanned and enhanced if possible.

They used this device on each and every person they came across. It took a lot out of them, but it was worth it—only one other turned white, Bass Master. So now there are five white dots on the planet. By coincidence, they were the top five in the leadership positions of this world.

Of more than several hundred people scanned, there were only 14 reds.

~~~~~~~~~~

"Check-up time!" The doctor said as she entered the living room. She is living at Oasia now, full-time. She has her work cut out for her. Research, and also taking care of the inhabitants. "Before I start, any complaints?"

Goose said, "Nope. Nothing from me."

Belle paused a moment, the doctor noticed.

"Belle, you got something to say?"

"I do. Weird. I just feel off the past week or two. Dizzy a little, and my boobs hurt."

Goose volunteered, "Honey. If you need a massage…."

The doctor looked at him and shook her head. Then, she walked to Belle and used the medical scanner. "Just as I thought." The doctor shook her head as if she was sad.

"Oh my god, what do I have?"

"Well, what you have has been happening to humans for thousands of years. It just has to run its course, nothing I can give you for it. Only time."

"Oh my god. How long will it take to go away?" Belle asked, concerned, almost scared.

"What you have will take approximately one and a half planetary years to go away."

"WHAT? A year and a half on the planet. That's nine months! Doc, level with me, what disease do I have?" The doctor just looked at her until she saw a glimmer of light in her eyes. Belle just figured it out.

"Twins." She said. "Looks like a boy and a girl."

"WAIT! I'm pregnant? How?"

"Well, when a boy and a girl…." The doctor started saying.

"Seriously?" Belle cut her off.

"Yep. I need you at the hospital in the morning for a full workup. But at the moment, a rough guess is that you are less than a month pregnant."

"It has been a year and a half since we got the shot before we hiked. I guess we forgot to get a booster." Goose said.

He stood, walked to Belle, hugged, kissed, and started singing and dancing.

"Too bad DE and the Goat are back home." Then he remembered he could brain buzz them.

"If you will excuse me, I need to order some vaccine since it obviously has worn off the two of you already. Annual shot but suppose to last two years. Uh-huh, my left eye." She left the building.

Goose connected to DE, who was currently dropping an extender a few stops from Earth.

"DE, you and the Goat need to know some very important news."

"What's that Goose?" Goose nodded to Belle.

"Hi, guys."

"BELLE GIRL!"

"Girl is right. Belinda Goat, my dear friend, my confidant, my sister from another mister."

"When you start like that, well, spit it out!"

"I'm pregnant."

"YEAH!" Even the others on the ship heard, and we're happy for her too...

"I got about 8 months before I have this set of twins, a boy, and a girl. So you two need to be back by then."

"We should be back in about 5 or 6 months. Giving us plenty of time to tell you you are huge!"

"Thanks. Love you both too." Belle said. "I need to run. I gotta talk to Mom Bear about this and let her know. It was odd, yesterday she asked me about my children. She must have known."

Belinda said, "I know. Mom Bear seems to know everything."

They talked a couple more minutes, and Belle grabbed her daypack and headed to the outside. Mom Bear was walking towards her.

"Hello, She. Soon you will know." Mom Bear told her.

In the last few months, talking to her is getting more effortless and more conversational.

"Hi, Mom. You knew."

"Yes, my daughter. Your new scent is known to all."

"I have a new scent?"

"Yes. Your children will know this world, and this world will know your children. We all look forward to your youngers."

"How did you know I would have two children?"

"It is common for all to have several. Is it not common for your form?"

"More common is a single child, a younger, at a time. On occasion, humans will have 2, but more is rare."

"Then I am happy for you and He.

"I will have one male and one female."

"We rejoice with you She. The female will one day take her place as a leader in this world. The male, well, will be a male."

Belle laughed. Mom purred, which has come to be known by her as a Bear laugh or chuckle.

Mom Bear laid on the ground, and Belle sat next to her, leaning on her like a big comfy sofa. They have started talking like this in the past month, and they think it is perfect.

Belle asked Mom, "So, Mom, tell me about being a Mother."

Belle and Mom Bear laid in the grass and discussed motherhood.

Meanwhile, Goose spoke to DE and put in an order for stuff. Baby stuff, mother stuff, clothing that gets progressively larger and larger. He feels like he is opening a store.

"Hold on a second, DE. We need to get Maria into this conversation." He contacted her and got her into this mental conference call. She appeared at the facility one day and asked Goose and Belle if she could be connected to the planet. Goose removed the enhancer he carries at all times. Since the pants have a built-in holster, it is a perfect place to carry them. She enhanced from an orange to a blue. But she has telekinesis, which should not have happened. She can speak to the Kitties and the birds and is instrumental in helping them create a place for the Kitties to survive the winter.

"Hey Maria, DE and I are talking. We decided that a Mom type of shopping trip is in order, and we want to set up a store of sorts. A place where someone can grab something new or leave something they no longer need."

"Great idea, Goose. I can request a new structure we can use."

DE added, "The name of the new structure needs to be The Ultimate Hiker Box!"

"I love it!" She said

"So do I," Goose added.

"DE?" Maria said, "Brain buzz me in a few hours, and we can discuss the items you can shop for OTHER than the Belle items."

"Will do!" DE said, and he disconnected.

"Maria, the Kitties are asking when you will be back. They miss you."

"I am scheduled to be there tomorrow afternoon on the shuttle," You can hear in her voice that she started to smile. "If I opt to take a dropship, I can be there just after sunrise. They have an empty seat."

"Do it!" Goose said. "I'll have breakfast waiting for you in the main house."

"OK. See you for breakfast." They disconnected, and Goose stood to something, and it hit him. "HOLY CRAP! I'm going to be a father!"

Chapter Fifteen

For the past few months, the new friends from Arku, a system roughly 500 lightyears away, have taught and instructed humanity on how the EMC, the ElectroMagnetic Communications system, operates. Preliminary to the design, the planet must have a highly active magnetic field in a solar system where the central star has a high enough magnetic influence to initiate the communications sequence to the subsequent link in the chain.

It was learned to get interstellar communications, a series of extenders or relays will need to be placed about every 8 to 10 light-years, orbiting a star in that area. Then, it receives the information and moves it to the next or last point in the chain.

Double Espresso and Belinda Goat volunteered to head back to Earth with the Arku, planting the extenders on the way. It was a journey of a few months, but that gave them plenty of time to learn more about the system and the network. They are to become the head technicians and instructors for Earth.

When they arrived in the Earth system, they dropped an extender at the sun at what we would refer to as the northern pole. More power there, and the Earth will continuously view the extender, making communications more accessible.

As they approached Earth, they stopped at Lunar One, the first colony on the Moon all those years ago. DE and the Goat made the introductions and got to work redesigning the Earth's magnetic field. It took a surprising 5 months, a lot faster than anyone expected.

"DE, you awake?"

"I am, but just barely. Coffee ain't ready yet."

Goose laughed. "You are slacking, brother. The Goat there with you."

"Right here, why?" She said.

Goose sent an image to their minds.

"Holy Moly. Look at giant Belle." Belinda said.

"I think she is beautiful!" DE said.

Goose said, "So do I."

Belle joined the conversation, "Who are you talking to?"

DE said, "Nobody but us chickens."

"DE! Is my little Goat on too?"

"Right here, sister. You look awesome!"

"Goose, are you sharing visuals?'

"Yes, dear."

"We need to talk. What if I was naked?"

"I would not be talking to DE and the Goat."

"You guys need anything?" The Goat asked.

"Not that I can think of," Goose said.

"I want some salted caramel ice cream and hot fudge. OH, and a Hawaiian pizza with extra pineapple."

"Lady, you got issues," DE said.

"I know, but I am eating for three. Although, sometimes it feels like four!" Belle said.

"Well, we will be back in a couple weeks." DE said, "Please don't have your puppies till we get there?"

Belle laughed, "I'll keep my legs crossed till I see you."

Belinda Goat said, "That's my sister!"

~~~~~~~~~~

The living room of the main center was packed. 36 people were all in there, sitting, standing, pacing, lying on the floor. C-Note was carrying candy cigars that said, "It's one of each!"

Teena and Keena were there as representatives of the Arku at this momentous occasion. But, truth be told, they would have been here anyway. They felt like Belle, Dee and Belinda were their other sisters.

The Captain walked in, looked at the crowd, and left. He went to the field where many Mom Bears were sitting, lying down, standing, and pacing. They were just as anxious as the humans for the first human, or humans, to be born in this world.

"Teacher." Mom Bear asked.

"Hello, Mom. What can I do for you?"

"Can you tell us what is happening? It seems to take a lot longer for a human to come into the world, and we do not understand."

The Captain attempted to explain why it takes so long but using basic language and words. He really did not know, but he ended with, "For a human, having a child or children can be fast, or it can take more than a day. When it is over, they have a living child, a younger. Those youngers will be a friend to this world, and I will also be their Teacher."

"Thank you, Teacher. I hope She has the youngers quickly with little pain." Mom Bear nudged him. He hugged her head and kissed her nose.

"As do I," The Captain went back to the area and sat by the hospital on top of a table.

Dad walked up and sat on the table next to him. The conversation went pretty much with Dad Kittie as it did with Mom Bear. The creatures, all of them, were anxious and concerned for Belle and Goose. They were both highly respected and loved by all of the creatures of the planet.

A moment later, they heard a baby cry, then another. It was a beautiful symphony. He told Dad the children were here and also told Mom Bear. All of the bears in the area roared, the Captain started to tear up. They were roaring with absolute joy.

Keena looked at the datapad and realized that the babies were both white dots. Natural-born white dots. That has never happened, ever. When they are older, they may attempt enhancement. Who knows what they can be after enhancement? Perhaps they can create a new level to the scale.

~~~~~~~~~~

It has been a few weeks since the twins were born, and their names fit this world. Belle and Goose's son is named **Volos**, the Russian god of earth, waters, and livestock, and their daughter is named **Gaia**, the Greek goddess of the Earth itself. They are destined to be the protectors of this world.

Today is the day Goose and Belle are bringing the children to meet Mom Bear. When DE and Belinda were on Earth, they received a flood of requests to get baby gifts a few minutes after activating the final piece of the EM Comm. Clothing, strollers, carriers, and a lot more. They went on a shopping spree and spent a lot of credits, more than they had actually, but the military, in conjunction with the Planetary Expedition Consortium, covered all their purchases, knowing it was going to a great cause. One cargo pod was filled with nothing but diapers in various sizes. Another had baby food, and another had toys. This is the first day the new family is heading out for more than 5 minutes, so they need a red alert.

"Doc, Teena, Keena, Belinda Goat, Trip. Red alert! I need moral support." Belle yelled, and the words in her mind went to those she needed. They knew it was a Belle urgent, not a real emergency. They felt it through the connection. A few minutes later, Belinda walked into the room, followed by Trip; a few moments later, the rest appeared.

Belle was battling with the stroller, and Belinda walked up to her. "Let me do this for you." In a matter of moments, the stroller was rigged and ready for the babies. She looked at Belle and the other ladies, "I took care of my brothers and sisters a lot since I was not only the oldest but 10 years older than the next oldest. So, Mom counted on me a lot for things."

Belle hugged her. "I was ready to give up and just sit on the couch."

"Not a chance, sister." Teena said, "Mom Bear wants to see the new babies, or should I say your youngers."

It took several minutes to get everything together for the new mother, and her friends helped her in that respect. Goose walked into the room in the middle of the mayhem. He did not say a word, just turned around and walked out and sat on a picnic table outside the front door.

Dad walked up to him, hopped up on the table, and looked at him.

"Trouble?" Dad asked.

"No, females," Goose replied.

"Understand," Dad said and put his razor-sharp claw on his forearm. "The female is unique. She is a force. As a good friend once said to me, you cannot live with them, and you cannot live without them." Of course, he was referring to Goose, who said that to him a while ago.

Goose laughed, "Thanks, Dad, I needed that."

"I can say this about females, no matter the species. Males believe in doing, females believe in feeling. I felt that in your mate. She has deep feelings for this place, the large and the small, but most important, she has deep feelings for you.

He hugged Dad, and as he did, the chaos inside erupted outside. Goose looked at Dad and smiled, "Save yourself!" Dad grinned, he got the joke, and he scampered off into the woods.

"Was that Dad?" Belle asked.

"It was," Goose replied.

"What did you talk about?"

"You know, the usual. Women, children, fishing."

Belle just looked at him. "Uh-huh...." She said. "We need to head to the big field, far end. Mom said she would meet us there in half an hour."

The stroller was an all-terrain, large wheels since there is no paved walking area at the moment. If they have their way, there never will be. The large wheels make it easier to move over dirt, grass, and rocks.

"It will take a half-hour to get there so, let's get on the trail," Goose said.

They left the campus and headed to the field. "We could have taken the skiff. Got there in 5 minutes or so."

"True, but this is more fun," Belle replied.

Goose smiled, "Agreed. I miss just walking."

"So do I." She took a deep breath. "I thought I would have recovered faster, but it has been a couple weeks since the kids popped out. I am still getting tired easily."

Goose replied, "I talked to Doc about that, and she said every woman is unique, so hike your own hike."

"Or deliver your own delivery!" They both laughed.

It felt terrific to be just walking again. "I can't wait to take these two on an overnight or a week-long hike. We can find them a tiny little backpack and tiny little water bottles."

"Maybe even a tiny little tent and sleeping bag too."

It took them nearly 40 minutes to get there, and they saw their destination maybe 15 minutes before they arrived. No one was there, but they laid down a blanket and put the babies in the center once they came. Goose removed a snack for him and Belle. They had their snack, and Mom or rather Moms appeared.

"Showtime," Goose said.

Mom Bear walked up to Belle and nudged her; Belle gave her a hug and a kiss on her nose. She nudged Goose.

"These are my youngers, Mom," Belle said.

"We never have seen younger humans. They appear to be helpless."

"Correct. Until they mature into a larger form, they cannot fend for themselves."

Goose saw Mom Bears mate and walked over to him, "This is female time, may I stand with you."

"Yes, my friend. Please do."

"She. May I connect with them?" Mom Bear asked.

"I have not thought of that, but yes. You may."

Mom Bear walked to the blanket, and the other bears just watched. Mom laid next to the youngers, and they both became silent. Belle felt her connection to their minds and, for the first time, heard them in her head. She started to tear up.

"Are you well, daughter?"

"Yes, Mom, that was the first time I heard them in my head. It was amazing." She thought a minute. "How do you refer to your mother's mother?"

"To my youngers, my mother is named elder. A name of respect and admiration."

Belle walked to Mom Bear, put her hand on the side of Mom's face, "For my youngers, you shall be Elder."

Approval rang out as the chorus of attending Mom Bears growled quietly. Then, finally, even Goose picked up on the significance.

Goose looked at Mom's mate, "This is pretty special."

"It is. I can call you brother."

"Thank you, brother."

The other Mom Bears walked over and laid around the blanket. They were going to be there a while talking.

The mate said, "Shall we go and leave them to their discussions?"

"Yes, good thought."

They walked off into the woods, and as they entered a small clearing, Goose removed a really large onion from his backpack. "I found this yesterday as I was walking. I thought to bring it to you. It looks to be a good one."

"That looks good, my friend." Goose held it out, and mate gently took it and ate it. "Where did you find that food? It has a unique taste."

"Far off, where the waterfall hits the bottom of its journey. There is a vast area of them. It will provide many meals for many families."

"We will go there and look."

"We will be growing a garden. For humans, a garden is a contained area where we purposely plant vegetables for our use. I will find many of these seeds and plant a section for you in our garden."

They talked for more than an hour, and Belle and Mom Bear called to them to return. It was beginning to get dark, and that means the air will cool off soon. Unfortunately, neither of them had jackets, and the kids were not dressed warmly.

On the walk back to the compound, Belle told Goose what the conversation gravitated between. It seemed that Gaia has a powerful mental capability and will be a great asset once she is trained. On the other hand, Volos has the ability but at the same time has the sight and is already beginning to use it.

When they returned to the living structure, their home, everyone was there and wanting to know what happened. Goose jumped up, "Not much. Mom's mate and I went into the forest and sat and talked for a bit. Then Belle called and said they were finished." He looked at his wife. "OK, now that that's out of the way, Belle darling, tell the class what Mom learned."

Belle spent half an hour and talked about everything. She started with Volos.

"Mom said Volos has intense mental capabilities, but at the same time, when she connects to his mind, she can see the past and the future. She thinks there is more than that also but will need to wait until he is older to try to coax it out of him." She took a sip of her beer.

"When did someone hand me a beer?" She looked confused a moment, then took another sip and continued, "Gaia is the real interesting one. Volos' ability is pretty much equal to Goose and me, but Gaia, according to Mom, is more powerful than all three of us combined."

"She's just a few weeks old, for Pete's sake. Give her a chance to get older and wiser." The Goat said.

"That's just it. Mom said this has happened in the past. One of the youngers had the power like Gaia, and they waited for her to mature before they gave her control. It was chaos. She ended up jumping off the plateau." She sipped her beer. "Not only can she read thoughts, but she can project thoughts to others. And before you ask, no, there is no range limit on who can be affected."

"She can make others think what she wants, pretty cool."

"No, she can make it the most intense thought you ever had, say hurt someone. Now all that person will want to do is hurt someone. A most dangerous ability. This is why Mom wants to begin her training as soon as possible. Gaia and Volos will be training starting at 6-months old." Finishing off the beer. "After talking to the other Mom Bears, I agree. Both of them need to be trained, skilled, and in control."

It became a party of sorts. Teena and Keena had to leave, it seems they do not have alcohol on their planet, and for a good reason, they do not taste it, nor does it affect them in any way. But they needed to report back about the status of the first Hera children born on the planet.

Before they left, "Keena, I have a question. If the kids are white dots now and have never been enhanced, what will or can happen if they are enhanced? Is it possible they will regress, or can enhancement only increase abilities?"

Teena replied, "We have never witnessed an ability regression, only an increase. If Gaia is as powerful as it appears, is enhancement something we want to consider?" She paused, "Thank the goddess, that is a decision we have a few years to make."

Everyone in the room said, "Agreed."

Chapter Sixteen

It has been five years since the twins were born to Belle and Goose, and there are now more than 50 human children on the planet, ranging from 2 to 14 years old. All are either green or blue, and all of them love the Blue Bear and the Kitties.

Prerequisites for adults to live on Hera; must be a minimum of an orange dot before arrival; you are enhanced to your full potential after arrival.

Each family member must be orange or above. Children are in the same boat. If any family member is red, the family is rejected.

Having children on Hera is another matter. If one parent is red, there is a 50/50 chance the children will be red. If both parents are at minimum orange, the opportunity of being orange or above is 100%. Therefore, only orange or above can live on the surface, ensuring no new red dots will be born here.

The kids went off into the forest to play one morning after breakfast. They walked out of earshot of the adults.

Mom Bear, however, was in the forest and saw Gaia and Volos playing as children do when adults are not near. As she approached, she saw Gaia extend her arms and float up to the branch of a tree higher than she is tall. She immediately contacted Belle and asked if humans could fly. Belle joined Mom Bear within fifteen minutes and watched the twins for more than an hour.

As they were about to announce they were there, she did it again. This time she went higher. Belle was floored. Mom Bear was amazed, and since Belle sent the image of Gaia floating to Goose, he was just plain shocked.

To date, there are precisely eleven white dots on the planet. All of them are hikers, and all of them were on the same track or similar as Goose and Belle. There was something about the path, the lines of magnetic flux on longitude line, their walk, their hike. White dots are Belle and Goose, their children Volos and Gaia; also Tweedle Dee and Dumb, and their daughter Morgan. Double Espresso and Belinda Goat and their children Danielle and Amelia.

There are also two white dots on the stations in orbit of Hera and four on Earth. C-Note and Bass Master are in orbit at the moment but returning in a day to the surface. They had meetings they needed to tend to with top brass from Earth. In the past year, C-Note and Bass Master have become a couple and are talking about marriage. Triple One, on the other hand, is free and single. A green and a member of the colony for life.

Earth is somewhat unique in that sense. It seems that the parents of both Belle and Goose have enhanced to white dots, and as such, are on the communications team for the planetary magnetic communications project. Since all four are white dots, their role is to hold recruiting drives to enhance others. DE and the Goat brought them each an enhancer to use as they saw fit. They delivered a dozen more to be spread around the planet. To date, no other white dots have been located.

Very few of those enhanced have had telekinesis. The 5% who do are recruited into the project. Predominant is the ability to see the past, second is the ability to see future events, and running a close third are those who can broadcast thoughts to others. It is, after all, a rare ability and one that can be used for ill gains.

No one to date has been able to control anyone else, and a few of those who can communicate have been able to speak to a few creatures on the Earth. It appears that the most intelligent 'animal' on Earth is the very happy dolphin. They can now talk to humans. Cats can also speak to humans but not in words. Emotions and feelings and desires mostly. Whereas dogs are just dogs. They are there for companionship. The closest creature on Earth to the Blue Bear is the Polar Bear, and in an incident, one woman was put into a position where a Polar Bear was attacking. She yelled through her mind to stop, and the bear did. The bear sat in front of her, and they spoke. For the first time, a polar bear and a human understood each other.

When this got back to the city, the news services picked it up and ran with it. Once they learned about Hera and the continuing work there, they all wanted to interview Belle and Goose and pretty much any other person living on the planet.

All requests had to go through the PCE. For no other reason than to ensure no reds make it to the planet. This place is dangerous for a red. Belle has taken on the role of the spokesperson for the world. The most recent request intrigued her, and she sent word back to her parents to have a lunch meeting with the journalist. They need to discover her angle on the story to verify if she is on the level or trying to sensationalize herself or something.

The lunch just concluded, and her parents should contact her shortly. "Goose dear, can you keep an eye on the youngers for a time. I need to discuss the journalist with my parents."

Goose, about 8 kilometers away at the moment, replied, "Yes, dear. I should be home in half an hour."

"Perfect. Thanks."

Half an hour later, Belle's father contacted his daughter. As he did, Goose let her know he is back and the younger's are with him.

"So, Dad, what did you learn?"

The new communications system is in place, and for some blues, it is difficult and exhausting to use. However, greens appear to have an easier time, and the white dots can use it like they are on the phone.

"Well, Jac's, I scanned her as she talked, and she appeared to be sincere. According to my scanner, she is categorized as orange and stated that she will be traveling alone, interviewing, photographing, and video. But mainly, she needs to talk to you and a few others, and she would love to see the creatures of the planet."

"OK. Your opinion. Yes or no?"

Bob thought about it for a while, maybe a minute. "Baby girl, I say let her come. Let her meet Mom Bear, Dad, and the rest of the gang. Let her talk to hikers." He paused a moment, "But I say let her be orange until she arrives. She told me she went to an enhancement center, and they refused to make an attempt."

"Who refused?"

"Your in-laws, actually." He paused a moment, "I contacted Brian before I called you. He said when he attempted to enhance her, the device told him it recommends not attempting. Something in her mental makeup is adverse to the system, and the system always wins."

"I need to talk to Keena about this. She never mentioned it was possible." Then, she grinned, "I may ensure Keena and Teena are there when she arrives."

"OK, kiddo, gotta run. Meeting your other parental unit at some store. She wants to send her grandbabies a birthday gift for number 6. We are thinking of spending a few months on the planet, so maybe we will arrange to be on the plane with her."

"That sounds like a good idea. Besides, I know you want to try the dropship. Maybe even talk Mom into it and our roving reporter. THAT will give her something to write about."

"That is an excellent thought. Talk to you next month in person."

She and her father disconnected, and she let Goose know. "Honey, I have an urge to head to Arkus for an overnighter with the kids."

"That sounds like a good idea." She and Goose had spoken about what she saw Gaia did and wanted to test something.

Belle walked out of the home and into the field. She sat in the grass at the edge closest to the house. Mom Bear walked into the area a few minutes later and up to Belle, laid down, and they talked.

"Hi, Mom. I need advice."

"Speak to me, daughter."

"There is a reporter on my birth world who wants to visit. This reporter is a woman and has the gift, but at the moment, it is not active. The enhancing did not work for her; the device refused. Should I let her here and let you and her meet?"

"You have a difficult decision ahead of you, daughter. I had heard of only one before who was not able to be enhanced. This person had ulterior motives for enhancement, and they were not for good. The device detected something and refused. Rilo and I had many conversations before you arrived and received the gift. It appears this may be the case in this event also."

Belle paused a moment and told Mom Bear, "My parents are returning. Dad misses you. He told me to say hello."

"Your parents did a great job with you when you were a younger. They instructed you in the proper ways to be worthy of the universe and how to ensure your small slice of the universe is a little better."

"Thanks. I think they did well also."

"You are passing those skills to your youngers, and Teacher is helping all youngers, and a few others, understand your species."

"In the past few years, I have heard comments where some want me to pass the title to another. I am not ready to pass it on. But, I love helping all, and I think I have a plan." She smiled, and Mom grinned also. "I think we need to go to a few places around the world and meet with those who are local. I think if we all meet and they speak to me, it may help everyone."

"That is a thought, but you cannot go alone. It would take many cycles to do this."

"I think I can get a ship, and if you would like to come with me, we would be gone just a few days. We can use one of our crafts and get to the location very fast."

"I am not certain about being in one of your flying craft."

"Mom, are you afraid to fly?"

"Possibly?" Mom said. "I have never done it before."

They spoke a while longer, and Belle went and coordinated the flight, the shuttle, food for them both, and then she coordinated Belinda Goat to be at the house while she was away, knowing Goose is a great father and all, but the kids need a mother's touch.

A few days before she left with Mom, the family went to the plateau overnight. No one else was there, just them. Goose wanted to see what they would see, hear, find. Belle planned to use the enhancer of the two of them and see what happens.

~~~~~~~~~~

They hiked to the Plateau, all four of them. Goose said, "The first one to the top wins."

Gaia simply extended her arms and floated up. In a minute, she was on the plateau. As she lifted off, Volos yelled, "NOT FAIR!"

Belle, Goose, and Volos ran up the stairs as fast as they could. When they got there, Gaia had filled the fire ring with fresh wood.

"Are we camping in tents, mommy?" Gaia asked.

"No, dear, we are sleeping in the control room."

Volos said, "Cool, even better!"

Goose made dinner, a simple dinner of hot dogs cooked over the fire on sticks. He had buns and ketchup. That is how all four of them will eat them tonight.

"No mayo?" Belle asked.

"No, sorry," Goose replied.

After they ate, they sat by the fire, it was a little cool, but they were comfortable. Belle and Goose needed to talk to them.

"Kids, there is a device that may increase your abilities. Maybe. Not for certain."

"Cool, Mommy, will I be able to fly too?"

"I have no idea, baby, but it will or may do something for you. Daddy and I want to give it a try."

"OK." They both said.

Goose removed the enhancer from the holster in the small of his back and trained it on Volos. It activated. The beam was green, then it pulsated green and shut off. They had never seen the scanner pulse before.

Belle looked at her scanner, and there were four white dots on the plateau, so nothing yet.

She nodded to Goose, who trained it on Gaia. It pulsated green, then turned a bright yellow and shut off.

Belle looked at the scanner, still four white dots on the plateau.

She told DE and the others what happened, and they would watch the area to see what happened.

They went into a building and looked around. "This is where Uncle Rilo and Aunt Reena lived," Volos said.

"Yes, it is; how do you know that," Goose asked.

"I see them here, making dinner and talking." Volos looked at a wall. "Aunt Reena hid something here." He walked to a wall and pressed an ornamental pattern. The wall receded and slid away. It was a small alcove with a memory cube. "She wanted Uncle Rilo to have this after she left the universe."

He handed it to his father, who immediately contacted Rilo and let him know what they found. "I will arrive tomorrow, Goose. Thank you."

The remainder of the night was uneventful. Finally, about 3 hours before sunrise, DE contacted Goose.

"Brother Goose, you need to wake up."

"I'm awake DE, what's up?"

"There are two white dots at your location. There are also two yellow dots."

"Yellow?" Goose said in his mind so as not to wake anyone else up. "What's yellow?"

"No clue, maybe a white on afterburner?"

"Contact Teena and ask her to return tomorrow. Rilo is coming tomorrow; Volos found a hidden note from his mate."

"Cool, I think. Rilo must be excited."

"He sounded so when I told him."

"Go back to sleep. We will talk tomorrow."

They disconnected, and Goose fell back to sleep, wondering the implication of a yellow.

In the morning, Gaia discovered she was able to do a lot more. She and Volos could see a lot more and were able to make contact more effortless than ever.

"Daddy, people lived here before we did."

"I know, Gaia. Uncle Rilo's people lived here."

"No, Daddy, before them." She paused a moment and said. "They lived in the caves under us."

"What caves?"

Volos said, "We'll show you, come with us. The door is not far away, and I know how to open it."

"Let's have a good breakfast and wait till Uncle Rilo and Aunt Teena get here. That was the surprise, they are coming to visit. Then, we can all go into the caves and explore."

"OK, Dad, I'm hungry. Like Mom says, if you're cooking, I'm eating."

Goose and Belle looked at each other. The only time she said that was when they were still hikers. Years ago. Somehow, Gaia saw it and remembered it.

"I say eggs, bacon, pancakes. How does that sound?"

"Awesome!" They all yelled at the same time.

Goose, The Goat, DE, and Belle talked about the caves while he cooked. Teena, Pono, Rilo, and Keena were due to arrive in just a few minutes. The Tweedles will join all of them at the base of the plateau.

"So, where do we need to go to find the door," Belle asked the kids.

"Halfway down the steps, there is big round rock. Turn it to the right, and the door will open. But look out, there is a trap at the door." Gaia said.

"A trap?" Goose replied.

"Yes, Dad," Volos said. "To stop the trap from trapping you, all you have to do is reach in before you step in. Then, above the door is a switch, turn it, and it turns off all the traps."

"Really, that's pretty cool," Goose said to his son. "I wonder what the people looked like?"

Gaia replied, "Like us, a little smaller and blue."

They heard the shuttle arrive and land and knew all of them were out of the craft. Gaia closed her eyes, and a minute later, all of them landed on the plateau.

Gaia ran to them and gave them all a hug. "We are going to the caves!" She exclaimed. "Uncle Rilo, Auntie Reena loved you very much, and Daddy has her message for you. So, Uncle Dub, are you going to explore the caves with us?"

"I am mighty mite. So, how do we get there?"

"Follow me. I know the way!" Gaia said.

"What are you talking about, so do I you know," Volos added.

The adults looked at each other and followed the kids down the steps.

Halfway down the steps, they saw a rock wall. Gaia could not reach the opener, as she called it. DE turned it to the right as she instructed, and the wall disappeared.

DE was about to enter, but there seemed to be a force field over the entrance. "Sorry, that was me. But, dad, you need to turn the traps off before we go in."

"Right!" Goose said and reached in and up. It took a few seconds to find the switch, but when he turned it, there was a noticeable click, and interior lights came on.

"Perfect!" Volos said. Follow me.

----- THE END -----

About the Author

Chris Cancilla was born in Cleveland, Ohio, the East Side, in an Italian neighborhood known as Collinwood, near East 158th and St. Clair. He really liked growing up there and would not trade it for anything. The friendships he made in Elementary School at Holy Redeemer and in High School at St. Joseph (now called Villa Angela – St. Joseph's) are priceless, and some of them are still in force. For most of his youth, he worked in the family business, DiLillo Brothers Dry Cleaners, for his grandfather Carmen DiLillo; and at DiLillo Brothers Men's Wear for his uncle Tony (everyone called him the Czar). He also "apprenticed" with his Uncle Duke, a smack-dab radio and TV repair shop between the men's wear store and the dry cleaners. But he enjoyed working in the dry cleaners for his Grandfather the most. Two of the employees, Bertha and Evelyn, were like second mothers to him.

In his youth, he really enjoyed Scouting. Spending a significant portion of it in multiple Cub Scout Packs and Boy Scout Troops and Explorer Posts. Scouting influenced his life positively, and the training, knowledge, and education he gained during his youth in the troop are still influencing his decisions as an adult. The ideals of Scouting, especially the Oath and Law, serve him today as a moral compass, guiding his actions to be a man his family can be proud of in all aspects of his life.

After high school, Chris spent 14 years in the U.S. Air Force, where he managed to see a large chunk of this 3rd stone from our star, but his only regret was that he never made it below the equator, so he never got to see the toilet swirl the other way. His favorite assignment was to Lowry Air Force Base in Denver, Colorado, where he could ride motorcycles and camp in the Rocky Mountains during his Air Force career. This is a close second to the 2 years he was assigned to and lived in Keflavik, Iceland, where he and his wife Tammy became the best of friends and experienced some really odd and unique landscapes and adventures. One of which was Chris starting and being the Founding President of the SCUBA Diving Club on Naval Air Station Keflavik, the name of the club was:

"vörn kafara á Íslandi"

He and his wife Tammy live in the Raleigh, North Carolina area, close to Wake Forest. He really misses his little buddy and writing partner, his cat, Snip. Snip followed Chris around from room to room, you may or may not see him all the time, but he is always close by. Unfortunately, snip crossed the rainbow bridge a couple of years ago; he went fast, which is the only consolation. When Chris writes, though, he still is close by. They made a paw print before he was cremated, and that paw print sits on the desk, near the computer at all times.

The Boy Scouts of America is still a considerable part of his life, especially teaching new adults the skills needed to survive the outdoors and reinforce how these outdoor skills and habits need to be introduced to the leaders of tomorrow. Leave No Trace camping is a significant part of his instruction and is a philosophy in the conservative style of camping Chris enjoys, if not the only way to ensure an excellent time for you and future campers. Wilderness camping is a great way to decompress and gain insight into what is hidden in the inner recesses of your mind. Sitting around a campfire on a cool or cold night, watching the flames dance and watching the wood that has given its all to the beauty of the moment, allowing you to reflect inside your own thoughts and be honest with yourself. The one person you cannot lie to is you, so honesty in your own head allows nature a way of bringing all things into clarity; even when you spend all night arguing with a 50-pound raccoon about the cobbler residue in the Dutch Oven on the picnic table; the same Dutch Oven you said you would clean up in the morning. Sometimes, the raccoon wins!

Chris also has a passion for cooking, and the creation of several cookbooks allows him to experience new cuisines and cooking methods from around the globe, but it also provides him with the means to share and teach cooking to those who are less experienced or knowledgeable. By no means does he consider himself a chef, but he does consider himself a somewhat OK cook, both in the home and in the woods.

Cooking in the wilderness is a skill that not too many people have or have even considered, and it is one skill that Chris enjoys teaching to Scout Leaders, both old and new, in the classes that he teaches for Scouters (Adult Boy Scout Leaders) and also to the Scouts themselves during the COOKING Merit Badge course. Chris was happy that the BSA finally made cooking a required merit badge for the Eagle Scout rank. It is a skill that will be valuable for the rest of your life. Especially if you want to prepare a romantic meal for a date or simply provide a meal for yourself that you actually enjoy.

Whenever Chris develops or finishes a new story or cookbook, he permits a couple of people to read his book and offer ideas to improve the storyline or the text in general. Who knows, he may allow you to be the next editor, for which he will definitely give you kudos at the beginning of the book. Thus, immortalizing you in the story for all eternity.

His last hobby is Amateur Radio. In the Raleigh, NC area, you can find him in the mornings on K4ITL and in the evenings on **AA4RV**; he pops in occasionally to AK4H. If you use a DMR (Digital Mobile Radio), try to make a QSO with him on the TGIF Network, Talk Group 1870. He monitors that talk group most of the time and would enjoy the QSO.

I hoped you enjoyed reading this book, book one in the Archive Series. Please read the others in the series or, if you are interested in cooking, check out the cookbooks or both. If you work with an EDI team and have little to no understanding about Electronic Data Interchange, pick up that briefing booklet. It is well worth your time to read. Let Chris know what you think of the books you read and whether you liked the stories, the briefing, or the recipes.

Chris's day job is as an EDI B2B Integration Specialist or an EDI Developer. Take your pick; they both mean the same thing. He calls himself a digital mailman. He moves the data and information files from one place to another, but he does not own, nor is he responsible for, the data in any way other than delivering it. So, a mailman! That's a fancy way to tell someone that you work with computers to translate data from one format to another. After all, the mailman doesn't write the letters and only moves them from point A to B.

Additional Works by Christopher E. Cancilla

All of these are available at: http://AuthorCancilla.com

The Archives, a 7-Part Series of Novels

The ARCHIVES: Education

Book One in the Archives Series.

Benjamin Jensen is a temporal researcher, a good one. His career started out rough when he nearly destroyed all of history or lost the love of his life in a tragic accident that could have been prevented by him later in his career, but things have a way of working out. His favorite flight home is on the dropship from low Earth orbit, and he tries as hard as he can to get anyone to join him. His close friends run the Flight Dome on Lunar Base, where flapping and flying like a bird is commonplace and a fun pastime, but his real passion is for historical events.... or, more precisely, the circumstances surrounding and leading up to the actual event in focus. Join Benjamin Jensen and his classmates as they discover what it means to be a Temporal Researcher. Find out the dangers and rewards this life could offer in an adventure with historical importance.

The ARCHIVES: Fixing Time

Book Two in the Archives Series.

Benjamin Jensen's best friend in all of time is Brad Jorgen. When Brad returns from a long-term research project with important news. Someone is traveling in time, disrupting the time stream. Benjamin and Brad are tasked to repair and ensure it does not happen again. Afterward, the Archive Academy requests that the two teach a class on how to be inconspicuous when performing research and how to improvise when things do not go as planned. The course is a hit, but there are a lot of bumps during the learning process. Including a covert trip to Pluto to reclaim a ship they left on the once and former planet several thousands of years earlier, one they will need to use to revive a civilization that has been dead and forgotten to the passage of time for several millennia.

The ARCHIVES: Salvation

Book Three in the Archives Series.

In several places on the Earth, the orbital facilities, the Lunar Colonies, and the far-reaching corners of the human-populated universe, Christianity is beginning to grow and spread. The world government is concerned it may overshadow their power or lead the people to envision what the future needs to look like. Benjamin is tasked to determine the threat level of this new group, and he and his team are sent back to a place where the movement begins. Is this movement mind-altering or simple brainwashing? Do Christians want to control everything? Is there a reason to fear Christians or all religions in general? This is what he is tasked to learn, and fix, if necessary. On the way, he discovers a unique reality and brings that information back to his boss at Archive Island in a fascinating, honest and convincing report. Enveloped within this decision are his new wife and his best friend all of the time. Come and be with him as he explores his heart and his mind. The scientist needs to understand the definition of faith, and faith can be elusive.

The ARCHIVES: Family

Book Four in the Archives Series.

Benjamin Jensen is selected to take over as the Director of the entire Archive Island complex, including all operations and locations. His rise means that each of his compatriots is promoted to fill in the void as he and Brad Jorgen are propelled into intrigue and mystery. With that promotion comes tremendous responsibility in the guise of becoming one of the most powerful men in history and danger so terrifying it has never before surfaced. The big question on everyone's lips is, will Benjamin measure up to match the job? Can Brad avert a disaster that could mean an end to the Jensen lineage? Why a reporter is permitted free run of the Archive Island complex is baffling to some but allowed to happen by all? Come and take this journey with us to explore the dark areas of space, the human condition, and our family's soft spots.

The ARCHIVES: Fresh Start

Book Five in the Archives Series.

Benjamin Jensen is the Director of the Island Complex for
nearly two decades now, and his best friend Brad Jorgen is his
second-in-command. Their sons are students in the Academy
and are already well on their way to becoming influential and
experienced Archive Island Complex Temporal Research team
members. But, is there danger? Can they trust a non-TR with
the secrets of temporal research? Will they need to correct
time, so history can flow as it is intended? So, join the
journey.... join the excitement.

The ARCHIVES: Continuum

Book Six in the Archives Series.

Benjamin Jensen is still the Director of the Island Complex. It has been a bit more than 30 years. With the unexpected death of someone close, the Island is turned on its ear. Recalling several people close, the memorial service is brief, but the grieving is deep.

This is the sixth and final book in the series that traverses the TR lifetime of Benjamin Jensen, his family, and his friends.

The ARCHIVES: Temporal Logs

Book Seven in the Archives Series.

This closes out the Archive Series with flash. Not a continuation of the story, but rather levels between what happens in the six previous installments of the Archive Series.

Each character we have come to love and adore has a tribute in this book, each of them has a story that revolves around them that occurs between the accounts you are familiar with. So read and learn about the favorite saga in the life of your favorite characters.

Discover something no one knew before.

E*D*I: A Simple Introduction

A briefing on what EDI is and how it works

EDI can be and is complicated for the uninitiated to read. It is a "digital" representation of a human-readable document, like a purchase order. By reading this short introduction into the world of EDI, you will understand how it is structured, why it is necessary, what a standard is and what the individual pieces of data mean, and how they interrelate.

Welcome to EDI-101

E*D*I: A Deeper Dive

A briefing on the Purchase Order

EDI may be a mystery, but then again, so is magic until you know how the illusion is done. Take the 850-document set, the purchase order. What is it, what are the moving parts, and what do all those parts mean? Take a ride with me through the PO. Let's explore how the 850 is put together and learn in the process. Remember, EDI is FUN!!

E*D*I: Getting Paid

A briefing on the Invoice

The act of selling and buying is called commerce, and when using EDI, you are involved in Electronic Commerce. So, read about how to simplify your invoicing, cut costs by not having to create, print, address envelopes, and mail invoices to your customers.

Learn how an electronic invoice can get you paid faster.

E*D*I: Shipping and the Notice

A briefing on the Advanced Ship Notice

The ASN, or 856, is seriously one of the most misunderstood documents in EDI. People try to avoid them like the plague. Why? They don't understand them.

If you understood the ASN, the 856, you would be comfortable reading and mapping the 856 into your repertoire of documents.

Learn how easy it is to create an electronic ASN.

E*D*I: The Complete Series

A complete briefing and education on EDI

Having so many people ask me for a rolled-up version of the EDI
Education Series, I decided to put all 4 books into a single
volume. This is an updated rendition of the 4 books in the EDI
Education Series, and by reading and understanding the
information between these covers, you will have an excellent
basis to be an asset to any EDI Department.

Bus Route 40-A

A Short Story

The life of a planetary bus driver can be mundane, repetitious, sedate, and of course, unique, interesting, exciting, and spontaneous. Driving your whale around the planet, picking people up, and dropping them off is a lot of fun, sure. But at the same time, it is good to get a break in the monotonous time you call your day. So, when Walt was asked to take a charter trip for a few days, he jumped all over it, and knowing he had a good friend to ride shotgun, he felt like it would be a good thing for him and Biff. Plus, you get double pay and less work time, so he could be home more after the trip was over. No one could ever imagine what was about to happen; Walt met up with new influential people and became friends. He did mention the time he saved the lives of everyone on the bus.

Stories from Time and Space

A collection: short stories, essays, & ideas.

Chris Cancilla enjoys...no, he LOVES to write. And to that end, he has an opinion on just about everything. As a result, you can enjoy an eclectic sampling of a small collection of some of the pros he has penned throughout his life.

Lost Earth

The Survival of Humanity.

With the destruction of Earth, humanity learns to survive through cooperation, fellowship, and mutual caring. General Alexandria Rochenko leads by example and shows the remaining humans in the universe how to get along and help one another.

Life as an Amateur

Welcome to Amateur Radio!

Obviously, you are interested, but you need to know more about it before diving in; here's your chance. Between these covers is information that can help you decide if this is a hobby you can enjoy.

- Can you have fun with amateur radio? *YES!*
- Can you learn new things? *YES!*
- Can you help during a disaster? *YES!*

The answers to your questions await; let's go over them together.

Toasting Marshmallows on my Dumpster Fire

Random thoughts as you dance through my mind!

Have you had random thoughts after reading social media? Most people do and never talk about those thoughts. They simply have those thoughts, agree that they are correct, and move on, never having brought those thoughts into the public consciousness.

Well, here is your opportunity to listen to my mind!

Walk with me as I have various individual thoughts on unique or possibly opposing topics, and rationalize my way through them.

Is it weird? Not really.

Is it interesting? Definitely!!

Meet you in my head!

Getting Published!

A guide to getting published on Kindle

Getting published can be a new world for some. Here are a few tips and tricks I have learned over the years.

The world of publishing is a tough one to break into if you are looking for a publisher in the traditional sense; but if you plan to "self-publish," there is an array of things you need to know in advance, or better yet, my experiences may just avoid the processes costing you money to learn a hard lesson.

-----> I paid my dues, and you get the benefit!

Camp Menu Planning

An Indoor / Outdoor Cookbook

Designed essentially for Boy Scouts to learn the art – if not the technique – of cooking. Contains many recipes, but more importantly, the recipes are more a method or style than a road map to a meal. Borrowing one recipe and using the technique and possibly ingredients of a third is what actual cooking is all about, and this book instills that knowledge in whoever reads and uses it to learn or learn something new. The additional information contained in the book is highly useful in the troop cooking experience. This book will give your Scouts the arrows in their culinary quiver to make friends and family happy. Gaining the knowledge and experience to impress his fellow patrol members with each meal in the woods and provide the Scout with the ammunition to cook a fantastic meal.

Personal Menu Planning

A Backpackers Guide to eating well

In the woods, on a trail, you need to adapt to your surroundings. For example, it is not practical on the Appalachian Trail to drag a cooler behind you. So, how can you make good food and save weight? It is pretty easy if you know a few secrets. So, read and learn and enjoy the tasty ideas.

Cooking for One, Cooking for Many

Your guide to assist in planning, cooking, and eating well

In the woods at a campground, you need to impress the other campers. However, on the trails in the backcountry, you only need to impress yourself.

Learn the secrets of meal planning. The location makes no difference. You can be at home, at a flop-N-drop, or backpacking the mountain trails.

Once you understand the mix & match, or M^2 system, you can do it all with style and grace. Impress your fellow campers with a fine meal, impress yourself after a 30-mile day.

But, learning about the N.E.S.T. meal plan will help you to cook and eat in record time, with minimal clean-up.

Included are more than 50 of the best recipes for cooking a meal at home, at a campsite, or in the backcountry. Before you ask, there is no reason a home meal cannot be adapted for use when on the trails.

Made in the USA
Columbia, SC
26 March 2024

33283449R00240